THE DEAD SEA CONSPIRACY

Teilhard de Chardin and the New American Church

THE DEAD SEA CONSPIRACY

Teilhard de Chardin and the New American Church

JAMES K. FITZPATRICK

WINEPRESS WP PUBLISHING

Printed in the United States of America.

Packaged by WinePress Publishing, PO Box 428, Enumclaw, WA 98022. The views expressed or implied in this work do not necessarily reflect those of WinePress Publishing. The author is ultimately responsible for the design, content, and editorial accuracy of this work.

Unless otherwise noted all Scriptures are taken from the Holy Bible, New International Version, Copyright © 1973, 1978, 1984 by the International Bible Society. Used by permission of Zondervan Publishing House. The "NIV" and "New International Version" trademarks are registered in the United States Patent and Trademark Office by International Bible Society.

The author gratefully acknowledges permission from HarperCollins Publishers to reprint excerpts from *The Divine Milieu* by Pierre Teilhard de Chardin.

ISBN 1-57921-393-6
Library of Congress Catalog Card Number: 2001091457

A.M.D.G.

To Katherine and Joseph Schittina

"The world can no more have two summits than a circumference can have two centres. The star for which the world is waiting, without yet being able to give it a name, or rightly appreciate its true transcendence, or even recognise the most spiritual and divine of its rays, is, necessarily, Christ Himself, in whom we hope. To desire the Parousia, all we have to do is to let the very heart of the earth, as we Christianise it, beat within us."

Pierre Teilhard de Chardin, S.J.

The Divine Milieu

Author's Note:

The story that follows is a work of pure fiction. Any reference to historical events, or to real people, living or dead, or to actual geographical locations, is intended only to provide the novel with a suitable setting in historical reality. It should be clearly understood that all names, characters, places, and incidents are either the product of the author's imagination or are used fictitiously, and that their resemblance, if any, to real-life counterparts is entirely coincidental.

Chapter One

I am not the guy you would expect to be in possession of the biggest secret in history: the greatest story never told. And I am not exaggerating. What I know—what I think I know, at any rate, you will have to judge—will change the world more than Einstein's splitting of the atom or the more recent invention of the personal computer, if word of it ever gets out. This much I know: It will alter the mind, the heart and soul, and the collective conscience of mankind.

What am I talking about? Well, here goes: I have information proving that Jesus Christ never rose from the dead; that the Gospel accounts of his miracles and Ascension into heaven are inventions of his early disciples, intended only to keep their cult going after the Crucifixion. Seriously.

Now, remember, I said *proving* it. There have been scripture scholars pushing this idea as a theory since the mid-nineteenth-century. Ernest Renan and David Friedrich Strauss were the pioneers here. H.L. Mencken worked the territory as well. But all they had to offer was what they thought was common sense and a predisposition to doubt that miracles ever occur. What I'm talking about is *proof*.

More than that, I have been told that the Jesuits, the Society of Jesus, the "Pope's Men"—at least some of them—have known about the secret for a good part of the 20th century. Yes, the Jesuits. The radicals. The intellectuals. The priests Maureen Dowd, in one of her columns in the *New York Times*, called the Catholic Church's "gadflies." (Dowd thought that high praise.) The so-called "Modernists." The liberal theologians who get the most heat from the hierarchy of the Catholic Church. Them.

The conservatives jump all over these guys, but considering the secret they hold, they might be the most loyal Catholics around. They have been trying to get the Catholic Church ready for the day when the secret gets out; to give the Church a meaning, a purpose, some dignity—now that it has lost its *raison d'être*, as they say in the old neighborhood.

How many Jesuits are in on the plot? I don't know that, not yet. But I do know who the "godfather," so to speak, was. (Although I guess that is an inappropriate label, all things considered.) Maybe you have heard of him. Anyone who studied in a Jesuit school in the 1960s or 1970s probably can guess. Pierre Teilhard de Chardin. Father Pierre Teilhard de Chardin, Society of Jesus. Teilhard de Chardin, S.J.

Talk about ironies! The Vatican silenced this priest in the 1950s because they thought he was depicting Christianity as a religion that would have meaning in the modern world only if it was a belief system with the power to transform our physical world; and because he pictured Jesus as a Messiah whose words could make this world, and only this world, a better place, a world where men and women could live in true, but strictly human and evolving "Communion" with one another. A "heaven on earth" I guess you'd call it.

Well, dammit, that *was* what he was saying! I know that now. (I think. Let's go slow with this.)

But, hell, what else could he do when he found out the secret? That, or tell the Pope and the bishops to close up shop and do what the British have done with their churches: run them as tourist attractions. No risen Jesus, no Catholicism. Conservative Catholic theologians are fond of that line from St. Paul: "If Jesus is not arisen from the dead, then our faith is in vain." Teilhard agreed, but not the way the conservatives hoped people would.

Q.E.D., *quod erat demonstrandum*: "The truth has been demonstrated." Teilhard understood. His theories about a world "Christified" through "Christogenesis" until an evolving mankind reached an "Omega Point" that would be the "Parousia" (the Second Coming of Christ)—it was all his attempt to ease the Jesuits and the Church of Rome into a new mission. They were code words meant to create a Catholicism that could continue without a risen Christ, without a hereafter, without a heaven and hell, or saints, or a personal, loving God with an "only-begotten" Son.

The Church and his beloved Jesuit order would have to find something new to do instead of "saving souls" in the traditional sense. The secret made the old notion of a religious vocation obsolete. Teilhard was convinced that he and his Jesuit co-conspirators could not keep the secret forever. Their task was to prepare the Roman Catholic Church and their own Society of Jesus for the Day of Reckoning, when the world would finally discover the truth.

The Catholic universities, the churches, and retreat centers, the religious orders, the sacred publishing houses, all these things could survive, he thought, if they adapted themselves to the new world. That was Teilhard's scheme . . . if I'm right.

There could be no more talk of heaven, of course, no more saints, no more prayers to a crucified Lord. But priests and nuns and popes and bishops could still be a light to the world, be examples of how men and women could live together in peace and in service to one another by accepting the teachings of the man called Jesus of Nazareth, even if his divinity was the invention of a bunch of Palestinian Branch Davidians.

Not in the same league as possessing the "Keys to the Kingdom of Heaven," but not bad either. Especially when there would be no alternative.

Chapter Two

I should tell you a little about myself before we go further. My name is Frankie Corcoran: Francis X. Corcoran; Francis Xavier Corcoran.

That should tell you a lot in and of itself. Irish Catholic family, Jesuit trained, in high school anyway. And I never got beyond high school.

Then how do I know all this stuff about scripture scholars and Teilhard de Chardin? Well, the high school I went to was not your ordinary high school. It was Regis Preparatory School, the Jesuit scholarship school in Manhattan: on Park Avenue, just off Central Park. And I went there in the early 1980s. Radical decade. So you heard about such things there. Quite a place.

You got in by taking an admissions test. All the little weenies from the Catholic schools in New York City and the surrounding counties would line up on a Saturday morning in the fall to take it. You got off the subway at 86th Street and walked two blocks back to this massive stone building on 84th Street between Park and Madison that must have been worth a zillion bucks. I am not kidding. We are talking Park Avenue, folks. Central Park, New York, New York.

And if you got in—which only a small percentage did—free tuition for four years, with the assurance that you were being admitted into a select company of Jesuit-trained young men who were going to rule the world, in the important things anyway. (Not that I ever heard of anyone really famous who'd gone to Regis. Maybe they are out there, but no one has let me in on the news. No presidents or senators or heads of Microsoft or anything. No *Who's Who in America*—that I know of, anyway.)

Not everyone made it through the place, of course. They threw out Pete Hamill. He says it was because he wouldn't toe the line for the conservative Jesuit priests of the 1950s and because the lawyers' and doctors' sons in the student body didn't appreciate his working-class genius. Who knows how true that may be? No one has ever accused Hamill of self-effacement.

Well, anyway, I got in and graduated, but that was about it. Four years of Greek and Latin and religion classes and enough homework to drive you crazy. But I did the work. I still don't know why. It just seemed like it was something you had to do to please my mother and avoid the wrath of the "Jebbies."

"Jebbies" was what we called the Jesuits. They were corkers. Who knew the most about American government? John Courtney Murray, S.J., Society of Jesus. Who was the most profound poet of the last two centuries? Gerard Manley Hopkins, S.J. Who was the thinker most sensitive to the race problem in the United States? John LaFarge, S.J. Who was the man who most correctly understood the concept of international law? Francisco Suarez, S.J. Which was the magazine that offered the most perceptive insights on American life? *America*, the Jesuits' weekly. Who was the most perceptive modern theologian? Karl Rahner, S.J. Who was the great prophet of the modern age? Teilhard de Chardin, S.J. And so on, and so on. These guys never let up.

It got to the point where most of us at Regis even printed a little cross with "A.M.D.G" underneath it on the top of all our homework and test papers. That was for "Ad Maiorem Dei Gloriam," the Jesuits motto, "For the Greater Glory of God." Now I can't remember them ever telling us to do that. They didn't have to. It was just expected.

Still, it all pretty much missed the mark with me. Oh, I recited the answers the priests wanted in Religion class, and printed

A.M.D.G. on everything I wrote (I had to catch myself to avoid putting it on top of my first few mailroom inventories on my first job on Wall Street), but my other interests were too strong for them to win me over completely.

I may have been the only graduate of Regis that year who did not go to college. But I doubt that many of my teachers were all that upset about it. I graduated near the bottom of my class—with no intention of wasting time at the colleges the Jebbies tried to steer you toward: Fordham, Georgetown, Holy Cross. It wasn't that I was a smart-ass or anything. I never gave my teachers a hard time. Truthfully, I was usually too busy nursing a hangover to have time for any serious classroom mischief.

You see then, as now, I was a hang-around guy. Even while at Regis, I used to cross Central Park with a few buddies on the last day of class before the holidays and down a few beers in the Dublin House on the West Side on 79th Street. The bartender there was the uncle of one of my buddies, one of those old-time Irish bartenders with silver hair and a fondness for starched white shirts and expensive ties and a string of dirty jokes about everything from Richard Nixon to Puerto Ricans to pansy interior designers. He let us drink in the bar's quiet back booths as long as we didn't make a scene. I can remember my first time passing through the saloon's imposing brass front doors (you'd think it was a delegate's lounge at the UN) and walking along the narrow space past the laughing men bellied up to the bar. To think that I was reciting Latin verbs at Regis while this was going on, all the jokes and sports talk and tall tales. Home!

Those afternoons were my introduction to the bar scene. It has been the backdrop to my life ever since. It is where I am most comfortable. No one trying to do anything but get drunk and engage in a little talk. Perfect. Places like the Dublin House and the Ranger and Knick games, beer in the bleachers at Yankee Stadium— I wanted the pocket change to become part of it all right out of high school, and not four years of scrimping to make it through some Jesuit college. I had some neighborhood drinking buddies who were making good bucks working in the mailroom at a couple of Wall Street firms. And they got me a job at one of them, too.

Am I saying I have a drinking problem? I don't think so, although when I read the descriptions of the tell-tale signs that the "drunk therapy" groups put out, I've got them all. But hell, if you take those "my-name-is-Harry-and-I'm-an-alcoholic" people seriously, the only time that it is OK to drink is when no one would want to drink! They tell you that you can't drink to get happy when you're celebrating, to drown your sorrows, to loosen up at a party, when you are alone, when you're nervous. What the hell is left?

Whatever. I don't think I'm a drunk. I drink a lot. But I am not an alcoholic. I never miss booze when I am not around a bar. I don't think about my next drink. I like bars. I like the people in bars. I like the talk in bars, the nuttiness, the raucousness, the I-don't-give-a-damn, in your face humor. I know people who swear the booze will catch up with me someday. We'll see.

In any event, for a few years I took the subway to my Wall Street job (Broadway-Nassau Street station) from my parents' apartment in Inwood. Back then Inwood was an Irish enclave in northern Manhattan, famous for drunks, union strong-arm guys, vocations to the nuns and priesthood, and some pretty decent basketball players . . . for white guys. I wasn't bad myself. One of the guys from the neighborhood even went on to play at the University of South Carolina when Frank McGuire was coach there.

Quite a guy, that McGuire. He was Inwood's favorite coach. The story goes that he told everybody that he could win the NCAA championship with five Irish guys from New York City's Catholic schools, and he did it—just once—with his North Carolina team, which beat Wilt Chamberlain's Kansas team in 1958. With a lot of help, I'll admit, from a sharp shooting Jewish dude named Lennie Rosenbluth.

The math skills and all-around orderliness I picked up at Regis paid off for me pretty quickly. I worked my way up from the mailroom to a position as a floor trader at Merrill Lynch. By the time I was in my mid twenties, I was making enough money to buy a co-op on West 95th Street, just off West End Avenue. I was tempted to donate ten grand or so to Regis just to rile my old teachers and the student government suck-ups who were still taking out student loans to pay their law school tuition. I never did though. Inwood preached the message that you don't kick a guy when he is down. You kick him to get him down, but not when he is down.

West 95th Street was just the right kind of neighborhood for me. Lots of bars and lots of bookstores and old churches and enough anonymity for no one to tell my mother—she still lives in Inwood—if I took home a tipsy secretary or Columbia co-ed who went ga-ga when I recited a few lines from Yeats or T.S. Eliot.

I did that once in a while—"got lucky," as they say. Still do, as a matter of fact, although now I specialize in thirty-something divorcees. But don't hold it against me. I know I am not supposed to do this, and I always feel guilty about it afterwards. And I don't chase married women, although I don't fight them off either. That's why it is important to have so many churches around. I can always find a confessor who doesn't know me when I want to get rid of the angst. And I still do that, too, in spite of my knowing the secret.

Why? What can I say? The Jewish guys I work with go to an analyst; I go to the most distracted and/or deaf priest I can find. You sort it out.

Look: What I am trying to get across to you with all these revelations about my "inner self" is that, even though I am no scholar, you can trust me about this Teilhard de Chardin Conspiracy. As a proud graduate of Regis, I was uniquely equipped to follow the contours of the secret when I found out about it that night a few short years ago.

Chapter Three

I t all began a year or so back when my brother Leo, a New York City fireman, and I were driving back from a ski weekend at Hunter Mountain in the Catskills. Leo is named after Pope Leo XIII. (If you met my mother this wouldn't seem very strange to you.)

I am into the ski scene. I don't ski very well, but I ski-lodge like a champ. Although I don't look as good as I used to, with the right fisherman's sweater and soft lighting, I can draw enough female interest to make a trip to the slopes worthwhile.

The lassies I attract may not pass for Cindy Crawford, but they're not dogs, either. In my mid-thirties now, I stand a few inches over six feet tall, am just a tad overweight (I run a bit), and am still equipped with all of my teeth and *most* of my hair: blonde, with a slight widow's peak. I've been told that I look like a young Nick Nolte after a few too many bar fights. I can live with that.

Anyway, that February night Leo and I were crossing the Newburgh-Beacon Bridge, just north of West Point. We had heard there was a traffic jam due to an accident on the Thruway just ahead. So we decided to head home by crossing the Hudson up by Poughkeepsie and heading south on Route 9. It was about 7 P.M. and snowing like crazy. Leo was driving, but wrestling the wheel, his Dodge Caravan slipping and sliding sideways over the icy bridge surface like a barrel on a ski slope.

I couldn't see more than a foot or two in front of us through the snowy swirl reflected in the headlight beams. Crusted with the white stuff, the bridge girders looked like props from the suicide scene in *It's a Wonderful Life*.

Nothing about the night seemed to bother the hokey suburban announcer on the local soft music station, though. He sounded like he was enjoying his report that the treacherous storm would continue through the night.

"Looks like no school tomorrow," the announcer said gleefully. "Be sure to tune in tomorrow at six to WHUD's Storm Center for all the school closings and cancellations. Brought to you by Geis Motors, your hometown Hudson Valley car dealer."

"Dammit, Frankie, I'm getting worried," Leo muttered, leaning and peering across the steering wheel. He was beginning to breathe heavily, in short bursts. "I can't see nothing, Frankie, nothing. This is bad. We've got to stop somewhere, or we'll get stranded up here."

Leo was two years younger than me, four inches shorter, and fifty pounds heavier. His lifestyle was catching up with him. I guess it is true: a steady diet of beer and processed meats leaves its mark after a while.

"OK, stop then," I answered. "No big deal. I can take a vacation day tomorrow. What about you?"

"I'm off anyway," he said, wiping the windshield with his sleeve. "My next tour at the firehouse ain't till two days from now. We gotta stop, no matter what."

"Do it, then. What the hell. There are a couple of motels—Holiday Inn or Ramada or something—right near where we exit onto Route 9 in Fishkill. We should be able to get a room there. We'll head out in the morning after they plow the roads. No big deal."

We got to the motel easy enough, a Holiday Inn, checked in, and went to our room. But I knew pretty quickly we would not be settling in for a long winter's night of television. As we passed the bar on our way to the room it was buzzing just about right—soft lights, some sad Sinatra songs on the jukebox, and the sound of slightly tipsy female voices in the air. The music of the spheres.

Leo stared at me over his shoulder with a cat-got-the-mouse grin. I guess we were not the only ones stranded for the night.

I sat on the bed in our room watching some hockey game between a bunch of no-names from Vancouver, B.C., on ESPN (nothing like when the Rangers and the Islanders would slug it out in the Garden back in the 1980s), waiting for Leo to shave and sprinkle himself with his English Leather cologne. He was going to be at his best when he made the move on whatever lucky female crossed his path at the bar. I chuckled a bit. He was my younger brother, and I felt about him the way an older brother is supposed to, but he was a piece of work.

My mother's Catholicism had made even less impact on him than on me. And the Jesuits never got a chance to shape his soul. He wasn't as good on the standardized tests as I was. He ended up going to LaSalle Academy, down near the Bowery. Not a bad place, run by the Christian Brothers, but nothing like the Jesuit schools. I got more homework in a night at Regis than he did in a week. At least it seemed that way from the amount of time he put into it.

Not that he was a bad guy. He had a warm smile, a hearty, backslapping barroom demeanor. His marriage lasted more than five years . . . not bad for our generation. He would give you the shirt off his back. Still, he had the morals of a tomcat. He was having sex with Washington Heights hookers when he was a high school freshman. He had a Dominican girlfriend around his firehouse throughout the duration of his marriage. He gave her and his wife the clap, which he'd caught from someone else.

He could be a little violent, too, when the wrong thing touched him off. A little? I'll say. I remember one afternoon in a playground up near Baker Field. Beautiful spring afternoon with the wind sweeping gently in off Spuyten Duyvil and the trees just beginning to bud. Leo was about fourteen at the time.

We had been playing basketball with two other of the old Irish crowd from Inwood and were sitting around taking a breather, four guys sharing two clear bottles of Miller before we took to the court again. Three black guys came onto the playground, bouncing a basketball, flipping it to one another, smoking Kools and talking trash. You know the drill.

The usual rule in these situations is for newcomers to challenge the guys who have the court; winners take over. We did it all the time in that playground, black guys, white guys, Spanish . . . it usually worked out. But this time these homeboys walked onto the court as if we weren't even there.

I was trying to come up with something diplomatic to say when Leo cut to the chase: "We got the court, jive ass."

I groaned. This wasn't going to be easy.

"You mean you *had* it," shot back the biggest of the black dudes. He was about sixteen, already over six feet, a mean-looking character. He pimp-rolled toward us, bouncing the ball and rolling his tongue over his lips as if he were about to bite into some Thanksgiving turkey.

He stood over us menacingly, wearing tan shorts—trimmer and shorter than the baggy styles of today—black sneakers, and white tube socks. You remember the look. His calves looked like the midsection of an angry python.

"Who you calling 'jive ass,' you little faggot?" he snarled. He added some of the four-letter words that you might expect. (You can use your imagination as to what *they* were. And do that with the rest of what I write, too. I still feel funny about putting the more vulgar details on paper. I keep thinking that my mother or some old priest at Regis will be reading this someday. I don't mind them hearing from me that Jesus is still in the ground somewhere around Jerusalem, but I don't want them to think that I am a lowlife. What can I say? St. Ignatius Loyola, the priest who started the Jesuits, used to say that if you gave him the boy, he would shape the man.)

Anyway, Leo didn't even look up as he smashed the beer bottle on the blacktop and ripped the jagged edge across the tendons of the black guy's calf. He went down as if he had been shot, blood pumping from his exposed vein like a smorgasbord fountain. Leo stood up, the basketball in one hand, the broken bottle in the other, and walked toward the other black guys. As calm as if he were selling magazine subscriptions, he told them, "You can have the court now. But you might have to get somebody to take your friend's place."

The black guys stared at Leo as if they had seen the devil himself. He had that look in his eyes—the one that makes even labor union goons back off, the look that says you are crazy enough to kill or be killed at the moment; that standing up to you means serious, serious business. They let Leo pass and rushed to help their friend, who was screaming and writhing in agony, trying to stanch the flow of blood with both hands.

We heard rumors afterwards that the cops were looking for Leo; that the black guy was crippled for life; that the drug dealer Nicky Barnes had vowed to cut Leo into parts and dump him into the Harlem River in revenge. I don't know if any of it was true. It was probably just street talk. Nothing ever happened, except that people pretty much stayed clear of Leo from that day forward. Me too, in certain ways, to tell you the truth. He is not all there. But he would trade punches with Mike Tyson without thinking twice to protect me. You can't ignore things like that about a guy.

Those were strange days in the New York playgrounds, the end of an era. When I walk by the playgrounds these days, all the kids look like derelicts. Even the so-called "good" kids want to come across like *gangsta rappers* or some body-pierced Chelsea slimeball. I met one of my boss's sons a few months back, as white as they come. He had more tattoos than a sideshow freak and a stud in his tongue the size of a lug wrench. He was heading for an SAT course that day to help him get into Princeton.

Back then, though, all the Irish and Italian Catholic school kids in Manhattan looked like little angels, apple-cheeked and barbered like models in an Ovaltine ad. You couldn't have beards or long hair in those schools. And you had a better chance of eloping with the Mother Superior of the local convent than of them letting you into the school building with an earring.

But by the time they hit high school those little Inwood angels had seen it all. Everything. They'd heard schoolyard studs bragging about their long afternoons with lonely neighborhood housewives, seen hookers having sex in the hallways of their apartment buildings and junkies sprawled on park benches with the bloody needle still in their arms. They had been there when union goons beat strikebreakers to a pulp. They knew where homosexuals would pay real cash money for them to do things that they wouldn't print in mainstream newspapers even today.

But come Sunday, the Catholic school kids would be there serving Mass in their red cassocks and lace surplices, in a scene that looked like the latest subject of a Norman Rockwell poster, holding the crucifix as if their minds were as innocent as a Disney farm boy's. And when they married, they looked for girls just like the girl that married dear old Dad and moved to someplace like Rockland County and joined the Holy Name Society in their parishes and acted as if the world were nothing like the way they knew it really was. You tell me about it.

We walked through the hotel lobby and around to the bar. I checked our reflection in a wall mirror. Leo was wearing his John Gotti-style knit shirt: dark, white piping, top button buttoned, his pot belly stretching the fabric above his belt. I was in a Black Watch plaid L.L. Bean shirt and a pair of tan corduroy pants. Irresistible. We hoped.

The lobby was what you would expect. I wonder if they train carpenters somewhere in Ohio to make all these Holiday Inns and Ramadas look the same: embossed dark green wallpaper, brass wall sconces, cut glass chandeliers, maple wainscoting, heavily framed paintings of fox hunts and farm girls in a fuzzy haze—like Charlie Russell trying his hand at Impressionism. I was sure that my bosses' wives—the world's best organizers of the seating lists for charity galas—would roll their eyes behind their Absoluts on the rocks at every plastic potted palm and Formica-topped dry bar in the place, but I was impressed. I always am when I see these joints.

I'll never forget my father's words when he took me, as a kid, to a Knights of Columbus Communion Breakfast at a place like this, just off the Saw Mill River Parkway in the Bronx. He was talking to one of his cronies, a steamfitter from High Bridge with a face the color of a slab of rare prime rib and a mane of white hair that Al Gore would kill for.

"Jackie, would you look at this place? Back home . . ."—he was talking about County Clare, Ireland—". . . even the British landlords didn't have vestibules like this." And nowadays the descendants of immigrants who wouldn't have been allowed to clean the kitchens in the rich folks' homes in the old country take these places for granted, think they're low class!

We entered the bar with our Inwood stroll: part John Wayne, part pimp. I don't know who came up with the script, but our crowd fell into the routine as effortlessly as a fashion model tosses her hair over her eye. What am I talking about? Well, you enter the room without looking at anyone there; your eyes roam from corner to corner, as if your major interest were the window treatments. All the while you are reaching into your breast pocket for your pack of Marlboros. Two steps more and you pop the cigarette into your mouth and let it dangle unlit while you return the pack to your pocket. You keep walking and looking around as you approach the bar, as if it didn't matter if Marilyn Monroe and Jimmy Hoffa were sitting there drinking margaritas.

The cigarette stays unlit; you talk through it, ordering your drink, letting it pop to the rhythm of your words. When the bartender nods in recognition, you snap your lighter, light the cigarette and blow a steam of smoke toward the overhead lights. Not until then do you deign to look around the bar, lord of your domain, holding the cigarette just under your nose, letting the rising smoke frame your face. Some Hollywood guys know the routine: Dennis Franz on *N.Y.P.D. Blue* is particularly good at it.

Within moments we both knew it: We'd struck gold. The women's voices we had heard earlier came from a cluster of twenty-somethings who had consumed enough liquor to no longer be worried about maintaining their Gwyneth Paltrow cool. They were with two men, salesmen types, a bit older. I didn't know, at first, if they were their husbands or just fellow travelers stranded in the storm. It didn't matter. After a few drinks, Leo and I would be able to get in on the conversation and hit on the women—discreetly, if they were married, or with ulterior motives if not. Either way would be fun. A night of drinks and drawing a glow from a slightly tipsy woman's laughing eyes. If there is a heaven, I'll take *that* as my reward.

Other than this group, there was only one other patron, a solitary drinker near the dark end of the bar, brooding over his beer and a cigarette under an amber Bass Ale sign. He looked like one of the local woodchucks: gray beard, flannel shirt, red suspenders. He paid no attention to us and I paid no attention to him. He could nurse his drink while I worked the ladies. *De gustibus non est disputandum.* The lounge itself was nice enough: dark and woody with a horseshoe-shaped bar canopied by a wooden rack of cocktail glasses waiting to be called to duty. The bartender would reach up for the appropriate glass when the time came to make a drink as if he were sliding an arrow from its quiver.

Leo and I settled in with our drinks, just two empty barstools away from the laughing men and women. We decided upon vodka and tonics so as not to overwhelm the ladies with beer breath. We're classy guys, right? We sipped on our drinks and smoked our Marlboros and casually let our eyes drift across to the revelers: two men, three women.

The women were not candidates for the *Sports Illustrated* swimsuit issue, but they were not bad. They could have been nurses or maybe sales representatives for a pharmaceutical company. You know what I mean. They were fashion conscious, but without the resources to do it right by the jet set's standards. Their clothes and shoes were from the better shops, but the better shops at the local mall. And their makeup and hairdos lacked that glow that you see on the trophy wives waiting for their drivers after the opening night at the Metropolitan Opera.

But that probably wouldn't have bothered these gals in the least; they were young and curvy and they knew it, dressed in various combinations of slacks and sweaters and gold necklaces. One in particular caught my eye, dark-haired and fashionably thin in a black sweater and slacks ensemble and with what looked like the results of a recent hairstyling session, all sorts of swirls and razor cut swathes setting off dangling gold earrings just a little too gaudy to be in good taste. I loved it. (So? Don't invite me to your next party.)

She seemed to be enjoying the attention of the men in the group, staring away in exaggerated exasperation every so often to communicate her disdain for one comment or another. But she would turn back confidently with a quick rejoinder to assure them that she was a woman of the world, that she had been around. Loud laughter followed each of her comments, especially from the two other women, who seemed to be enjoying their companion's ability to hold her own with the men in barroom banter. If there is such a thing as an *alpha female*, this gal was one. She was in her element. Donald Trump or Brad Pitt probably wouldn't send the limousine for her, but she was the queen bee in this hive.

"Listen to the one in the black sweater, Frankie," Leo half-whispered while tapping on the bar and motioning for two more vodka and tonics. "She thinks she's hot."

"Me, too," I answered.

"Hell, no one is as hot as she thinks she is."

"Yeah, and by closing time you'll be offering her your pension for an hour in the sack."

"That's true." Leo nodded pensively as if I had asked him about Federal Reserve policy. "But you never accused me of being picky at closing time before." He looked up with a slight grin. "But she's the type that won't give me a tumble until I get her drunker than she is. I need you to warm her up. You're more her type. Why don't you turn on the society boy charm?"

"How do you know one of those guys she is with isn't her husband?" I said while rubbing the lemon peel around the edge of my drink.

"Come on, we have a couple of hours to find that out," Leo shot back with an air of feigned disappointment. "But I don't think they are. She's enjoying their company too much." He smirked a bit at the depths of his observation. "Right? But, look, I don't want you to walk over and give her the key to our room. I'm not uncouth. Just break the ice for me. And if I don't get anywhere with her, the other two ain't bad. I'll let you keep her."

I chuckled into my glass, unsure if he wasn't half-serious. "I don't know about that. I don't think I'm ready to be in one bed while you get over some woman in the next. I can't even picture it. Just thinking about it gives me a clue to what Shakespeare meant by the double-backed beast."

"What kind of beast?"

"Nothing, nothing," I laughed. "Just joking."

"Hell, you read too much," he answered with a dismissive wave of his hand. "Come on, let's join the group. I want to get a closer look at those tomatoes."

The second vodka seemed to have done the trick for Leo. He was confident enough to walk over and introduce himself. I had been rendered superfluous.

"Hey, you folks stranded, too? Some storm, no?" Leo was nodding and smiling in sequence to the three women and two men. "My brother Frankie here and me were heading back to the city and couldn't make it. I'm on the job with the fire department in New York and he's a Wall Street guy, rich as sin."

I shrugged my shoulders in protest. "My brother is exaggerating, folks. My name is Francis Corcoran. I hope you don't think we're being pushy. We are just being sociable."

The two men in the group reacted warmly enough. It was one of those times that you either act like a good sport or get confrontational. They were not ready for confrontation. They were in their forties and getting soft around the middle. I reached across and shook the hand of a man in a tan sweater on the nearest barstool. But he was just a prop. I moved past him and shook the hands of the others in the group, saving the alpha female for last. When I shook her hand I gave her the soulful look that I had relied on from Inwood bars to Morningside Heights coffee shops to East Hampton beach houses. It didn't always work, but it was the best weapon in my arsenal. And it worked often enough.

"Nice to meet you," she answered, biting her lower lip and reaching for her drink, acting as if we had just shared some secret that the rest of the group would be denied.

Was I on first base? Too early to tell. You know how it is: For a lot of women that heavy-lidded first stare is just a way of communicating what they think is a fashionable sophistication. But before I could make another comment, Leo was making a move around my shoulder, positioning himself next to her while he ordered a round of drinks for his newfound friends. The game was afoot.

Which was OK by me. I could sit back for a while and watch Leo play the working class hero who had the skinny on everything from who killed John Kennedy to oil companies who faked the whole energy crisis to the Freemasons who ran the Vatican. He didn't know anything about these things, of course, beyond a rapid-fire blurb meant to indicate that the mass of mankind was in error on the topic. But that didn't matter. He didn't care about any of it. It was barroom banter, in the same category as match tricks, meant only to make him the center of attention and to draw women into his orbit. "Get them laughing. Get them talking. Rolling in the hay comes later," was his way of describing his *modus operandi*.

Everything went as planned. The little group became a model of saloon *bonhomie*, a slightly tipsy, giddy, wisecracking collection of strangers in the night. Loud laughter accompanied Leo's little routine: an imitation of Shirley Temple's buck-and-wing, Jimmy Cagney's death oration in *White Heat*, a few Monica Lewinsky jokes.

From the bar's windows I could see the snow continuing to pile up in the hotel's parking lot. It was a pretty sight. The woodchuck with the beard and the suspenders three stools down seemed to like the sight of the snow, too. He ordered another beer and shifted his barstool to get a better angle to watch it swirl. Leo's booming laughter and tall tales seemed of no interest to him.

The alpha female was enjoying Leo though. She liked being his foil. "That's crazy," she would say. "No way." "Baloney." "Don't go there . . ." (She used the last quip repeatedly. Who started that one? Dr. Laura?) Leo wasn't insulted. It didn't matter whether she agreed with him or not. As long as she was laughing and talking to him, everything was on track. He was making his move. *Tah-dah.*

It turned out that the three women were high school teachers from the area. They had been at an educational conference at Vassar College, just a few miles up the road, and were on their way home when the storm became too dangerous for them to continue. Like us, they had used the motel as an emergency stop for the night. They had called their husbands and explained their predicament and the hubbies agreed that staying over was the best option. The two men sitting with them were salesmen staying at the hotel for a few nights while seeing clients in the area. Not exactly in the same league with the group in the *Canterbury Tales*, but good enough for the task at hand.

Did the fact that the women were married make any difference to anyone? None. The small talk started out innocently enough. Nothing out of line. Then, lubricated by the hooch, it moved forward to the level of suggestive double-meanings. And now it was traversing into some outright flirtation. Leo sensed the progression. I could tell he was bristling with anticipation of what was to come.

Me too. The alpha female with the gold earrings was getting better looking by the minute. Things were getting interesting. I couldn't keep my eyes off the spot where her rear end bunched up against the vinyl of the barstool. Black slacks were never filled better.

Then Leo ruined it all . . . *in an instant.*

"Of course when you get an abortion you kill a baby," he blurted out. "What the hell else is it?"

I never found out how abortion came up. In fact, I never knew that Leo had any feelings about the fate of the unborn. And he probably doesn't. But once he got rolling he dragged out every argument that the Catholic pro-lifers use to demonstrate the humanity of the fetus. He was in rare form, describing at what month of a pregnancy the fetus begins to move, when its heart beats, when it feels pain, when its fingernails sprout. I guess he thought he was impressing the gals with how quick he was on his feet; with the fact that he was an independent thinker.

Wrong. Very wrong. The women turned on him like barracudas. They were social studies teachers, and they had the feminist line on abortion down pat. Leo went from being an engaging saloon raconteur to something lower than a garden slug. Maybe if he had cut his comments short, they would have cut him some slack, but when he went on and on and on . . . it was over. And, of course, I was destroyed in the process, too; guilty by association. I would sleep alone. (I agree with him that the fetus is a human life, but, hell, I know it is unwise to bring it up to a feminist when you're hitting on her. Come on!)

Such is life. The conversation soured quickly. When he realized what was happening, Leo tried to undo the damage by buying a few more drinks, but it was too late. The spell was broken. He got the cold shoulder and a lukewarm goodnight as the women turned to leave. When they left, the two salesmen gulped down their drinks and left as well. They were angry with Leo, too—you could tell—but said nothing. Apparently they had had some high hopes as well, which sank in the wake of Leo's polemic. The room grew heavy with silence.

"You want another drink, Leo?" I asked, trying to lift the somber mood that had now overtaken him.

"Damn, Frankie, I didn't know they would get that angry. It was just talk. What the hell did I say?"

"Forget it. It's late anyway. Besides, they were married. They were probably going to go to their rooms about now anyway."

"Yeah, maybe. But I thought it might be with me draped around that one with the big earrings."

"Nah, she was just a tease," I said with shrug. "She knew what she was doing. It was all just bar talk."

It was then that I heard the muffled laughter from the woodchuck with the suspenders in the corner of the bar. Apparently he and the bartender had gotten a kick out of the scene they had just witnessed. The bartender looked up and saw that I had noticed them. He walked over to us, still smiling. He was a short, roly-poly fellow in a white shirt and black bow tie, with strands of once-blond hair plastered down across his head.

"Hey, hey, fellows, calm down. No offense. You want another drink?" he said good-naturedly. "You might need something to soothe the pain after getting shot down like that. You looked pretty close to getting some tail."

"This is a new one for me," the woodchuck added. He lowered his head and laughed into his beer. "This beats all. Extraordinary. What is your Cardinal going to say? I wish I had that dialogue on tape. What are you two? Right-to-Lifers out for a night of drinking and whoring?" He shook his head and laughed again as my brother and I stared at our shoes.

Chapter Four

I looked across at the woodchuck. He was smiling in a friendly way. He meant no harm. No reason to get all upset. Hell, I agreed with him. It must have been a funny scene to watch.

The woodchuck spoke again: "I don't meant to be rude. But *are* you two pro-life people? I'm serious."

"No, we're on our way from the Nocturnal Adoration Society," I answered. The Nocturnal Adoration Society was a Catholic men's group you don't hear about much anymore, but they used to arrange for their members to pray for an hour each, in a night-long vigil in front of the altar and the Blessed Sacrament—the exposed Communion Host—in Catholic churches once a month or so. My father was a member when we were kids. I filled in for him a couple of times. I don't know why I brought them up. It was just my usual way of trying to get one-up on a barroom smart-aleck. I had no idea if the woodchuck would even know what I was talking about.

It turned out that he did.

"No you are not. There is no chapter around here anymore."

"How do you know?" I responded.

"I know." He waved as he turned back to his beer, signaling that he had no desire to keep the conversation going.

Which was fine with me.

I turned to Leo while downing the remains of my vodka. "Come on, Leo, finish your drink. We've got to get some sleep. They might have the roads plowed pretty early. Even if they don't, I have to be up early to call work to tell them I'm not coming in tomorrow."

"No, not yet, one more, Frankie. Just one," Leo answered, tapping the bar with his forefinger to get the bartender's attention. "I've got to cool down a bit or else I'll start banging on the door of those babes to let me in."

"OK, it's on me," the bartender said. He had moved into his tip-optimizing mode. "But just one more, guys. I know it's only eleven o'clock, but that's some damn storm out there. I live nearby, but I'd like to close up and hit the road."

"OK, OK, just one more, one more," said Leo, pointing energetically to our glasses. "Then we'll go. You got my word. Give the smart-ass at the end of the bar another beer too, on me."

"Smart-ass yourself," the woodchuck shot back, barely raising his eyes from his cigarette. "But I will take another. I'll worry about who bought it for me when I sober up tomorrow. You can call me a smart-ass if you want, but I'm not the one who drove away the women by spouting all that Catholic claptrap."

For the first time I took note of the fact that there would be a considerable amount of sobering up to do for this character. His head was bobbing a bit and he had lit a second cigarette while the previous one sat at almost full length on the ashtray.

"Whaddya mean, claptrap?" Leo shot back. "You don't think that it's a kid inside a woman when she's pregnant? Then what is it?"

"Leo, come on," I pleaded. "Let's talk about something else— the Knicks, the old Dodgers, UFOs—anything."

"Hey, Frankie, give me a break. Dammit, you're the one who convinced me that it's got to be a kid. Don't you believe that anymore?"

"I don't remember telling you that, but I don't care what it is. They can do what they want." I didn't really mean that, but I did mean that I didn't want to talk about it. I was tired of this stuff. I had listened to Baby Boomer and Generation X women talk about abortion rights for years now. There was no way anyone was going

36

to change their minds. They want abortion available to them-selves—just in case. Even the ones who say they are opposed to abortion want that, if you ask me. Nothing and no one is going to tell them otherwise. I believe the fetus is an unborn child. I think they do, too, but they don't want their lives ruined by an unwanted pregnancy and they vote and that is the end of the story. Period. *No mas.* Life goes on.

"I don't care, either," Leo added emphatically, "if by that you mean I lose any damn sleep over it. But don't tell me it ain't a baby. Those broads knew that. That's why they got so riled up at what I was saying."

"When is it a baby?" the woodchuck cut in. "At two months, six months? When?"

"Sure as hell at nine months and they abort them that late," Leo responded.

The woodchuck slid across three barstools with the same thrust and lift that people use when sliding down the pew at church. He ended up on the stool right next to us. He emitted a wet smell, like a rain-soaked dog.

"What about at three months? Would you allow it at three months?" he asked. The drink was causing him to have a hard time with some of his consonants, but he was still able to speak coherently.

"Maybe I would allow it at two or three months," said Leo. "I seen the pictures of what it looks like then. It might not be a real kid that early."

"Your precious church does not allow it even then," the wood-chuck answered. "And you were haranguing those women a while back about all the things that occur at two and three months into a pregnancy—heartbeats and fingers, all the rest. Do you believe all that or not?" He drew heavily on his cigarette in two emphatic bursts, as if it were an old war movie and the sergeant was about to put out the smoking lamp.

"What do you mean *our* church?" I said. "My brother and I never said we were priests or theologians or anything."

"Then don't embarrass yourselves with your barroom homi-lies," said the woodchuck. "Look what good it did you. You chased off the fair damsels with all that Catholic mumbo-jumbo. My name is Carey, by the way. Desmond Carey." He reached out to shake our hands.

His hand was not what I expected. With the flannel shirt and suspenders, I thought he might be a manual laborer of some kind, maybe a landscaper or a member of a town road crew. But his hands were long and soft, the kind that never did anything heavier than lift a teacup.

"I'm Frankie Corcoran. And this is my brother Leo," I said. "And I don't think it's mumbo-jumbo, by the way. Not all of it." I was less worried about the Catholic Church's reputation than mine.

"You don't? Come on, you two don't make sense," said Desmond Carey, the woodchuck. "Look at yourselves. You are drinking to excess and you just tried to seduce some married women. What would your Holy Mother the Church tell you about that? You tell those women it's immoral to get an abortion, but you think it is all right to have sex with them and perhaps get them pregnant. That's smart."

"Hey, we don't think it's all right to sleep with married women," Leo insisted. "Who said that? We do it, but we know it's wrong." He laughed in a self-congratulatory burst. "The church is right about sleeping around. Just because I can't live up to the rules don't make the rules stupid."

"Oh, my God," Desmond Carey answered, shaking his head in despair. "You are one of *them*."

"Them?" I said, genuinely puzzled.

"Yeah, what's a them?" added Leo.

"You're Catholic school robots," responded Carey. "Brainwashed imbeciles, still repeating the little slogans some ignorant nun without a high school education taught you. What college did you go to?"

"We didn't go to college. Didn't need it," I replied quickly, as if I had just caught him in an error.

"What high schools, then?" Carey responded confidently. "I know your type. Somebody taught you these Catholic word games."

"We went to school in Manhattan; my brother to La Salle down near the East Village. I went to Regis up by Central Park."

The change that came over Desmond Carey was immediate and unmistakable. Something about the names of our high schools unnerved him. He exhaled heavily and looked down at his beer. "Regis . . . my God, Regis—the worst of the worst, damned Jesuit automaton, smart-ass with all the answers and not a bit of common sense. You poor fool. You realize of course that are going to go through life scarred by all that insanity."

"Don't worry about that. I didn't pay much attention to the Jebbies when I was there," I assured him. "What do you know about Regis, anyway?"

"Too damned much. I used to teach there. I used to be a Jesuit."

"Cut the crap," I said with a half-grin. I thought this was the lead in to a joke. I was waiting for the punch line.

"He was," the bartender assured me. He was leaning over the bar now, apparently enjoying the conversation. "Father Desmond Carey, onetime priest, full-time drunk." He patted Carey on the shoulder to assure him he meant no harm. "He used to teach in the seminary just five or so miles up the road, before he saw the light."

"What seminary?" I asked. Considering what my mother was like, and all the religious magazines we used to get at our house, I thought I would know if there was a Catholic seminary somewhere near here.

"Yeah, what seminary?" Leo added for moral support. "The seminary is down in Yonkers, Dunwoodie. There's no goddam seminary near here."

"Used to be," said the bartender. "It's a school for chefs now, the Culinary Institute of America, straight up from here on Route 9 in Hyde Park, famous place. But before that, this guy used to teach there." He patted Carey's shoulder again. "They trained priests there. I'm telling you the truth."

"When were you at Regis, Corcoran?" Desmond Carey asked with a tinge of sadness in his eyes. You could tell that he was not sure this was a topic he wanted to pursue.

"I graduated in 1982."

"It was closed by then," said Carey.

"What was closed by then?"

"The Jesuit seminary, St. Andrew's on the Hudson. We closed the building in the early 1970s and sold it to the Culinary Institute."

"Who's *we*?"

"I told you. I was a Jesuit priest. I taught philosophy at St. Andrew's."

"I don't believe it," said Leo emphatically.

"I don't care if you do or not," Carey answered. "My God— what's the difference? It was more than twenty years ago when I left the Jesuits. I've been teaching courses at community colleges and at Catholic high schools around here ever since then and been a clerk in a Barnes and Noble bookstore and now I am enjoying spending my Social Security money on beer and cigarettes. Who cares what you think? I think I'll bid you gentlemen adieu."

Carey rose to reach for his coat, which had been slung across a nearby barstool. He slid straight to the floor as if someone dropped him down a coal chute. He sat there like laundry from a cut clothesline.

"Oh, my God, he's drunker than I thought," exclaimed the bartender. He reached across the bar to hold up Carey's head. "Help me out here, fellows."

Leo and I tried to give him a hand. We reached down to steady Carey's shoulders. His flannel shirt felt damp and greasy, as if it had not seen a dry cleaner's in quite a while. I was not sure if it was the shirt or Carey's matted gray hair that was the source of the wet dog smell.

"Where does this guy live?" I asked the bartender. "He can't drive. That's for sure."

"Not far. Usually I call a cab for him when he's as drunk as this. But there won't be no cabs coming out tonight," said the bartender. "Look at that snow. I'd drive him myself, but my tires are bald and there's a big hill up to his apartment."

"I'll walk," Carey muttered over his shoulder. "Just get me up. I'll walk." He reached up for the bar rail and hoisted himself like a boxer rising for the eight-count, on one knee first, then all the way up. He leaned his back against the bar and took a deep breath and then began walking toward the door.

He was bobbing and weaving slightly, but there was little chance that he would fall again. Leo and I walked alongside him anyway, like farmers escorting a newly birthed calf. He was OK, until he got to the front door of the bar. When he opened it, a blast of icy air and swirling snow poured over us. You couldn't see more than a few feet over the mounds of snow building on the decorative shrubs separating the parking lot from the motel walkway. A plow was moving across the parking lot thrusting up even more snow, criss-crossing the overhead lights with its headlight beams. Desmond Carey staggered backwards as if he had been hit by a heavy ocean wave.

"Desmond, my boy, you ain't gonna make it nowhere walking through all that snow," said Leo. "No way."

"Can you guys give me a lift?" Carey asked near-plaintively, suddenly aware of his predicament. Drunk or not, he knew he could not walk into the storm.

"Hey, really, I'm sorry," I answered. "We would like to help. Really. But the reason we're staying in this place is because our car couldn't handle the snow. No way we can make it to where you live and back. We don't know the roads around here."

"Damn it," blurted the bartender. "What the hell am I gonna do now? I got to get outta here before I get snowed in, too, but I can't leave old Des staggering around in the snow."

I looked at Leo. He shook his head and laughed. He knew what I had in mind.

"OK, Frankie the altar boy, OK," Leo muttered, pretending to be more annoyed than he was. "Go ahead."

"How about if we let him sleep in our room?" I suggested to the bartender. "No one would know. We'll let him sleep it off on the floor. Tomorrow morning when he sobers up and the roads are plowed, he can drive home."

The bartender looked toward the hall leading to the front desk, then at us.

"I'm screwed if anybody finds out," he said furtively.

"Who the hell is going to tell? My brother and me are the only ones who are being inconvenienced. And we can take a guest into our room if we want. Right? What's the big deal?"

"I guess," the bartender responded with an air of relief. "What about you, Desmond? You OK sleeping on the floor for the night with these guys? They look as if they won't make a pass at you."

Carey nodded. "I'd be grateful to them. I really would. I drank more than I realized."

"Let's go then," said Leo. "You want us to hold your arms up or can you walk to the elevator on your own?"

"I can walk." Desmond Carey nodded twice as if he had just deciphered one of mankind's great mysteries. "I can walk."

And he could—as long as we moved slowly and moved breakable items out of his path. We walked through the door leading from the bar to the hallway and down the carpeted hall toward the elevator that would take us to our room on the second floor. Inside the elevator, Carey leaned his head back against the stainless steel wall of the cab and breathed heavily, patting his pockets for his cigarettes. He found a crumpled pack in his shirt pocket with about five or six butts remaining. He smiled at the remaining cigarettes like a father pointing out his first born through the nursery window. "I got enough for the night" His world was complete. "Too bad we don't have a pint of Jim Beam."

"Jim Beam?" I frowned. "I'd say you've had enough for the evening."

Carey lowered his head into his flannel shirt and emitted a mixture of laughter and phlegm-rattling cough. "You're the Regis boy, right? You Irish Catholics are too much—boozy whoremasters hell-bent to save the world from its sins. But it could be worse. Probably you would be true degenerates without that phony church scaring the hell out of you. I guess it is better to be intimidated into civility by a myth than to end up living like Charles Manson. You poor imbeciles."

"Poor imbeciles?" Leo leaned across and stared him in the eye, pretending to be angry. "That's the second time you called us imbeciles. You shouldn't talk like that to the guys who saved you from being found tomorrow propped against a light pole frozen stiff like one of those prehistoric mastiffs they dig out of the ice in Alaska."

"Mastiffs?" Carey laughed. "Do you mean mammoths?"

"Whatever," Leo shrugged.

"But you're right," said Carey. "Good manners cost us nothing. I bet the nuns told you that, too. It just rubs me the wrong way when I see people living their lives worrying about your Jesus and your church, when it's all a fairy tale."

"Says you," Leo answered.

"Says me," said Carey. "But I know what I am talking about."

We set up two pillows and a bedspread on one of the room's chairs for Carey. Then I headed for the shower. I was all for being charitable, but I had no intention of giving him one of the beds. He was old, but not so old that he couldn't survive a night on a chair, or on the floor if he preferred. There are limits to my good will. I figured Desmond Carey would be snuggled in his bedspread, dead-to-the-world when I came out of the shower.

Wrong. He was holding court. My brother was the audience.

"Frankie, come here, come here, listen to this, listen to this—listen to what old Des has to say." Leo was perched on the edge of his bed. Desmond Carey was leaning back in one of the room's red leather chairs like the Buddha, smoking, wrapped up in the red and white diamond-patterned bedspread, his feet, still in their wet wool socks, propped up on the hot air vents from the window heater unit. He seemed to have sobered up a bit.

"OK, what's he got to say?" I asked, rubbing my hair with a towel.

"Tell him, Des. Tell him what you know."

"I've said too much already," said Carey. "I sometimes talk too much when I drink. Perhaps I should get some sleep," Carey answered, pulling the bedspread further up around his shoulders.

"Frankie, you know why he thinks the Catholic Church is all wet? Remember what he said?" Leo said excitedly. "Because he knows it is all a con job, a two-hundred-century-long con job. He knows that. He can prove it. He's got the goods."

"Yeah, yeah, I'll bet. How does he know that?"

"I'll tell you how," said Leo. "He knows where Jesus' body is; that he never rose from the dead; that some of his followers faked it all just to get people to follow them. The first Apostles were hucksters, Frankie, con-men."

"Please, I never said that, not that," Carey muttered. "Some of the disciples believed that he was the Messiah, the Son of God. But there were others who didn't think their contemporaries would believe it unless they invented something magical about Jesus' death. They thought they were doing something admirable—helping people believe in Jesus who wouldn't believe in him otherwise."

"OK, OK, great. I'm going to hit the sack. You guys mind if I put out the lights and get some sleep?" I answered as calmly as if they had just told me the scores of the Knicks' game.

"Frankie, didn't you hear him? Do you know what this guy is saying?" Leo demanded.

"Come on, there are more stories like that than about where Elvis is hiding. It's old hat. Guys have written books about it, about Passover plots and conspiracies and first century mystery cults for centuries."

"And they come pretty close to the truth, Mr. Corcoran," Carey assured me from inside the folds of the bedspread. "Especially David Friedrich Strauss."

"Says you."

"Says I."

"Frankie, will you listen to him," Leo argued. "He says he can prove it."

"You used to believe the guy who said there was a sea serpent in Lake Champlain," I replied. "He said he could prove that, too. Come on, let's get some sleep."

"Tell him, Desmond," implored Leo. "Tell him what that priest—whaddya call him? Tie-hartz?—found out."

Desmond Carey looked up at me from the bedspread like a turtle peeping out of its shell. "You're the Regis boy, no?"

"I'm the Regis boy," I answered with an air of resignation. Apparently I would have to hear this story before I got some sleep.

"Then you have heard of Teilhard de Chardin."

"Vaguely."

"What do you know?"

"Oh, man, do I have to do this?" I said.

"Not to make me happy," said Carey. "I've already said more than I should. Good night." He scrunched down into the bedspread.

"Come on, Desmond, tell my brother," Leo implored. "Tell him the story."

Carey peeked up from his bedspread again. "I asked you what you know about Teilhard."

I sighed. "I know he was some French Jebbie that got in trouble for his theories back in the 1940s and '50s."

"What did he say that was so objectionable?" said Carey. "Do you know the basics?"

"Not really," I answered.

"I'll simplify for you," said Carey.

"Oh, thanks," I replied.

"I did not say that you are dumb, Corcoran. You probably have made more money on Wall Street this year than I've made in my whole life. It is just that you have no background in this area."

"OK, go ahead."

"Teilhard's theory was that evolution was a fact of life, that the world we know was shaped by the evolutionary process, pretty much as Darwin described. But here's the key: what he also said is that evolution is now in the stage where humanity has the responsibility of carrying the process forward. We are conscious beings. The world of the future will be what we humans make it. In other words, evolution is now under human control, our control. So it is the task of Christians to take Christ's message of love and human solidarity and use it to remake the world, to Christify it, create a communion of all mankind, what Teilhard called a Christogenesis."

"OK," I nodded. "Big deal. I can remember the Jesuits spouting that stuff to me when I was at Regis, all that jive about remaking all things in Christ."

"Then, Mr. Corcoran, why did the Church condemn his theories? They did, you know. They ordered him to stop teaching." Carey pushed back a wet strand of gray hair across his forehead. "Well?" His eyes half-closed and he nodded drowsily.

45

"What is this, a surprise quiz?" I answered impatiently. "You going to give me a gold star if I get it right? I don't know why."

"Because Church authorities believed he was preaching a fully secularized Christianity, a world without a risen Christ—no heaven, no hell, no angels, no saints, no Jesus and Mary floating up on the clouds. This world, the material world perfected by human love and human creativity was the only heaven mankind would ever know. When that perfection was realized, when mankind succeeded in creating a world remade by human creativity and love, that would be what the Church calls the *Parousia*, the Second Coming of Christ. Teilhard called it the 'Omega Point.' Christ's love would 'come to life' again at that time, if you will. Someone once described it as the 'final triumph of the divine love revealed in Christ.' The authorities accused Teilhard of being a materialist, an empiricist, of believing that the physical world we perceive with our senses is the only reality. Some even accused him of being a Marxist."

"And, I know, I know . . ." I answered, ready to pin him to the wall. I knew these goddam Jebbies. "The bishops and pope and everyone thought that because they were too dense to appreciate another Jesuit genius, right? They couldn't grasp his deeper understanding of what Jesus was all about?"

"That's what his supporters alleged," Carey replied. "They launched a public relations effort to save Teilhard, to make him into a misunderstood spiritual giant, a man of God trying to express the Christian faith in a vocabulary suitable for intelligent modern men and women. But, ironically . . ."—Carey leaned across and looked me right in the eye with a mischievous twinkle—"the silly old Bronx priests and their spinster spear carriers were right. Teilhard was describing a world without the risen Christ. He knew there was no risen Christ. You see, he knew where the body was buried." He winked and pulled the bedspread up around his face. "And now, if you will excuse me, my good men, I will take your leave."

Desmond Carey closed his eyes, this time determined to close the conversation for good.

"Frankie, did you hear him?" Leo asked.

"I heard it."

"Well?"

"What can I say? Let's get some sleep, too. He's not going to say anymore tonight anyway. He thinks he's left us breathless." I cupped my hand and stage-whispered across the room to Carey inside his blanket: "Right, Desmond?"

"You are right, my good man," he stage-whispered back.

"What if he's right?" Leo continued.

"What if he is? What difference would it make to you? You drink and screw around as much as you want when you think Jesus is watching you. If he isn't, you can do it all without worrying about burning in hell. You should love it."

"Smart-ass."

"See you in the morning."

Chapter Five

The morning was a pleasant surprise—clear and sunny, believe it or not. The storm had left a blanket of snow on everything in sight, but not a trace of its presence in the morning sky. I got up earlier than Leo and Desmond Carey, at about six-thirty, to go to the lobby. I didn't want to wake up the sleeping beauties when I called in to leave a message on my boss's tape, letting him know I wouldn't be able to get to work. He'd rant and rail a bit, but I hardly ever took a day off from work. I was a Puritan in that regard, if in few others. Besides, all would be well in a day or two, after I racked up some big sales on the floor of the Exchange.

Leo and Carey were still sleeping when I got back to the room. I parted the curtain slightly to watch the orange plows moving across the roads outside the hotel, cutting wet blacktop channels for the morning traffic, which was heavier than I thought it would be. The kids who were hoping for a day off because of the snow were going to be disappointed.

I walked quietly to the bathroom to shave. When I returned, Leo and Carey were up, looking at the morning news on CNN, both wrapped in their blankets like roadside Indians in a Gene Autry movie. Talk about unlikely scenarios.

"I guess things worked out OK," I said. "You two slept like babies, except for the snoring. It sounded like an outboard motor shop in here."

"Mr. Corcoran, permit me to thank you once again for your kindness." Carey spoke quietly, half-bowing in a near-formal way. He had sobered up and was clearly embarrassed by his situation. "I do not do things like this. Forgive me."

He was a different man. He carried himself with the demeanor of an elderly librarian.

"It looks like you'll be able to drive home OK," I answered quickly in an effort to change the topic. I hate to see a grown man grovel. Most of the time.

"They're plowing out there. You should have no trouble getting your car on the road."

"I'm sure, I'm sure," Carey answered. "If you will just let me use your bathroom to clean up a bit, I'll be out of your way."

"Hey, Frankie," Leo interjected, "Old Des here don't want to talk about last night. I've been trying to get him to talk some more about that French priest he told us about. But he's clammed up."

"Mr. Corcoran," said Carey quietly, "I've been trying to tell your brother that I said more than I should have last night. I drank too much."

"I know. I've done the same, many a time," I said diplomatically. "My brother and I have been listening to bar talk all our lives. We all say dumb things once in a while."

"What I said was not dumb. It was the truth, Corcoran. It is just that I should not have told you about it. There is a difference."

"Come on, you're telling me you know where Jesus is buried? Give me a break."

"No, that is not what I said," Carey bristled. "I never said that I was the one who knew. I said that Teilhard de Chardin knew where the body was buried."

"And he told you? Why you?" I asked.

"Not me personally. But he told quite a few fellow-Jesuits, who told me. I know about fifty Jesuits who know. No doubt there are more."

"Why are you telling us, my brother and me?"

"I shouldn't have. But I did last night. My mistake. I can't unring the bell. But no one will believe you if you tell them, so I am not worried about that. It is just that I do not appreciate being treated like the village idiot."

"But you said you could prove what you are saying. Were you serious?" Leo asked.

"How is he going to do that?" I quipped. "Do you think he has some videotapes he can sell us?"

"You really do have quite a bit of Regis in you, Corcoran," said Carey. "You think you have all the answers."

"Come on, Carey, relax," I answered. "I don't want to pick a fight. Clean up and we'll make sure your car starts and we'll be on our way. Let's be friends."

"You don't believe me about Teilhard?"

"I don't believe you about Teilhard."

"You can be quite insufferable."

"Oh, boy, maybe you were a Jebbie," I responded. "You think you can twist words into whatever you want them to be. Look: I am not arguing with you. Relax, big fella. You can believe whatever you want. No big deal. I don't care."

"But you think that I am a deluded old man."

"Oh, man, I don't care," I said, placing my shaving kit back into my suitcase.

"I can prove it," Carey said calmly. "But it is a long story. Why don't you follow me to my apartment and I will tell you things that will change your life. I'll make breakfast for you and your brother and we'll talk, if you are interested. How does that sound to you?"

"Let's take him up on the offer," said Leo. "Des says he can prove it. Let's hear his story."

"What? You want to do that? Have breakfast with Father Desmond here?" I asked in disbelief. "That doesn't sound like you. You want to sit and drink coffee and talk about Jesuit theologians."

"What the hell . . . why not? We got all day. Hey, Desmond, you make good eggs and coffee?"

Carey answered without a pause: "If do, if I must say so myself."

Well, to make a long story short, we decided to go to Desmond Carey's apartment for eggs and coffee and the inside scoop on his Jesus conspiracy story. I came to the conclusion that Carey was a lonely old man who was not used to having an audience like Leo and me. Nothing wrong with humoring him. We were not the sharpest knives in the drawer on theological questions, but at least we knew what he was talking about. I imagine that most of the people he came across in the Dutchess County bars where he hung out would think he was talking about some new imported wine if he mentioned Teilhard de Chardin. At least I had heard the name before and could follow what he was saying, for the most part. The fact that I went to a Jesuit high school seemed to make a difference to him. And the way Leo hung on his every word must have made him feel like Mary Higgins Clark at some ladies club luncheon.

So we followed Carey's old Ford Taurus up the road to his apartment. It was located above a garage behind an old white colonial house, down a winding driveway through a thickly wooded area. We got there just as the plowing service was leaving. We parked next to the pile of snow that the plow had pushed up against the side of the garage. You got to Carey's apartment by walking up a rickety old wooden stairway bolted to the side of the garage. We had to push the snow out of the way with a swipe of our feet as we climbed the stairs.

But it turned out that the apartment was not bad, warm and neat, with knotty-pine paneling and a wide-planked wooden floor. Carey must have had a thing about Indians—oh, I'm sorry, Native Americans. The walls were covered with what looked like Navaho blankets and pictures of Indian men and women staring into the desert sun. Georgia O'Keeffe would have liked it. (I think. What do I know?) It was cozy. Leo and I sat on worn and lumpy old chairs that almost swallowed you whole, something in the twentieth-century Salvation Army thrift shop genre. The heat poured down on us from an overhead blower that had obviously been added to the room when the landlord decided to turn the area above his garage into an entrepreneurial venture.

And the eggs and home fries were good. So was the coffee. Carey served us first and then joined us, sitting with a plate of eggs and fried potatoes perched on his knee.

"Where should I begin?" Carey asked, sipping his coffee from a mug shaped like a dwarf's head. He seemed to be enjoying his new role of wise village elder.

I let my eyes roam the bookcase behind his chair. It was little more than pine planks, painted white and nailed together. But it was neatly done, obviously the work of a trained carpenter; and large, covering the entire wall. You could track the history of Carey's life in the sequence of titles. It confirmed for me that he actually had been a Jesuit. There were some books from his loyal Jebbie days—Frederick Copleston's *History of Philosophy*, a copy of Bernard Lonergan's *Insight*, T. S. Eliot's *The Idea of a Christian Society*. Some from what you could call his transition period—two or three of Teilhard's books, one by Dorothy Day, a copy of Michael Harrington's *The Other America*. Then a few samples of his current alienation from all things Catholic—*Liberation Theology* by Gustavo Gutierrez, something by Alan Dershowitz, Hillary Clinton's *It Takes a Village*, books generally reflecting the views of those who seek to use the power of government rather than prayer to remake the world.

"You know, Desmond, you can skip a lot of the details with us," Leo volunteered. "Just tell us about how this priest found the body, and how he knew it was Jesus—that kind of thing."

"Is this what they call *cutting to the chase*?" Carey chided. "So be it." He sipped his coffee. "Do you two know anything about the Dead Sea Scrolls?"

"Not me," said Leo.

"A little," I said. "They were old versions of the Bible, found in Israel in a cave somewhere."

"Close enough," said Carey. "They were found in Israel in the late 1940s in a place called Qumran, near the Dead Sea." He picked a bit at his eggs and potatoes, took a few bites, and said, "Do you know *why* they aroused so much interest?"

"Nope," said I.

"Me neither," said Leo.

"The old parchments were accounts of an ancient Jewish sect called the Essenes. Many scholars believe that Jesus was a member of this sect. Some speculated that they would provide information about how Jesus developed his understanding of his religious mission—that perhaps we would discover something that would indicate whether Jesus really thought he was the Son of God or whether that notion was invented by the writers of the Gospels."

Carey paused, and stared at us, clearly for dramatic effect. "There were some who believed that the scrolls would indicate that Jesus was selected by the Essene leadership to make the claim that he was the Messiah in order to build the sect's following among the Israelite people; that he did not believe he was divine until that moment."

"Which would mean that he wasn't divine," I interrupted.

"Precisely," said Carey.

"But the scrolls didn't show that. If they did, we would all know about it. It would have been headline news," I said.

"The scrolls we know about do not show that. The scrolls that have been hidden from us are something else again," said Carey calmly. "I am referring to the scrolls that Teilhard de Chardin discovered and hid."

"This is getting good," said Leo, leaning forward. You would never guess that Carey was talking about something that would make Leo's entire system of religious belief an outright sham. Leo acted as if he were hearing nothing more than another hot revelation about the love life of Princess Diana. "How does this Tie-hard get mixed up in the story?" he asked.

"Until the time of the Dead Sea scroll discovery," Carey continued, "Teilhard was a largely obscure French Jesuit doing archaeological research in China and the Gobi desert. He was known within the Jesuit order for his speculative philosophical works on evolution—*The Phenomenon of Man* and *The Divine Milieu*—but few outside the order knew anything about him. He wrote these books in the 1920s and 1930s, but was forbidden to publish them . . . for all the reasons we discussed last night. If you remember, there were those who thought Teilhard was describing a world without the transcendent, without a personal God and a risen Christ. Well, whether or not Teilhard was suggesting such a thing back in the 1930s can be debated. But he certainly was after he discovered

Jesus' body. That is the point. He began to preach a Christianity that was entirely horizontal in perspective, a Pantheism one might say, a religion without an afterlife and a spiritual dimension beyond the world of the senses."

Leo finished the last scrap of his eggs and placed his plate on the floor. "How did he get to see these Dead Sea Scrolls?"

"I was just about to get to that," Carey continued with a studied, patient smile. "Teilhard had returned to France from China in 1946. He had not been able to leave China until then, and had been a virtual prisoner in China during the World War II years, the Japanese occupation. He was over sixty-years-of-age by the time he returned to France, but still at the peak of his powers intellectually. He was respected for his archaeological expertise. When the Dead Sea scrolls were discovered, he was secretly sent by Church authorities to examine them. Whatever you want to think about Rome and the Jesuits, they recognize who their talented people are, even those they have forced into silence. With a team of Israeli and Protestant scholars, he worked on analyzing the scrolls. But he did so under an alias, so there is no official record of his involvement."

"The people he worked with must have known who he was," I said. "By the 1960s his face was popping up all over American magazines. My high school Jebbies showed me full-page pictures of him from *The Saturday Evening Post*. And once you saw his face, it was hard to forget it. Didn't they say they tried to make Max Von Sydow look like him in *The Exorcist?*"

"Yes, that's true. He was a distinctive-looking man," said Carey. "Quite a character. Do you know that rather than serve as a chaplain in World War I he volunteered to be a stretcher-bearer? The French government gave him a military medal and the Legion of Honor for his bravery. Probably his colleagues at Qumran did recognize him. But so what? They probably considered it some Vatican public relations move—not wanting the rebellious priest to get too much favorable media attention. Unless you know what I know about Teilhard's discoveries, no one would be concerned about whether he was in Israel for a while working on the Dead Sea scrolls. There were many scholars who moved in and out on the project."

"And what did he find out?" I asked.

Carey placed his half-finished plate of eggs on a nearby table, leaned back, and continued: "The team of scholars working on the scrolls was under the supervision of the Israeli government. Qumran is located within Israeli territory, on the northwest bank of the Dead Sea, twenty miles east of Jerusalem. There were Protestant, Catholic, and Jewish scholars on the project. Teilhard was just one of the group. But one day as they were exploring the caves, he came across a dagger, hidden under a large rock near where several of the scrolls were uncovered. It is hard to say what possessed him—what he did was not ethical in professional terms. He should have reported all of his findings to his team leader.

"But he didn't. He slipped the dagger inside his shirt and took it back to his room. He had seen something on the dagger that aroused his interest. You see, it was a Roman soldier's dagger, still in its sheath, with the familiar S.P.Q.R. carved in bronze on one side, the outer side that would be seen by the public if it were worn in the usual place on the hip."

"What does that stand for again?" I asked. The initials rang a bell, but I was not sure.

"*Senatus Populusque Romanus,*" he answered. "The Senate and the People of Rome. It was the official insignia of Rome, appearing on many buildings, official documents, and military guidons, on the escutcheon beneath the familiar decorative Roman eagle. Roman military officers would have it emblazoned on their more formal swords and daggers; some tattooed it on their arms. What was of greater interest, however, was what was carved in smaller letters inside the top edge of the sheath, where it would not likely be seen by anyone but the owner of the knife."

"Which was?" I asked.

"I.N.R.I." Carey paused as if I should fall off my chair. "A Regis boy should know what that stands for."

"It was the sign on Jesus' cross," I answered.

"And it means what?"

"I forget."

"It was what was placed on the cross by the Romans, to mock Jesus and his claim to be the Messiah. I.N.R.I., *Iesus Nazarenus Rex*

Iudaeorum. Jesus of Nazareth, King of the Jews. Teilhard was intrigued, as you may imagine. What, after all, would a Roman soldier be doing with I.N.R.I. carved on his weapon?"

Carey folded his arms and continued: "Well, later that night, back in his apartment, Teilhard examined the dagger in private. The sheath turned out to have a narrow compartment, within which there was a small map marked 'Sepulcrum.' That's Latin for burial place or sepulcher. At first, Teilhard thought the map would be to the site of the Church of the Holy Sepulchre in Jerusalem, the church built over the spot where Christians believe Jesus was interred and where he rose from the dead. What he found was something very different. It was a map to a location on Lake Tiberias, what is sometimes called the Sea of Galilee in the Gospel accounts. It is about fifty or sixty miles north of Jerusalem."

"And he thought—what? That this was where Jesus was buried?" I asked.

"It is not as illogical as you might expect. Jesus was crucified in Jerusalem and interred in Jerusalem. That is where Christians believe he arose from the dead. But the Gospels, Luke and John, especially, tell of him appearing to his disciples, even eating fish with them, on the shores of Lake Tiberias. You may remember the scene. The disciples do not recognize Jesus at first. He is forced to show them his wounds and talk to them of his days as their leader to convince them he is who he says he is. Hasn't that ever struck you as strange? Why wouldn't his followers have recognized him?"

"Got me," I answered. "Tell me, why?"

"I am getting ahead of myself," said Carey. He rubbed his hands across the sleeves of his flannel shirt as if he were seeking warmth from the fabric. "Let us go back to Teilhard and his map. Teilhard decides to check the site indicated on the map. He travels by car with two laborers from Qumran to Lake Tiberias, near the ancient city of Chinneroth."

"And he finds Jesus' tomb," I said.

"He finds Jesus' tomb." Carey paused and raised his eyebrows. "Yes, he finds Jesus' tomb. The map turned out to be what it claimed to be. Now you must keep in mind that what I am telling you now is a second-hand account from Jesuits who were given the details by Teilhard. I was *not* there to hear Teilhard's account myself. But the story goes that the body was buried in a desolate spot, in a grave that Teilhard was able to unearth with the help of his two Arab diggers."

"How did he know it was Jesus who was in the tomb?" I asked.

"There were documents with the body that indicated his identity. I will get to them in due course. Moreover, the bones—encased in a stone casket and preserved surprisingly well by the dry desert heat—bore the markings of once having been broken in exactly those places where you would expect them to be if the body was truly Jesus'. The wrist bones and the bones of the feet showed clear traces of once having been shattered by nails. The bottom rib on the left side had been broken just the way a bone would be if sheared by a driven lance. Teilhard was certain about what he had found."

I still didn't believe any of Carey's story, but I was getting into it anyway, like one of those cable television programs about Atlantis or the Bermuda Triangle.

"Well, as I said," Carey continued, "the map Teilhard found was in Latin. So were the documents he found in the tomb. They explain why the disciples did not recognize the risen Jesus when he appeared to them at these scenes in Galilee. The traditional explanation is that his risen body was different from the earthly body—a glorified body. Not so. Teilhard's explanation—how much from what Teilhard learned from the documents with the body and how much from speculation, I do not know—was that Jesus had changed his appearance, that he had dressed as a Roman, shaved his beard and cut his hair Roman-style, short and combed forward in the manner of Julius Caesar. His disciples had never seen him without his full beard and shoulder-length hair. The change was dramatic. That was why they did not recognize him at first. You see, he was being protected and hidden by wealthy Romans who were associates of Joseph of Arimathea."

"Who?" asked Leo. (*I* would not have had to ask that. I remembered who Joseph of Arimathea was.)

"Joseph of Arimathea was the man who provided the Apostles with the tomb where Jesus was buried in Jerusalem," Carey explained. "The Gospels do not tell us much about him, except that he was a respected member of the Sanhedrin, the Jewish high court. But the fact that he was able to persuade the Roman authorities to permit him to take the body from the cross and arrange for the burial indicates that he was a close associate of influential Romans. That was why the map in the dagger and the documents in the tomb discovered by Teilhard were in Latin. These Romans were the ones who buried Jesus on the shores of Lake Tiberias. The dagger belonged to one of them. Teilhard's theory was that they gave the dagger to someone in the Essenes after Jesus' death because these Romans were aware of his role in the Essene movement. And the person in the Essenes to whom they gave the dagger decided that the map and the dagger should accompany the manuscripts we now call the Dead Sea Scrolls."

"Did these Romans believe Jesus was the Son of God?" I asked. "Were they disciples, too?"

"In a way, in a way. Teilhard's theory was that they believed he was the Son of God the way we all are sons of God when we perfect our humanity, when we live lives selflessly, seeking to transform the world through an unconditional commitment to our fellow men and women. The Roman disciples thought Jesus a brilliant moral teacher, that he had discovered the key for living a good life, to finding peace and meaning in our worldly existence. And, of course, they thought he had been executed unfairly. They were the ones who managed to get the Roman soldiers guarding the cross to take Jesus from the cross before he actually died—Jesus had friendly relations with certain Roman centurions, if you remember—to fake a death report and then move him to Joseph of Arimathea's tomb. They were the ones who bribed the guards stationed at the tomb to allow them to roll back the stone, remove Jesus, and nurse him back to health."

Carey sipped on his coffee and paused, as if pondering whether he should go on. "You know there is a clue in the Gospels about how it was done—in Matthew 27–28."

"I'm listening," I said.

"Read it yourself, if you doubt me. Matthew states flatly that the high priests were on to what happened. They accused Jesus' followers of bribing the Roman soldiers on guard to let them roll back the stone to the tomb so that they could remove the body. It turns out that that was pretty close to the truth.

"The high priests did not think Jesus had survived the Crucifixion, of course. They thought the disciples simply removed the dead body and then hid it so that they could begin spreading the story about a resurrection. They did not know that Jesus was still alive when he was entombed and when he was removed from the tomb. They did not know about the Roman military's involvement."

"And none of the other Gospels mention any of this about bribing the soldiers?" Leo asked.

"No. Not a word," Carey answered. "My guess is that someone thought it would not be wise to plant these seeds of doubt. They made sure the story did not appear in later accounts. Teilhard's story was that Jesus lived out his days in the company of these wealthy Romans, for the most part in the area around Lake Tiberias."

"For how long?" I asked.

"Not that long," Carey said calmly. "The Crucifixion had weakened him severely. He died around 40 A.D. in his disguised Roman identity. His Roman disciples decided that the secluded spot on the shores of Lake Tiberias would be an ideal location to bury him without arousing suspicion. They arranged it all."

"And the guys who wrote the Gospels and Peter and the first Christians knew all this?" Leo asked. "Come on—why would they let themselves get martyred and eaten by the lions in the goddam Coliseum if they knew it was all a hoax?"

"I did not say that! Not all of them had to know. Joseph of Arimathea and the Romans in league with him knew. Who else knew, I can't say. I don't know if Teilhard knew that, either. Remember, I have never seen the documents that Teilhard took from Jesus' tomb."

"But you are convinced anyway that it was Jesus' body that he found?" I asked.

"I am. It is why I left the priesthood," Carey answered without any show of emotion. "It does not matter to me if the first Apostles believed in the Resurrection of Jesus, or not. They may have been sincere—in error, but sincere. Centuries of Christians have believed that Jesus rose from the dead. They were sincere, and many of them intelligent. Sincerity is not the operative word here. The fact of the matter is that Jesus' body is in the ground in northern Israel. That changes everything. Their Christian faith is based on a lie. What is it that St. Paul said? 'If Jesus is not risen, then our faith is in vain?' Well, he is not risen. I have talked to Jesuits who were close associates of Teilhard. Everything I have told you came from them. These men would not lie to me. I sat through many long and sincere discussions with them about what we should do with this information now that we had it. Their priesthood—their very lives—were all changed immeasurably by the information provided to them by Teilhard. They would not have faked such a story. They had nothing to gain."

"You know," Leo cut in, "this sounds like that stupid movie with William Dafoe playing Jesus."

"You are speaking of Kazantzaki's *The Last Temptation of Christ*," Carey said with his lips pursed, as if he were surprised that Leo would have been aware of the movie. "A bit overwrought, but pretty close to the truth in the important things."

"Does every Jesuit believe this?" I asked.

"No, no, please. I told you that already," Carey responded. "Teilhard told people he trusted and people he thought able to deal with the magnitude of the revelation. And the people he told then told a select group after Teilhard's death. I was one of the latter group. Looking back on the priests I met who were apprised of Teilhard's discovery, I would say that those who were let in on the secret were what you might consider 'worldlier' Jesuits, the intelligentsia of the order, if you will, men who were more likely to deal with the truth without becoming hysterical. But they were the leaders of the order. Their task became to redefine the order and the Catholic Church itself, to prepare for the day when the world would discover the truth."

"Hey, Desmond, how about if I take a little more java?" Leo asked.

I laughed inwardly. Leo had changed the topic as calmly as if he had been discussing football scores.

"By all means, by all means," said Carey with a slight bow.

Leo poured the coffee for us and returned the pot to the stove.

"OK, Desmond, let's say I buy what you are saying," Leo said after his first sip of coffee, ". . . why didn't all the Jebbies who got the word leave the priests the way you did?"

"Many of them did," Carey said. "The number of defections in the Jesuit order in the 1970s was enormous. The order lost about a third of its priests in the United States between 1965 and the mid 1990s. That was no coincidence. It was about that time that the information was being disseminated. That is when I found out."

"All the priests who left knew about Teilhard's discovery?" I asked.

"Not all. I am not sure exactly how many were motivated by Teilhard's discovery. I suspect that many who left knew nothing about Teilhard's secret—that they left because of the changes in the order brought about by those who did know. Those who knew the secret tried to redefine the Jesuit's mission as a strictly worldly mission. My guess is that many of the priests who left decided they could be social workers and political activists without living lives of poverty, chastity, and obedience. Why make the sacrifice of living a religious life, if you discover that your work as a priest is to be indistinguishable from a layman's?"

"Is that why you left?" I asked.

"Well, I was one of those who knew the secret, of course. That makes a difference. But, yes, it just did not make sense to me to continue the charade and live the discipline of a religious life if the central belief was a lie. I had always been tempted by what the Church calls the 'sins of the flesh.' There was no reason any longer to deny myself those pleasures. I wanted to marry, have children, live a life of what people call the *bourgeois* pleasures. I was confident that I could secure teaching positions that would allow for that. So I left."

Leo leaned forward. He was getting confident enough with Carey to tease him a bit. "Did you get as many women as you'd hoped?"

"No, I did not," Carey answered. "I never married. In my younger years I indulged in what might be called 'one night stands,' sometimes with prostitutes. But I have lived a lonely life." He motioned to the walls of his apartment as if he were waving a tired greeting to them. "I have lived alone in places like this since I left the Jesuits. I would not call it a happy life. Some might call it a wasted life. I don't care. I am beyond such worries."

"Maybe you would have been better off if you'd stayed," I noted sincerely. "I used to hear a lot of laughter coming from the dining room where the priests had lunch at Regis. It never seemed that bad a life to me."

"I have thought that many times myself. I enjoyed the camaraderie of the religious life. I really did. But I could not live the lie. I could not live as a priest once I knew the secret. In any event, I left the order. Once I left, I was not about to crawl back and ask them to take me back just because my life never turned out the way I'd expected. Even though the order would have accepted me back. Do you know that they have permitted a few prominent Jesuits who left the order to marry, and who botched up their marriages, to return to the order?"

"How could they do that?" I asked. "The Jesuits don't let divorced men join the order."

Carey chuckled. "But you see, they weren't divorced. Their marriages were considered invalid because they were still priests when they took their marriage vows. And they did not marry in Catholic ceremonies. So they were free to rejoin the order. Neat, no?"

"What about their wives?" Leo asked. "I bet they didn't go for being dropped like that."

"I bet not," Carey agreed. "But I don't think the directors of the order brooded too much about them. In any event, I burned too many bridges when I left. I had been outspoken in my rejection of Christianity, root and branch."

"What did you say when you left? Did you tell them what you knew about Teilhard?" I asked.

"No. I said nothing. But I did not have to say anything to some of the priests living in my community when I left. My God, they were the ones who told me about the secret."

"*Whose* God?" I snickered.

"Touché."

"Why did the priests who stayed stay? If they knew about Jesus' body, there would be no reason for them not to hit the road, too," I said.

"Good question, Corcoran. You are showing some traces of your Jesuit education after all! Maybe all that money the Jesuits expended on your education at Regis was not a complete waste. But there is no one answer. Now, remember, I am not aware of the total number of priests who know about Teilhard's discovery. I can speak only for those in my circle who had been informed."

Carey rose from his chair, peered out the window to check the weather, and then returned to his place. He pursed his lips as if he were trying to find just the right words for what he was about to say. "I would say there were two types who stayed after learning the secret."

"Who were willing to stay priests after knowing that Jesus never rose from the dead?" Leo asked with a puzzled look.

"Yes, precisely," said Carey. "First there were those who might be called the true *Teilhardians*. They bought the notion that this secularized Christianity was a higher and more mature Christianity, a Christianity stripped of its childish superstitions, of its otherworldliness. They developed a new understanding of their vocations, of what it meant to be a priest. They decided they could live as Jesuits in a world without a risen Jesus."

"A Society of Jesus without Jesus?" I asked.

"Well, yes. You mock, but that is it precisely. There have been people heaping praise upon Teilhard all over the academic world for providing just this insight. Why should it surprise you that there were Jesuits who sincerely bought into this new vision of a more mature Christianity?"

"Who were the others who stayed?" I asked.

"The group who were just too accustomed to their lifestyles as Jesuits to leave, especially once they were past middle age. Where were they going to go? It can be nice to never have to worry about paying rent or doctor's bills, you know, to never worry about being out of work, to have a secure teaching position at a prestigious university, to have comfortable living quarters in some of the most desirable urban neighborhoods in this country, to enjoy the companionship of an intelligent group of men, always available for good conversation and commiseration. They were able to go on, doing relevant work, living lives of service to mankind in spite of the secret. The Jesuit life has its charms. I miss it, often."

"If it is so good," I asked, "why aren't they getting new vocations these days? Maybe a religious life without a religion doesn't sell."

"It could be. I don't deny that. Look at me," Carey agreed.

"But you never thought of going back?" Leo asked.

"I told you. I could not go back. I could not live the lie. But I guess there are Jesuits who decided to live with the necessary compromise. I can come to no other conclusion."

"But, look, I still don't see why you were so convinced that Teilhard was right about what he found in the tomb," I said. "What were the documents he took from the burial spot that were so damn convincing?"

"You could call them the Fifth Gospel. The final Gospel, the *ne plus ultra*. Jesus' own words transcribed by Joseph of Arimathea, a Gospel that ends once and for all the claptrap about devils and miracles and angels. Jesus was aware that his followers were beginning to put to paper exaggerated tales about his miraculous powers and claims to divinity, what we call the Gospels. Which was not unexpected, I imagine. Once Jesus' disciples were convinced that Jesus had risen from the dead, it would not be surprising if they would want to paint the case, so to speak, to provide even more miracles to corroborate Jesus' supernatural powers. Jesus wanted to correct these misinterpretations of his life. This was the Fifth Gospel, Jesus' Gospel, that Teilhard found. Oh, yes, one more thing: Teilhard also took Jesus' right hand."

Chapter Six

J esus' *what!*"

"You heard me correctly, Corcoran," Carey replied. "Teilhard took Jesus' right hand. Jesus' right hand and a Gospel account that dispels centuries of superstition and myth-making about who Jesus was and what he taught. That is what Teilhard had in his possession. As well as the Roman dagger inscribed with INRI."

"His hand! Come on . . ."

"His hand. Teilhard wanted something that would provide incontrovertible evidence when coupled with the Arimathean Gospel—a hand with nail wounds in the wrist, a hand that would carbon test to 33 A.D. Why would it shock you that he took the hand? He was a trained archaeologist. He knew how to care for such a discovery. To whom should he have given it instead? The Israelis? Why them? You would not be shocked if he took possession of Julius Caesar's hand."

"But this is Jesus' hand!" Leo exclaimed.

"What did you want him to do? Kneel and treat it as a sacred relic?" said Carey. "It is the hand of a first-century Palestinian rabbi, no more, no less. That is the point. Teilhard's discovery ends all reason for treating Jesus as some divinity. As a great teacher with the power to inspire generations to come—yes. A great man, perhaps the greatest who ever lived, but not a god. There was no reason for Teilhard to wait for violin music in the skies. He took the hand. And I know where it is. I told you I had information that would change your life."

"You've seen this hand?" I asked.

"No. Teilhard showed it only to a handful of fellow Jesuits. One of those he showed it to, however, told me of seeing it. He also told several of my closest friends in the Jesuits. I have no doubt that he was telling the truth."

"Why?"

"Because he was in great anguish when he told me. His life, his very being, was changed forever. One does not fake such things. I later met some of the other Jesuits whom Teilhard informed. They were equally tormented."

"And you know where the hand is," I said.

"I do. Yes, I do. In fact, you spent four years of your life within a stone's throw of it. It is thermostatically sealed inside a safe— behind a false wall at Regis."

I laughed out loud. "OK, OK, I thought you were serious at first."

"I am quite serious, Corcoran. Quite."

"Behind a fake wall at Regis? Come on. Where?"

"I don't know exactly where, but it is there. In the 1950s, you see, Teilhard stayed for a while with the midtown Jesuit community near Regis. You remember, of course, that the Jesuits also operate Loyola High School in that vicinity, as well as their church on Park Avenue around the corner from Regis, St. Ignatius Loyola. You know that."

I didn't know if I should laugh again or send for the guys in the white jackets. I was sitting in a room over a garage, listening to a gray-haired woodchuck in a flannel shirt and suspenders telling me that Jesus' hand is hidden behind a fake wall in my old high school. I looked across at Leo. I couldn't tell from his expression if he was dazed or awestruck.

And I wasn't sure what I believed, either. But I decided to play along. "Why did he hide it there?"

"A few of Teilhard's Jesuit confidants had access to the building one summer in the early 1950s when the school was closed and otherwise deserted. It was just after he returned from Qumran and was doing some work with the Wenner-Gren Institute, a Manhattan think tank that sponsors archaeological research from its headquarters on Fifth Avenue. He was working out of their offices. The story goes that Teilhard hired some masons to build a brick veneer somewhere at Regis. It is said to match perfectly the existing infrastructure of the building, probably in an out-of-the-way place in the basement or attic. I don't know for sure. He placed the hand, the Roman dagger, and the Arimathean Gospel behind this fake wall—and, most importantly, the map to where the remainder of Jesus' body stills rests along the shores of Lake Tiberias."

Carey paused to sip his coffee before continuing: "He also included a diary of the entire story about how he'd found the hand and the Gospel. Which is important: It is a diary in Teilhard's own words verifying the discovery and the validity of the new Gospel. Moreover, he translated the Gospel into English and French, with the assistance of Jean Danielou. Do you know who he was?"

"Not a clue," I answered.

"He was a Jesuit Scripture scholar of great note, respected by traditionalists and liberals alike. His involvement gives even greater credibility to what I am telling you. In any event, Teilhard cemented everything over so that no one would know what he had done. Think about it: it is a very safe place. Even if renovations were to be done, no one would change the stone and brick structure of the building. The hand will remain safe as long as the building remains standing, and if you know that building you know that it will be standing hundreds of years from now. It is built of massive blocks of granite and limestone."

"Did this Danielou leave the Jesuits, too?" I asked.

"No, he stayed. But afterwards he lived a lifestyle that indicated he harbored few fears about life in some hereafter. He died in the apartment of a Parisian woman who had been his mistress."

"And Teilhard and the other Jesuits in on this thing decided to keep all this secret?" I asked. "Forever? Keep everyone in ignorance?"

"That, my good fellow," said Carey, "is what those of us who knew the secret debated with great intensity—great intensity. Whatever you think of us, we have consciences. Some of us believed our primary responsibility was to the truth, to mankind, to liberate Christians from the lie they are living. Others felt a great responsibility to the Catholic Church and the Society of Jesus. They did not want the information to be made public until the new secular role for the Church and the order could be established and accepted by the masses without great disillusionment. They wanted the order to play the role in preparing Catholics for their new worldly mission, for life in the secular city. Not an unreasonable concern, I would say."

"Man," said Leo, "they've been taking their time. If I got this right, it is over fifty years since this priest robbed the grave. Don't you think the world is ready yet? Is there anything to these stories about Satanists in the Church? Maybe these priests are devil-worshippers who want to use this information to destroy the Church and they're just waiting for the right time."

Carey smothered a laugh and waved his hand as if to brush aside Leo's idea. "No, no, please, it's nothing like that. There may be some Satanists somewhere in the Church. I don't deny that. I've heard the stories. But that's not what we are dealing with here. The Jesuits I am telling you about may have lost their faith by the standards of your sixth-grade nun, but they are not devil-worshippers. Please . . ."

"Then why are they covering this up?" Leo asked

"Look," Carey shot back, "I was one of those who pushed for a speedy resolution of the dilemma. Many of my fellow Jesuits agreed with me at the time. There were many heated debates over just that point. We were voted down. It is one of the reasons I left the Church when I did. But I am no longer a Jesuit, so I am unaware of what those who currently know the secret are planning to do. I don't even know how many modern Jesuits know where the hand can be found. But I am confident that it is a sizeable group."

"Hell," Leo responded, "it is pretty obvious that they don't want anyone to know yet. If they did it would be all over the papers and television."

"Indeed," said Carey. "It will be the biggest story in the history of the world when the information is made public. But I simply do not know what they intend to do. The people who know could be planning to reveal the secret tomorrow; or not in their lifetimes. I just don't know. I sometimes wonder myself. When I see Jesuit theologians pushing for new understandings of when Jesus discovered that he was divine, or introducing new interpretations of the Virgin Birth or what is meant by the Resurrection, I suspect that the day may be near when the information will be released. But, you are right. They are staying their hand. Why? I don't know. Maybe it has been decided that the world will be better off if no one ever knows. And frankly, I don't care anymore."

"You better off now that you know?" I asked.

"I am not sure. I was a happier man when I believed that life had some transcendent meaning—if that is what you mean. Ignorance is bliss, as they say. It is no accident that the atheist intellectuals such as Sartre and Camus were such dreary souls. It is not true: One need not assume Sisyphus happy."

"What?" I asked.

"Oh, I'm sorry. A bit of a theological inside joke. Let me put it this way: Children are happier when they believe in Santa Claus. Mankind will have to learn to live with this revelation, just as they adapted to the idea that the sun and the moon do not control our lives."

"But, look, you don't really know any of this for sure," I said. "Some Jesuits you know told you something about what Teilhard de Chardin is supposed to have told them. And you believe it all. Hell, you wouldn't buy a car with that little information, and you change your whole life because of it? It doesn't make sense. You would think you'd at least have to see the hand and test it and see that Fifth Gospel. Sounds to me like you were just looking for an excuse to leave the Jesuits and the Church and this was it."

"Could be," said Carey with a slight shrug. "I told you I wanted to enjoy the normal pleasures of life—to experience a woman's love. I longed for that when I was a priest with an intensity that you will never believe. It can be a lonely life being a priest. I would see men and women in the park with their children, see them embracing and laughing as their children ran across the grass—and I ached, literally ached with longing for those joys."

"But Desmond, my man," Leo said with a wink, "you know those marriage vows that keep those couples together don't make any sense either if Jesus is a lie. Why should that lug and his lady in the park stay with each other if their vows to the Father, Son, and Holy Spirit are just words that they say? 'Till death do us part?' Why?"

Carey nodded in agreement. "I hope you will believe me when I tell you that such concerns were at the heart of the discussions I sat through for years before I left the Jesuits. I am sure that the modern Jesuits who know the secret are making a point very similar to yours—in their own theological shoptalk, of course."

"Which means what?" Leo asked.

"Oh, you know—the scholarly language that theologians use to explore the role that religion and the belief in a Supreme Being play in the human psyche—about the 'ground of our being' and the *ens in re,* and so forth."

I motioned with my hand over my head to indicate that he was losing me.

"These are terms that theologians use to define the role that a belief in some transcendent arbiter of truth and eternal rewards and punishments plays in history. Christianity has played that role in Europe and the United States, and increasingly across the world. Do you know that there are more Christians now in Asia and Africa than in the United States? Do you think this planet will be a better place if people no longer believe that they will be accountable when they meet their Creator after death? Without the proverbial 'fear of God' and the belief in some sort of natural law? The stakes in all this are enormous."

"You're saying these Jesuits know the truth, but the rest of us shouldn't. Is that the way it works?" I asked.

"Don't blame me. I'm not one of them anymore. I have no control over these matters. I would have released the information twenty years ago. I don't believe in the risen Jesus. I don't preach to anyone. If anything, I try to convince people to rely on their own resources, to take Jesus' message of love and community and make it work in your life—*this* life. Forget the hereafter. And . . ." Carey leaned forward, "I know that Jesus would agree. Remember, I know about the Fifth Gospel."

"You know squat," I said, surprising myself with the anger in my voice. "You never read it. You never saw the map to where Jesus' body is. You believe something someone told you about what Teilhard de Chardin hid at Regis. It's crazy. There is no reason to believe this stuff is true. Why didn't you at least go there to check it out before you flipped your whole damn life?"

"It is not that easy. You would have to know where to look for the fake wall and the safe. And that information is also hidden in a secret place. Teilhard recorded the directions to where the fake wall is located at Regis and also the combination for the safe that he hid behind the wall. After his death that information was put in a safe place."

"Wait, wait," Leo blurted impatiently. "You're saying the fake wall where Jesus' hand is hidden is secret and so is the information about how to find the fake wall. Then this is a dead end. No one can prove this unless they blow up the whole goddam building at Regis."

"No, no," said Carey. "There are only a handful of Jesuits who know exactly where the hand is hidden. But those who know about the hand and the fake wall also know how to find the directions to its location. They know where the directions and the combination to the safe are hidden. If they decided to inform the public, they could get to the directions in a day or less. But here's the key—no one person can do that without making all of the Jesuits who know about the secret aware of what he is doing. You see, they did not want any one individual flying off the handle and making the information public, not without first consulting with the rest of the Jesuits who know. When the secret is revealed, it is to be a corporate decision of all those in the order who are privy to it."

"Let me get this straight," I asked. "Only a few Jesuits saw the hand and the Fifth Gospel and they know personally where it is hidden? But a lot of others know *about* the secret—know that it is somewhere in Regis. And all of them know where to find the directions that will show them where the fake wall is at Regis."

"Yes," he answered. "That is how it was set up."

I looked out the window. The sun was rising in the mid-morning sky, changing the shadow patterns along the driveway to Carey's apartment. It had melted the plowed areas down to smooth expanses of wet blacktop, but snow was still piled thick on the grassy areas. A pleasant scene. We had been talking and drinking coffee for over an hour now. I didn't know whether to encourage Carey to go on with his story or to end things and head back to Manhattan. I was fascinated by what the old coot was saying but suspicious that he was off his rocker.

Either way, there was nothing I could do. I didn't want to waste too much more time. But Leo looked as if he could listen forever—as long as the cigarettes and coffee did not run out, anyway. And Carey was in his glory, clearly reveling in the attention we were paying to him.

"Well, are you going to tell us, Desmond?" I asked. "Where are the directions to the fake wall at Regis hidden?"

"About five miles from here."

"I'm listening."

"They are in Teilhard's casket."

"Which is where?"

"In the old Jesuit cemetery where he is buried at St. Andrew's on the Hudson, on the grounds of the modern Culinary Institute of America. It is in Hyde Park, just outside of Poughkeepsie, just up the road from here. Teilhard died on Easter Sunday in 1955 while living with the New York Jesuits. There is talk that someday his body will be returned to France, but so far it is just talk. The cemetery is still maintained by the order."

"This is getting goddam goofy, Desmond," I said. "Are you telling me there is a Jesuit graveyard on the grounds of the Culinary Institute?"

"Of course there is. Did you think they would dig up all the bodies when we sold the grounds to the Culinary Institute? Actually, it is quite picturesque. It lends a certain charm to the property. There was no reason for the Culinary Institute to be concerned about it. All the students know where it is. It is only a stone's throw from the highway up there, just off Route 9."

I looked at Leo. He stared back at me with slightly raised eyebrows in a mixture of fascination and skepticism. I stared back at Desmond Carey. He was leaning back in his chair, puffing his cigarette and grinning a cat-got-the-mouse grin. He was pleased with himself, with the way we did not know what to make of him.

"Well, would you like to see it?" he asked.

"See what?"

"Teilhard's grave."

"You're telling me the directions to where the fake wall is located at Regis are in his casket?" I said.

"Yes. I am not lying. They are. Teilhard's closest confidantes thought that would be the safest place to hide the information. I suspect they were being a bit melodramatic, too. Some Jesuits can be that way. These priests were great admirers of Teilhard, almost what people would call a cult following nowadays. As I understand it, everything is inside a metal case about the size of a cigarette pack placed alongside his body. Ingenious, no?"

"No," I answered. "If the information is on a piece of modern paper it will rot away pretty quickly."

"That will happen if those who are aware of the secret decide to let it happen," said Carey. "My understanding is that the information is to be made public sometime before anything like that occurs. But, since I am no longer in the Jesuit order, I can't say that for sure. The younger Jesuits who know may decide to keep it a secret forever. I don't even know how many Jesuits under the age of forty have been told. Almost all of Teilhard's confidantes who had firsthand knowledge of all this are dead now. And the group who are my age, who learned the secret from them, are not long for this earth. In another ten years, most of them will also be dead."

"And then the world will stay ignorant of all this forever," said Leo. "You think they have the right to keep this secret?"

"I don't know about the *right*—they have the *power* to keep it secret if they want," Carey shrugged, as if it mattered little to him one way or the other. "Do you want to see the tombstone? We can be there in twenty minutes." He sat back in anticipation of our answer.

"Yeah, let's go," I said reflexively. I half-regretted my answer almost as soon as I spoke the words. "What the hell. Let's take a look. OK with you, Leo?"

"Yeah, what the hell," Leo answered. "Let's take a look. This could be interesting. Maybe we can even find a saloon afterwards for a beer or two."

And so it turned out that a half an hour later we found ourselves in Leo's van, driving up Route 9 on our way to the Culinary Institute and Teilhard de Chardin's gravesite. Route 9 is one of those interchangeable thoroughfares you can find all across the country these days. I haven't been to that many cities—places in New Jersey, Virginia, Pennsylvania, San Francisco, mostly for meetings for my company—but they all have a strip like this, the proverbial "malling of America." We drove through Fishkill first, then Wappingers Falls, spots made famous by Tawana Brawley and the Reverend Al Sharpton a few years back, then into the outskirts of Poughkeepsie. And it was all the same—indistinguishable franchise shop America.

No one said much. We smoked and exhaled through small openings where we had rolled down Leo's van windows and peered out at the passing scene. One after another: McDonald's, Burger King, Pizza Hut, gas stations that seemed to specialize more in beer and lottery tickets than car repairs, a large white mall rising from a hill on the left side of the road, a Ground Round, a Denny's, some individually owned restaurants here and there, an Indian restaurant with a mock Raj exterior, dry cleaners, and cheap florists behind grimy windows in flat and ugly strip malls. No beautiful and spacious skies, no amber waves of grain that I could see.

Then the setting changed, just before we entered the heart of the city of Poughkeepsie. The road swerved down towards the Hudson River, opening a vista of old railroad yards along the water's edge and a gnarly expansion bridge, linking Poughkeepsie with the rocky outcrops on the western side of the river. It gave hints of what the area must have been like when factories around here actually turned out products that would be shipped up and down the river from this spot on barges and railroad cars.

We cut in and out of the grimy heart of the downtown area before we knew it. That seemed to be by design, as if the powers-that-be had decided this was to be more a city to drive through than live in, now that the malls and the McDonald's had contoured the suburban stretches beyond the city limits into the places where life for the middle class was lived.

"There it is," Carey said, pointing his arm past Leo's face from his spot on the back seat of the van. "There on the left." We had just passed Marist College and a few small mock-Irish bars that seemed to be there to cater to the college crowd. "Just up that hill. There it is—St. Andrew's on the Hudson, the Culinary Institute of America."

And there it was. I must admit: Quite a sight. The Jebbies of the first half of the last century knew how to erect a building to last, clearly convinced that they were a permanent and important part of life in this country and wanted their institutions to reflect that role. I wonder what the older Jesuits, whose vision was responsible for places like this, thought when they saw them being sold to cooking schools.

The campus was separated from the highway by a curving field-stone wall that looked as if it had been there since Ichabod Crane's days, which, I guess, was the idea. But now an incongruous green sign with gold lettering, much like those you see outside Manhattan bistros, proclaimed "Culinary Institute of America." I wonder what the sign looked like back when this was still a Jesuit seminary. If I remember anything about the old Jebbies, it probably was a simple white item with black lettering and a stark black cross.

The buildings peeked at you through a wall of wind-tossed evergreens atop a small incline on the western side of the road. We drove up a twisting driveway, past an empty white security guard station until we found a small visitors' parking lot. From there we could see the full outline of the old seminary buildings. Hollywood could not have done a better job: weathered red brick surfaces accentuated with limestone capitals and cornice moldings; a slate roof adorned with copper-sheathed belltowers and cupolas verdigris-streaked to perfection. A delicate line of lancet windows graced the upper floors. Not every building was part of the original seminary. The Culinary Institute had added several new structures, easy to spot because of the newer brick and less ornate architecture. But whoever was in charge of the new construction had good taste. The architect had blended the new buildings into the look of the old.

"Up this way," Carey motioned. "The cemetery is just past the old classroom building. Great restaurants in there now. Progress, eh? You should try them someday." Carey began to breathe heavily as we walked up a slight incline toward the school. He reached for a cigarette to help things out.

As we approached the center of the campus, you could see the Hudson River off to the west. It curved into a small inlet at the foot of a hill stretching down from the main dormitory buildings, as if the river had been put there to provide a setting for the school. With yesterday's snow still coating the grounds, it was breathtaking, a perfect location to learn how to raise a soufflé. I'd pay to see the scene from a boat heading down the Hudson.

"It is over there, just around that building on the right," said Carey.

We had just passed an administration building, some more dormitories and a classroom building. Everything was quiet, with very few people moving about the campus. Classes seemed to be in session.

"There it is," Carey announced proudly. "Right there."

He pointed toward an open area behind a loading platform for the school's kitchens and a large green garbage dumpster: a cemetery, enclosed by a decorative wrought iron fence nearly blue from age and weather streaking. In the river wind, drooping evergreen limbs whisked across the fence's spiked top rail.

Carey was right. There was no reason for the directors of the Culinary Institute to concern themselves with the presence of a cemetery on this campus. It was quaint, picturesque, and unobtrusive. The tombstones were low, small ovals of uniform size, protruding like tree stumps in the snow. Probably most of the people who passed in and out of the campus never even noticed the spot, and those who did would think it a pleasant vestige of life in the Hudson Valley towns of old. I wouldn't be surprised if the school's chefs entertained the idea of using the setting for some white wine and cheese parties.

We walked to the wrought iron fence and peered in. A heavy lock prevented us from going any further. Carey became uncharacteristically solemn. No more smart-ass talk. This was, after all, where many of his best friends were buried. No doubt there was a time when he thought that this would be his final resting place.

"Know anyone in there?" I asked.

"Indeed I do," he answered quietly.

"Not a bad place to push up daisies," said Leo.

"Not bad at all," Carey agreed. "A whole generation of Jesuits from this part of the country are lying before you. Do you want me to recite some names?"

"No, don't do that. We wouldn't know them anyway," I replied quickly. I had sensed that things were on the verge of getting mushier than I was in the mood for.

"You're right," said Carey, not taking offense. He glanced from tombstone to tombstone and twitched his nostrils a bit, the way you do when you want to keep the tears away.

I wondered what he was thinking. The men buried here had lived their lives in dedication to a religious belief that Desmond Carey was now convinced was a fraud, a lie. Men of talent, ambition, high intellect, they had sacrificed the pleasures of life that most men live for, in order to save their souls and live an eternity with Jesus and the saints, the *Beatific Vision* the Church calls it. And they had done great things, built universities, written scholarly books, and lived their lives in foreign missions caring for the poor, in service to the lie. In fact, seeing as how most of these priests were the sons and grandsons of Irish immigrants, the cream of that crop in fact, you could call it the ultimate paddy-hustle.

"Which one is the grave-robbing priest?" asked Leo. "Which tombstone?"

"Well, the snow has me a bit disoriented," Carey answered, "but I think I can show you. Follow me now . . ."

He thrust his gloved hand through the iron rails and pointed as if he were counting heads in a classroom.

"Count with me . . . OK? One, two three . . . you with me? Got it?" He continued counting until he was nearly at the far end of the cemetery, the side opposite where we stood at the gate. "Now count across to the left. One, two, three, four . . ." He continued counting until he located the gravestone he was looking for. "There . . . *there it is*. The graves were dug in chronological order, starting from where we're standing. Teilhard died in 1955. That placed him fairly deep into the rows."

I was able to pick out the gravesite, even though each gravestone was exactly the same size and shape, just a small stone oval. No carved trumpet-blowing angels or sprawling Crucifixion scenes like those you find at crooked politicians' and mobsters' mausoleums. Everything uniform and dignified, reminiscent of the tailored black cassocks worn by the Jesuits of old. No crimson capes and birettas for them. The prestige came from being a Jesuit, not parading like an Austrian archduke at a court wedding.

"What do we do now?" I asked. "Go buy some shovels?"

"Don't even jest, Mr. Corcoran," Carey replied, "That is not why I brought you here. I wanted only to show you that I am not some village blowhard. That is Teilhard de Chardin's grave."

"I repeat: So what do we do now?"

"You do nothing. Go home and live your life the best way you can with the information I have given you," said Carey. "Not many men know what you now know."

I glanced around the grounds. Everything was still silent. Not a soul in sight, except for what might have been one of the kitchen help: a middle-aged portly man in a dark windbreaker, with one of those round and florid Irish faces and eyeglasses with one darkened lens. A "smoked" lens is what I think they call it. I had seen eyeglasses like it before, but never knew what the one darkened lens was for. I still don't.

He was standing by the garbage dumpster off to our right, on the river side of the graveyard. I assumed he was dumping some kitchen waste, yet he glanced over at us repeatedly. Probably there weren't many visitors to this spot on the campus. But he showed no intention of asking any questions. In fact, he turned his face toward the dumpster when I looked over at him, as if he did not want to draw attention to himself. Which was fine with me.

"Well, Desmond, we've seen it," I stated quietly.

"Do you believe me that Teilhard is buried here?" he replied.

"No reason not to. This is where they bury Jesuits and he was a Jesuit. I'll suspend my judgment about the rest of the story."

"Why?"

"I already told you. All you know is what someone told you about what is in that grave. I think you should have held off from making up your mind, too. I believe that you believe what you said is in there with Teilhard's body. Is that good enough?"

Carey waved his hand in front of his face, as if to wipe away my comments. "I understand," he replied. "It really does not matter. Some day you will discover that I was telling the truth. I am confident of that."

"I think we'd better go, Desmond," I said. "It is past noon. My brother and I have to get back to the city. It's a long drive."

"I can't interest you in a beer or two?" Carey asked, clearly eager for a few more hours of conversation.

"No, no, we can't. We've got to work tomorrow. Right, Leo?" I looked across at Leo. His face was placed against the iron rails of the fence, like a boy at the zoo.

"Yeah, yeah . . . I guess we gotta go," Leo said, looking up at me and then at Carey. He seemed deep in thought. I didn't expect a Jesuit graveyard to turn him so solemn.

Chapter Seven

I learned soon enough on the ride home that solemnity had nothing to do with Leo's mood at the graveyard. Other thoughts had entered his mind. It wasn't until we were barreling down the Major Deegan Expressway just past Yankee Stadium that he made them known. He was biting on the filter of his Marlboro and squinting into the mid-afternoon sun as he spoke. There was still a wisp of snow left, covering the debris along the side of the road and in the grimy canyons of the public housing projects along the Harlem River. Not quite Currier and Ives, but a lot prettier than the usual collage of beer cans and old tires.

"Frankie, what should we do?"

"About what?"

"You know what. Do you realize what Carey told us?"

"The world's greatest secret, if it is true," I answered. "I guess we'll never know."

"What do you mean, we'll never know? You mean you're gonna just forget what you heard; go back to life as usual?"

"Yeah, why not? It was bar talk, something from *The X-Files*. We don't even know if Carey was ever a priest."

"No way. He was. You know that. He knew too much about the Jesuits. Even the bartender said he was a priest—that he taught in that place before it became the cooking school. I believe that. The bartender told us that way before the old coot told us anything about Jesus' hand. The bartender didn't know about the hand. There was no reason for him to give us a line. What—do you think the two of them were in league against us? That they planned all this just to jack us up?"

"That's easier to believe than what Carey told us," I answered as Leo maneuvered across the Willis Avenue Bridge and toward the loop leading to the East Side Drive. Afternoon traffic wasn't that heavy as we cut and weaved our way downtown.

"That's the point, dammit. Anything is easier to believe than what Carey told us. We just can't go back to our lives as if we'd never heard what he said."

"What difference does it make to you? When was the last time you worried whether Jesus really rose from the dead and is sitting on a cloud somewhere?"

"Frankie, I'm not talking the state of my soul here. I'm talking bucks, big bucks. Do you know what this could be worth if we got that map and the hand? The book companies and television networks would offer us a zillion bucks, Frankie, a zillion. You got money up the kazoo, but I don't. What do you make on Wall Street anyway?"

"Not that much. Four-hundred K last year," I answered, "plus capital gains."

"Capital gains? What the hell is that?"

"My portfolio."

"What's that worth?"

"Come on, Leo, have some mercy."

"A million?"

"More or less."

"Dammit! You know what I make on the job? With overtime, just about sixty grand. I'm pinched for bucks, with the alimony and all. We can't just forget all this, Frankie. We got to check it out. It could set us up for life, with more money than we've ever dreamed of."

"What do you want to do? Dig up the goddam grave?"

"Damn right! There's got to be a way. If people can rob banks, someone can figure a way to get into that grave without anyone knowing. It can be done. We know guys from the old neighborhood who could put us in contact with the right people."

"Then what? Let's say we find the directions to that fake wall at Regis. What do we do then?" We had just exited at 96th Street and were heading cross-town. The new domed Islamic mosque on First Avenue rose up before us at the crest of the hill. "We walk in and ask the Jebbies at Regis to let us knock down a wall and look around a bit?"

"First things first. We get into the grave and see if the metal case with the directions to the fake wall is in there with the body. Once we get our hands on it, we decide what comes next. If those directions are there, we'll find a way to get to the fake wall. For a few million bucks I'll figure out a way to get behind that wall. You can bet your ass I will. I'm a fireman, goddam it. I can fake an inspection or something. I'll find a way."

Leo moved in and out of traffic, then cut across the 97th Street transverse through Central Park. A few trophy wives were walking their longhaired dogs past the reservoir, heads back and jaunty, as if the park had been put there as a backdrop for their afternoon stroll.

"Frankie, look . . . just think about it, will you?" Leo implored. He was double-parked outside my building, waiting for me to get out and unload my ski gear. "This is serious stuff here. We got to talk to someone about this, someone who'll know what we should do next. Ask around. See if one of the swells at your company knows a book publisher or somebody in the media we can talk to about what to do."

"Come on, you want me to tell someone about what Desmond Carey told us?" I asked.

"No, come on. Give me a break, Frankie. You're the smart one in the family. You can figure out what to say. Just tell them that we have access to some information about Jesus' life, something groundbreaking. Tell them enough to get them interested. You don't have to mention the hand or the body. Just say you know where there is a new Gospel, something like that. Once we're sure we can trust them, we can tell them the rest."

"Let me think about it, OK? There is no one I can think of off the top of my head in the publishing business. I'll have to reach out a bit."

"Just promise me you'll think about it. Really think about it. I'm gonna ask around, too. We can't let this lie, Frankie. It's too big."

"OK, OK, I'll think about it. I'll give you a call in a few days. But don't be bugging me every night until then. I'll make some calls. I'll get back to you. But don't go telling every smart-ass in your firehouse and every drinking buddy you know about what we heard."

"Hey, you don't have to tell me to keep quiet. Are you for real? I'm the one who's thinking the big bucks here," Leo replied. "You keep your yap shut, too. We can't let anyone know what we know. Nothing. Absolute secrecy."

By the weekend I still had not called Leo. I left a message on his answering machine to assure him I was on the case. Which wasn't true. I was still stumped about what to do next, even though I had come to the conclusion that Leo was right; that this was the chance for us to make more money than we'd ever dreamed of. The old-timers I worked with on the Street convinced me that there would be down years when Merrill Lynch was likely to lay off guys like me, the bottom feeders in the company. We could not pass this up.

Did I worry about the religious side of things? Just a little. I was still a practicing Catholic, but mostly out of habit. I didn't brood about the things that worry the theologians. I figured I could leave the big religious questions to them. They'd probably be debating what to make of the hand and the Fifth Gospel and the body on the shores of Lake Tiberias for the next hundred years, the way they do with that Shroud of Turin, leaving plenty of time for Leo and me to structure our trust funds with our newfound fortune. And I convinced myself that no harm would be done, that my mother's old Irish Catholic cronies wouldn't believe that it really was Jesus' body, that they probably wouldn't even pay attention to the story when it came out. No one would be hurt. And Leo and I would make a serious bundle.

If . . . if we could figure out a way to get into Teilhard de Chardin's grave up at the Culinary Institute, that is. And if we found the directions to the fake wall at Regis in the casket. And if that fake wall really had a thermostatically sealed hand of someone buried on the shores of the Lake Tiberias. And if there really was a map showing us how to find that body. I could keep track of a pocketful of buy and sell orders on futures contracts all day long on the floor of the Stock Exchange, but I didn't know how to tie these strings together.

I am not sure why, but I decided to roam around the neighborhood near Regis that Sunday. I thought it might help me to sort things out, provide the right backdrop to my soul-searching, maybe even afford me an opportunity to check out the structure of the building in hopes of figuring out where the fake wall might be. There was an eleven o'clock Mass at St. Ignatius Loyola, just around the corner from the school on the corner of 84th and Park. I could go to Mass, and then get a cup of coffee and drink it on one of the benches by Central Park across from the Guggenheim Museum. Not a bad way to spend some time, even on a chilly winter Sunday morning, and even if it didn't help me come up with any ideas about how to find the hand. Some great looking women stroll by that side of the park heading towards the walkway that divides the Great Lawn from the Reservoir. Ah, Sunday in New York.

I took the subway from the upper West Side to Times Square, shuttled across to Grand Central and took the No. 4 Train up to the 86th Street station, my daily route to Regis in the old days. I climbed over a panhandler in the stairwell and exited onto 86th Street. It was one of those dazzlingly New York mornings when the sun's rays carve Manhattan into stark relief, every block and stone and mullioned window crisp and clean in the brisk air. I arrived at St. Ignatius Loyola just a few minutes before Mass.

I hadn't been inside St. Ignatius in years, not since my high school graduation ceremony, in fact. What a day that was. My mother was bursting with pride that her darling boy had graduated from "Regis, the Jesuit scholarship school" (she always described Regis that way to her biddy friends in Inwood), but was heartbroken that I was one of the few in the graduating class that year that did not go on to college. She also knew that I had come home pie-faced the night before after closing up one of the bars in Inwood with my drinking buddies.

Even the big bucks I was making on Wall Street did not make up for my failure to go to college and "use the brains God has given you," as she put it. She would have loved for me to become a priest, or maybe an officer in the Marines. She would have my picture on the wall—in my cassock or my dress blues—next to the Pope's and John Kennedy's if that had happened. Pushing paper on Wall Street, no matter how lucrative, struck her as a sell-out, even though she would never hurt my feelings by putting it in those words. What can I say? She is no dummy, Margaret Mary Corcoran, née Flanagan, of County Clare. A pain in the neck sometimes, but no dummy.

The architecture of St. Ignatius overwhelmed me, just as it did when I first saw it as a schoolboy. I'm no expert, but I have always thought it the perfect church. They say that it is a replica of Gesu, the Jesuits' Church in Rome, a domed Romanesque structure like the ones that Michelangelo used to design. It consumed a half block of Park Avenue real estate. The massive stone walls and brass entrance doors that opened with the ease of a screen porch in the Hamptons caught your attention first; once inside, your eyes were drawn to the clerestory, the huge expanses of stained glass widows along the roof line and the shafts of color they poured into the air above the sanctuary, illuminating the kaleidoscopic array of frescoes stretching from ceiling to floor. The vaulted ceiling, supported by soaring tan marble columns, arched high above the nave, seemingly defying the laws of gravity. Don't ask me who paid for it all. Whoever footed the bill, it was worth it, in architectural terms alone.

In addition, it did what it was supposed to do. It helped me pray. It really did, evoking the feeling that there had to be more to life than the physical world around us. I slid into a pew halfway down the center aisle. The church was about three quarters full, with the kind of congregation you would expect on Park Avenue. More mink and camel hair coats and silk scarves than you could count, but also a sprinkling of florid-faced men who could have been cops from the neighboring police station and Hispanics who looked as if they worked in the kitchens of the local restaurants. Park Avenue or not, this was a Catholic Church, and it was Sunday, and the congregation was there because they *had* to be there. No one questioned whether you "belonged." Social class seems to have a lot to do with why Protestants became Baptists or Episcopalians, but the Kennedys and the Buckleys have to stand in line with their maids to receive Communion.

I tried to pray in preparation for Mass. I always do . . . go through the motions at least. I can't explain to you the full meaning of the Mass and what Catholics mean when they say that the bread and wine are changed into the body and blood of Christ, but I believe that something happens, that the ceremony is a way of getting close to the meaning of life, of loving God above all things and our neighbors as ourselves for the love of God. How exactly, I don't know. But I know smarter people than I am—like the Jesuits who taught me in high school—who believe that the Catholic Church is what it says it is, who believe that the Mass is serious business, the secret to the mystery of the universe. That's been enough to make me want to stay what they call a "practicing Catholic." Plus I feel at home in these churches. I still do, in spite of my way of life.

I wasn't able to stay as focused on my prayers as I intended, though. My mind roamed back to the idea that Jesus' hand might really be behind a wall in a high school building just around the corner from where I was kneeling. What would that mean if it were true? Could the Catholic Church go on, with some new less spiritual identity, the way Teilhard de Chardin taught? Would the people who love Jesus and live their lives by what he taught act the same if his body was in the ground somewhere in Israel? Would people still love their fellow men and women—those who do—the way Jesus taught men to? Things are bad enough in this world. What would happen when the fear of God was no longer in the equation for millions of Catholics? What would it be like if that changed?

I looked up as the priest and the altar boys strode down the center aisle to begin the Mass. I rose from my seat, made the Sign of the Cross, and nearly fell to the floor.

The priest was a heavy-set man with a ruddy face and eyeglasses with one darkened lens—the guy who had been watching Leo, me, and Desmond Carey at the Jesuit graveyard at the Culinary Institute!

I slid sideward to get behind the floppy hat of the woman in the pew in front of me. I was at least twenty rows back from where the priest stood at the altar, but feared he might notice me. I've heard priests say they know where the "regulars" sit when they say Mass; that they can tell when someone is missing, that the congregation is never just a blur of faces to them. No question, from this distance I could see his face clearly enough to remember him. I was sure that he could do the same if he happened to spot me.

I wasn't sure why I was nervous about allowing him to spot me. He couldn't read my mind about what Leo and I were planning to do with Teilhard's grave. For all he knew, we were just friends of Desmond Carey who had been given a tour of the old seminary. Still, what was he doing at that graveyard in Hyde Park? Why would a Jesuit from St. Ignatius Loyola Church in Manhattan be roaming the Dutchess County countryside a week ago? I tried to keep my face half covered as he swept his glance across the congregation and recited the opening prayers to the Mass.

"The grace and peace of God and our Father and Lord Jesus Christ be with you."

I joined in the response: "And also with you."

The priest moved through the early stages of the Mass, from all appearances filled with sincerity and piety: "Lord God, Lamb of God, you take away the sin of the world: have mercy on us. You are seated at the right hand of the Father . . ."

I couldn't help but wonder: If this priest was one of those who knew the secret, what did he mean by "seated at the right hand of the Father?" If he knew about the body by the shores of Lake Tiberias, why would he say these things with ardor? Was it all a con? Had he convinced himself he was doing something noble by pretending to believe, until the rest of mankind was ready to be enlightened?

The same thoughts arose during his sermon. It centered on our obligation to bring Christ "to life" by caring for the least of our brethren; on the need to carry the message of love from the Mass into our daily lives; on the futility of living a solitary life of prayer if we ignored the "needs of our brothers and sisters." He stressed that we could not be the people of God if we did not live our lives with a "fundamental option for the poor."

He raised his eyes and arms toward the great domed ceiling and raised his voice dramatically: "Those who reverence Christ's presence in the tabernacle must also reverence Christ's presence in the poor, the homeless, in AIDS victims!"

It was the kind of thing I had heard from Jebbies hundreds of times before, but it took on new meaning for me now. Was this what Desmond Carey meant, about how the Jesuits who know the secret are trying to change Christianity into a religion that has no meaning beyond making life on this planet better for our fellow men and women? In the past when I heard these sermons, I always thought that the point was that we would not get to heaven without living a life of service—that a concern for the poor was what Jesus wanted from us, a Jesus who was alive and looking down on us, and who would reward us for our behavior. But was Carey right? Were they really talking about a world without a life after death, without an actual heaven and hell and a personal God? Was the only eternal reward we would ever know to be the improved world we could help create, right here on terra firma, by living a life of human love?

Was this priest with the weird eyeglasses one of those who were trying to get Catholics ready for the day when a personal God and an individual reward or punishment in the hereafter would be taken from them—when the secret would be released? Was the plan to fill the world with years of sermons like this—to prepare Catholics to accept a Christianity without the spiritual dimension?

I watched his eyes as he intoned the words of the Consecration, when Catholics believe their priests turn the bread and wine into the body and blood of Christ: "Dying you destroyed our death, rising you restored our life. Lord Jesus, come in glory." What was he thinking as he closed his eyes, deep in thought? *Lord Jesus, come in glory?* From where? When? How?

I made sure that I received Communion from one of the lay Eucharistic ministers. No way I was going to look this guy in the face as he distributed the Host. But I watched him as he methodically placed the Communion Host into the hands or mouths of the line of communicants, repeating over and over the words, "Body of Christ." If he knew the secret, he had to pretend to take this moment more seriously than he really did.

Then it struck me: *Maybe not.* If he were a true believer in the new man-centered Christianity, receiving Communion was the key to what the new Church would be all about. As they say, you are what you eat. If we eat the same bread, we become one body, the bread we share becomes us. Maybe these new Jebbies consider receiving Communion a symbol of the new spiritual unity of mankind that Desmond Carey said Teilhard de Chardin was trying to inspire, a spirit of unity formed by the message of love taught by Jesus. Is that what they mean when they say Jesus becomes the bread and the wine, and we become one with Jesus by receiving the Host?

Come to think of it, a priest who believed in this new worldly religion without a heaven and a risen Jesus probably could interpret everything that Catholics believed to make it fit for himself. Think about it. Baptism? An initiation into a holier life through becoming a new member in the human community of love. Confession? You reconcile yourself to your brothers and sisters, the community. Right? You could go on and on . . . reframe *everything.*

I made sure to avoid the priest after Mass, exiting by a side door instead of standing in line to shake his hand and exchange pleasantries. Even this Catholic glad-handing after Mass took on a new light for me. Catholic priests never pressed the flesh after Mass when I was a young altar boy. We used to say it was a Protestant thing; that the Protestant parsons had to be friendly to get the crowd to come back next Sunday for services, but that Catholics had no choice but to come back. You could cover Catholics with fire and brimstone and demand more loot in the collection basket and they would be back the next week, under the pain of sin.

Could it be that the priests who pushed for this new consumer-friendly handshaking after Mass were laying the foundation for the new Catholicism, where human interaction would be more important than in the old days; one where the priest would be less a channel between mankind and the Creator than a facilitator for better interpersonal relations? Is that why they keep talking about the "people of God" these days? My mind was literally racing.

I'll tell you this: this priest with the strange eyeglasses seemed to enjoy his new role as neighborhood social director. He shook hands with exuberance, smiled a politician's smile, and fussed over the children in the crowd as if he had never seen one before. And the Park Avenue swells came from his receiving line with the feel-good-about-yourself smiles you see on the ladies in the audience when they watch Oprah hug some aging rock star who has just lost twenty pounds on her new diet.

And why not: It was a beautiful Sunday morning, and they had heard the Word of God, received the Lord in Communion, indulged in a *frisson* of guilt over having so much when there were those with so little in Appalachia and Rwanda, and were now on their way for Bloody Marys and brunch at Le Bistro du Nord or Le Régence. "Peace be with you."

I strolled down 84th Street toward Regis. The stone walls and stately trees that formed the eastern boundary of Central Park could be seen two blocks ahead. In fact, Central Park's great lawns used to be the place for our warm weather gym classes at Regis. I paused for a moment in front of the school. It blended perfectly into the serried ranks of granite and brownstone townhouses and office buildings in the ritzy neighborhood. I stood there for a while, reminiscing about the years I hurried through the building's lacquered entrance doors and up the stairs to my Latin and Greek classes. I tried to figure out how the hell Leo and I could ever get into the place to knock down a wall to get at Teilhard's secret cache.

It would not be a piece of cake; that was for sure. Even if we knew *exactly* what wall to break through, it would take a couple of hours to complete the task of locating the safe and getting away with its contents. We would have to find a time when the building was empty and some way to get inside without setting off the alarms that were sure to be activated, and a way to do our work quietly enough so as not to alert anyone in the vicinity.

I was not sure if some Jebbies actually lived in the building. Most of them lived in a community house around the corner by their church. And what about custodial staff? What time did they arrive? Were there workers who cleaned the building in the overnight hours? Might there be others who were in the building on weekends, along with some faculty members to supervise athletic events, school plays, and the like? It would not be as hard as breaking into the Morgan Bank but, I repeat, no piece of cake.

On the other hand, there was an upside. If we were caught during the break-in, the legal ramifications might not be that worrisome. Probably I could make up some story about an alumni prank, say I was doing it on a dare. It would be embarrassing as hell but not enough to get us any jail time. Not a bad risk/reward ratio, I thought.

The actual mechanics of breaking in? Well, I was not a complete novice in such matters. I was no cat burglar, but in my teens had indulged in a few break-ins: into a neighbor's house to get some weekend hooch, swimming pools in Riverdale on hot summer nights, and once into a local public school over the Christmas holiday to use the indoor basketball court. What I am saying is that I knew my way around skylights and basement windows. But Regis was not freestanding. It butted against neighboring structures as massive as itself. There were no overhanging tree branches reaching close to side windows that I could jimmy. And there was no way that I could see to get onto the roof to look for the attic door that you found atop most Manhattan buildings. In addition, this would be a well-lit street all through the night. No way to lurk in the shadows to carry out the boost, not on Central Park East.

I got my coffee in one of those new boutique coffee shops and carried it to a spot on Fifth Avenue just outside the park. I stood sipping it, watching the pedestrian traffic moving north and south along the Upper East Side's famous Museum Mile. I made up my mind: I was going to find out, one way or the other, if Jesus' hand was in that building. Case closed. Now only the details remained.

Chapter Eight

There was a message from Leo on my answering machine when I got home after my excursion to Loyola and Regis. I can't say that I jumped for joy when I heard his voice, seeing as how I wasn't ready to get into any details with him about all our grave-robbing tomorrows. I had picked up my copy of the *New York Times* at the newsstand in Grand Central Station and was planning to spend a quiet afternoon reading it, then enjoy an evening at the bar at Cleopatra's Needle drinking vodka and tonics, listening to piano jazz (once in a while played by the actor, Michael Moriarity—not bad, either), and making small talk with a few of my friends from the Street. Two or three of them were always there on Sunday night, drinking enough to be fun but always on their way out of the door before 10 P.M. so that we all could get a good night's sleep before Monday's opening bell on the Exchange. It was our version of the Protestant ethic, even though we were all Catholic school-boys gone bad. Even a couple of married guys would spend Sunday evenings with us once in a while. We all drank vodka to make sure no one smelled the booze on our breath the next day on the job. How's that for dedication.

There was an urgency in Leo's voice: "Frankie, we got to talk. I've got some news. Call me back when you get in."

Which I did.

"Hey, Leo—it's me, Frankie. What's going on?" I asked without enthusiasm.

My lack of gusto did not deter him: "Frankie, I'm glad you called. Something just hit me. I figured out who we can ask about our problem. I don't know why I didn't think of it before." He was speaking from his apartment in the Bronx, not far from the Bronx Zoo.

"Who?"

"John Sullivan."

"Who's John Sullivan?"

"John Sullivan. Come on—you remember him from the neighborhood—the numb nuts from over by Isham Park. Remember? The guy who was always talking about the laboring classes and the dispossessed of the earth. He was just a little older than you, went to NYU?"

"The guy with the long red beard?"

"There you go—that's the guy. But he doesn't have the beard anymore."

"Why him?" I asked.

"Listen to me: I met him about six months ago," he answered. "He works now with the Catholic Worker people, down on First Street. You know the holy rollers I'm talking about?"

I did. It was the late Dorothy Day's organization. Some of my teachers used to bring in their newspaper *The Catholic Worker* to get a discussion going in religion classes on things like social justice and private property rights and whatnot. At first I was surprised that Leo knew about the group, but then I realized that the Catholic Worker soup kitchen was just around the corner from LaSalle, Leo's old high school, down near the Bowery. He probably saw them a lot in that neighborhood. They sometimes held discussion groups to convince Catholics that Christ's call to love our fellow men and women should be interpreted as a commitment to social activism for the poor. I never had a problem with that idea . . . as long as they didn't get in my way of making a buck. (Hey, somebody has to make the money first before the more socially conscious among us can spread it around.)

Leo continued: "Here's what went down, Frankie. I met him at Mom's arts and crafts fair at Good Shepherd, in the church auditorium. I stopped by to see what she made to sell at the fair—just to make her feel good. Like I care about her crocheted Irish doilies, right? Anyway, Sullivan still lives in the neighborhood, a working class hero. He had a table there himself, selling crap that some Indian tribe made—to raise funds for a Catholic Worker center out West. You know, the usual drill—change purses and rosary pouches with fringe and beads all over the goddam place."

"And?"

"And he told me that one of the things he did at the Catholic Worker was help Indian authors make contact with New York publishers. He said he landed a few contacts for Indian poetry. Great beach reading, I'll bet. Anyway, he could be just the kind of guy we need; I'll bet he already knows about this Teilhard character. He's one of these *Jesus-loves-the-little-children* kind of guys. He'd go gaga over this new Gospel that Desmond Carey was talking about. It'd be right up his alley."

I paused for a second. I was not sure if I should tell Leo about the priest I saw at St. Ignatius Loyola that morning being the same man we saw up at the graveyard at the Culinary Institute. But I did: "You know what, Leo?"

"What?"

"I went to Mass over by Regis today. Guess who the priest was?"

"Who?"

"Remember that guy we saw by the garbage dumpster when we were checking out the graveyard at the Culinary Institute? The guy with the glasses with the smoked lens?"

"Yeah, barely."

"Well, he was the priest who said the Mass I went to this morning."

"So?"

"You don't think that's strange?"

"No. Why? It's a Jesuit cemetery. Someone from the order has to maintain the place. Maybe he was visiting some long lost buddy's grave. Priests have friends whose graves they might want to visit, don't they?"

"I guess," I answered. "Why did he stay back from us by the garbage dumpster like he didn't want to be noticed when we saw him? You remember that?"

"I guess he wanted to wait until we were gone for his private moment with the deceased. How the hell do I know? What's the big deal?"

"Nothing, I guess. You're right. So what do you want to do with John Sullivan?"

"Set up a meeting. Talk to him about contacting a book company."

"Go ahead then. Call him, go meet with him," I shrugged.

"No way, Frankie. You've got to come, too. You know how to talk about all this stuff better than I do. I'll call him to set up a meeting, but you've got to come, too."

"How much are we going to tell him?"

"It's like I was saying the other day—just enough to get him interested; enough to convince him that a publisher would want to look into what we have to say. But nothing about the hand or the body until we know that things are falling into place."

"Which means what?" I asked.

"I don't know. You tell me."

"OK. I'll do what you said last week. I'll tell him the part about Joseph of Arimathea's Gospel—that we know how to get our hands on it. We'll tell him that and see how he responds."

"That's why you've got to do the talking, Frankie. I don't know shit about this Joseph of Arimathea. I'll say the wrong thing, or too much. How about I give him a call and we meet him some afternoon when you get off work at the Exchange? His office at the Catholic Worker is only a few subway stops from Wall Street, right near the Bleecker Street station. I'll meet you there. I'll pick an afternoon when I'm not at the firehouse."

Which is what we did. A week or so later, I got off the subway at Bleecker Street. Leo was already there, having taken the train down from the Bronx. He was hunched over a cardboard container of coffee and a cigarette inside a storefront, hiding from the wind.

If I must say so myself, he looked like a Bowery regular in the late winter dusk.

He greeted me with his usual solicitousness: "Hey, Frankie, dammit, you look like a real suit. I got to admit it. I bet you fool them down there on Wall Street, got them thinking you live someplace like Darien or Scarsdale with a lemon drop wife and a Cocker spaniel."

"Nice to see you, too."

"Did Mom ever see that coat?" He reached out to stroke my camel's hair overcoat. I had bought it at Moe Ginsburg's on sale, but I guess it was pretty posh by Leo's standards. "She'd wonder how many sweaters for the kids in Appalachia you could buy for the same dough."

"Baloney. She saw it. She thought it made me look like a gentleman."

"Look like one, maybe."

"OK. You win. Does Sullivan know we are coming?"

"Yeah," Leo answered, poking his cigarette into the dregs of his coffee and tossing the cup into a wire trash basket. "He didn't know who I was at first, but he remembered me from the craft fair at Good Shepherd I was telling you about. And after I told him a few stories about you from the old neighborhood, it was like 'old home week.' You were pretty famous in your day, you know. He mentioned the time when you were about sixteen and you and Teddy O'Malley drove off with the police car from outside the Holy Name Society meeting. Remember? When the two cops went inside to swig some beers? When the two bulls came out and found it gone, they ran down Broadway with their guns drawn trying to find it. What a pisser."

I chuckled a bit in response. I did remember. It was a funny day. And we never caught hell for it. The cops could not make a stink over what Teddy and I had done without admitting that they had left the car running while they downed a few beers. Besides, we parked the car just one block away, where they would find it without much problem. The incident passed quickly. The fun was in hiding in the hall of one of the nearby apartment buildings and watching the cops come out and realize that their patrol car was gone. For a moment or two, they looked as if their lives were ruined forever, which they could have been if the car had been really gone. But they deserved some anguish. They were loudmouths who played good Catholics and solid citizens while taking monthly payments from one of Nicky Barnes' lowlife street pushers.

We walked the two blocks from the subway station to the Catholic Worker headquarters on East 1st Street, just off the Bowery. The building had seen better days, nestled between some boarded up and graffiti-smeared buildings. It was a brick structure, but with the bricks painted a glossy red, giving it the texture of the men's room in a run down saloon. It was probably worth a pretty penny though, considering the way real estate values have boomed on the Lower East Side.

A streaked and grimy street-level window, framed by a sill as cracked as a Death Valley riverbed, offered passersby a view of a stained and dilapidated old sofa and a couple of Formica tables where the soup and bread were distributed to the neighborhood homeless—the men everyone called *Bowery bums* in the days before political correctness set in. The building's only identification was a small blue sign above the window identifying it as the Catholic Worker's St. Joseph's House.

There was a time when I thought the seediness of the building was an affectation, a way of demonstrating authentic poverty to Dorothy Day's donors. Hell, how much does a can of paint and a bucket of Spic and Span cost? But no more. The place looked genuinely desolate, like the haggard men hustling change from the passing cars a block away on the corner of Houston Street.

John Sullivan was waiting for us in a tiny office, just a small green metal desk, a couple of busy bulletin boards and a rickety bookshelf. I would never have recognized him if I had bumped into him anywhere else. The bright red hair I remembered had thinned and aged to the color of blush wine. He also had put on a lot of weight.

But he still had his old affinity for authentic workshoes and blue denim shirts with prominently displayed activist buttons in support of his favorite causes. It used to be buttons about strip mining and banning the bomb back when I was a teenager; now it was Abu Mumia-Jamal and global warming. But, hey, why scoff? I'll bet there are social gatherings where buttons like that can break the ice with the black-sweater-and-Birkenstock-type babes; save an hour or so of buttering-up conversation. Just one look at your shirt and they know you are a sensitive soul that they can sleep with without losing their self-image. Just like a power tie does for the yuppie movers and shakers, with the requisite reverse spin.

"Well, well, it really is the famous Corcoran brothers," said Sullivan, looking up from a manila folder. "Good to see you again, Leo. And Frankie, you haven't changed much except for the wardrobe. My God, you really have come up in the world. Is that the *GQ*-look?"

"Nice to see you again, John," I answered, reaching across his desk to shake his hand.

"Won't you sit down.?" Sullivan pointed to two chairs that looked as if they had been bought at a going-out-of-business-sale at a failed catering house, wedges of cracked black plastic and pock-marked chrome. Leo and I folded our coats over the backs of the chairs and sat down.

We exchanged a few more reminiscences about our families and the old neighborhood, adding a bit of background on what had taken Leo and me to our current states in life. Sullivan went into some of the work he was doing to further the beatification of Dorothy Day and end police brutality against the homeless. Leo and I acted as if we were impressed. It didn't fool him. Something I'd said had put him on edge:

"I must say that you seem to have bought into the cash-nexus society, Frankie. Does it trouble you to be spending your days making more money for millionaires when there are homeless people sleeping over subway grates just a stone's throw from where we sit?"

"I can't say that it does. I seldom meet the people whose orders I place on the floor of the Exchange. Except once—a young widow who was able to buy a co-op in Forest Hills and put her daughter through college with the money she'd made on the portfolio her husband set up with my firm. He was a cop, killed on the job. She thought I was a goddam prince."

"OK, OK . . . no offense intended, Frankie," Sullivan backed off. "Please, don't take me wrong. Everyone needs employment. I understand that. In many ways, the system exploits you as much as the assembly line worker."

"Interesting thought," I said with what I guess was more disdain than I intended. I really could not have cared less what Sullivan thought about my social conscience.

"I think this conversation is heading in the wrong direction," Sullivan answered with a smile. "I did not mean to sound officious. Why don't we start over? I understand from Leo that I might be able to help you in some way. What is it?"

Leo looked over at me, clearly signaling me to do the talking.

So I did: "Well, John, I don't know how to say this exactly, but . . . well, tell me, what do you think it would be worth if someone could come up with a new Gospel, one written by Joseph of Arimathea?"

"Oh, my God, you two haven't been taken in with the Holy Grail nonsense, have you?" Sullivan raised his eyebrows and shoved his double chins into each other by lowering his jaw. "It is fairy tale material. It is what that Indiana Jones movie was all about. People have been spreading those stories since the Middle Ages. It is what Sir Gawain and Sir Galahad were supposed to be searching for, all of those legends."

"I'm not talking about the Holy Grail, just an authentic new Gospel, a Fifth Gospel written by Joseph of Arimathea, one that records Christ's words word-for-word."

"Impossible."

"OK. But what if someone could prove it?"

"You?"

"No. But what if I could provide material from someone who could, information from the records of Teilhard de Chardin?"

"What do you know about Teilhard de Chardin?" he asked with an expression that implied we shouldn't even know the name.

"Not much . . . just that people who know about these things would be likely to trust his word if he said the Gospel was authentic."

"Let me get this straight," Sullivan continued while inserting some papers and manila folders into the top drawer of his desk. "You're telling me you have a Gospel written by Joseph of Arimathea, the verifiability of which is attested to by Teilhard de Chardin?"

"And by another Jesuit—Jean Danielou," I answered. "He helped Teilhard translate the gospel."

Sullivan raised his hands as if he had just met a stickup man with a gun. "You must be joking—a new gospel translated by Teilhard de Chardin and Jean Danielou? *Please . . .*"

"That's exactly what I am saying," I continued. "Leo and I aren't theologians or anything, not even close. But we ran into someone who convinced us that this material exists. We know a hustle when we see one, probably better than you do, John, and we're convinced that the guy who told us about the Fifth Gospel was telling us the truth."

"Have you seen this Gospel?"

"No. But it was described to us. It is supposed to be Jesus' own words, meant to expose the exaggerated claims about his miracles and whatnot. Joseph of Arimathea copied it down, like a secretary, word for word."

"Wait a minute . . ." Sullivan spread his arms wide in exasperation, as if he were waiting to catch a beach ball. "Do you know what you are saying? You are telling me that Jesus was seeking to correct the other Gospels—Matthew, Mark, Luke and John. Don't you realize that those accounts were written years after his Crucifixion?"

"We do," I responded.

"Bingo!" added Leo.

"How, pray tell, could Jesus have written them, then?" Sullivan asked. "He had already, as they say, ascended into heaven. He was not around to write anything."

"What do you mean 'as they say'? Don't you believe that Jesus ascended into heaven?"

"Let's not get into that," Sullivan replied quickly. "I believe in the spiritual meaning of his Resurrection. But whatever I believe, Jesus was not around to dictate *anything* to Joseph of Arimathea after his Crucifixion. That's clear, whatever your interpretation of the Resurrection and the Ascension."

"What if I have information that he survived the Crucifixion? That Joseph of Arimathea found a way to get him out of the tomb and nurse him back to health?"

"Frankie . . . Leo . . ." Sullivan strained to appear sincere. "I don't want to be condescending to you. Seriously: I know that you are not dummies. Obviously someone has impressed you with this story about a new Gospel. But, believe me, people have been telling tales like this forever—about the Holy Grail and the Knights Templar and Masonic intrigues and the location of the lance that pierced Jesus' side . . . It's pure bunk."

I leaned across the desk and fixed Sullivan with my hard-guy glare: "John, you said you didn't think we are dummies. Then give us a little credit. I know all about all that Holy Grail crap. I've got cable. We are not talking about anything like that. All we are talking about is a new Gospel recording the words of Jesus after he survived the Crucifixion—no magic spears or potions or anything of the kind. And we are talking about the word of Teilhard de Chardin to back up that everything is authentic."

"Impossible."

"You said that."

"I'll say it again: Impossible."

"What if we could prove it? Do you think a book publisher would be interested?" I leaned back in the chair and softened my stare.

"Are you kidding? It would be the most important book of the last two thousand years. Publishers would be lining up with their checkbooks."

"This is getting interesting," Leo observed. "Do you mind if I smoke?"

"*I do* . . . of course, I do," Sullivan exclaimed. "Come on: I can't let you smoke in here."

"Shit," Leo muttered, stuffing his Marlboros back into his breast pocket. "If I farted, you would pretend you didn't notice, but if I want to smoke a cigarette you act as if I'm cracking a can of tear gas."

"This is a no-smoking office. That's the way it is," Sullivan shot back. He had taken the high moral ground. No "I'm OK, you're OK," do-your-own-thing non-judgmentalism this time, not on second-hand smoke.

"OK, OK, Sully," Leo answered with a smile. "Lighten up."

I shifted the discussion back on topic: "John, look, here's what we're saying: We think we have access to what sounds to us like proof that this new Gospel is authentic. What do we know? But even if all we have is enough to make what the lawyers call a *prima facie* case, wouldn't it still make a great book? If the Bible scholars shoot down this new Gospel, it will be long after everyone has bought our book. Wouldn't that be enough to get a publisher interested?"

"My God, if all you have is some new writing by Teilhard de Chardin, they would be interested. If it is speculation of his about a new Gospel that demythologizes the older Synoptic Gospels, that would be groundbreaking. It would be very valuable. But how would you two have this information? That is what I don't get."

"We are not willing to say. Not yet," I responded. "But, believe me, no offense, John, I wouldn't be spending my evening here with you if I didn't think we had something worthwhile."

"Well, what is the next step then?" Sullivan asked. "What can I do for you?"

"My brother tells me that you have some contacts with book publishers, that you made connections for some Indian poets. Do you think you could put us in contact with people who would be interested in this new Gospel?"

Sullivan leaned back in his chair. He squinted and pursed his lips and nodded, as if he had just come upon a great insight. "You know, I could, with exactly the right person. His name is Norman Barlow, one of the young lions at Lantern Press. He loves religious exotica. He made money for them on stories about Indian shamans and Egyptian fertility cults. There is a market for that kind of thing. I'm sure that he would love to do a book on a new Gospel, as long as you have something that will give it credibility. He needs at least a semblance of authenticity or Lantern won't touch it."

"We can give him that," I said. "That's exactly what we are offering, something solid. I promise you that."

"But you won't tell me what?"

"Not yet."

"Very mysterious, I must say, for the Corcoran brothers. You two were never known for being circumspect."

"Well, we're going to be as circumspect as hell," said Leo, "until someone puts some bucks on the table."

"Barlow deals in big bucks," said Sullivan. "He won't give you the time of day unless what you have to offer convinces him there is money to be made. He doesn't deal in books for the university library circuit. He wants themes that he can sell on Oprah's and Rosie's shows."

"Which ours is," I said without hesitation.

"Which yours would be—*if* what you come up with has credibility. I repeat: credibility is the key. You can't come up with tall tales told by some barroom philosopher about a cave in the woods with the Holy Grail. I'm warning you about that. You'll be out of Barlow's office before you know what hit you."

"How can we get to see this Barlow? Can you reach out for us?"

"I can. But . . ." Sullivan began to squirm a bit in his chair. "Would there some formal involvement for myself?" He suddenly developed an interest in arranging some pencils in a desktop holder.

"Involvement?" I asked. "I don't follow."

"Well, I'm going to have to spend some time opening doors for you with Barlow." Sullivan looked up from the pencils.

Leo cut in: "Hey, Frankie, don't you get it? John wants a piece of the action. Some role for himself in—what did he call it?—the cash-nexus society."

"I am not talking a formal agent's fee," Sullivan responded with a pained expression. "*Please* . . . I would donate a considerable portion of any finder's fee that you gave me to the Catholic Worker."

"What was the finder's fee the Indians gave you when you put them in contact with Barlow?" Leo asked, clearly pleased with the turn of events.

"This is different," said Sullivan. "You two are not from the victimized vectors of this society. Both of you make more money than I do. If you stand to make big money from a book offer I open up for you, I think it would be proper for me to be compensated for my efforts."

Things were on my turf now: "Anything we sign over a hundred-grand gets you a big one. How's that?"

"Big one?" Sullivan asked.

"A thousand dollars."

"That would be reasonable," Sullivan responded quietly.

"Reasonable! I'll say it's reasonable," Leo snapped. "A thousand dollars for a phone call? You never had a better offer in your life. My brother is being generous. There are other ways to contact a publisher than through you, you know!"

"I said the offer was reasonable," Sullivan answered quickly. "What is it you want from me? I would be grateful for a thousand dollars. I think that would be more than generous. But you won't regret it. If you sign with Barlow, I believe that he will assign an editor to work with you who will please you very much, a wonderful woman named Helen Bergeron. Barlow is a wheeler-dealer, but Helen is an exquisite woman. She specializes in books on religious themes. You'll love her, not a dishonest bone in her body. She is a Eucharistic minister at her church up in Westchester . . . Pleasantville, I believe. But she was originally a Bronx girl, from a parish over by Parkchester. You will find it easy to deal with her."

"I don't get it," Leo replied. "Why do we need this woman if Barlow-whatever-his-name is going to give us the bucks?"

"Barlow is a manager at Lantern. Helen Bergeron would actually work on editing the book. She will put you in contact with the ghostwriter who will work with you in packaging everything. You will need someone to provide a professional narration for where the information about Teilhard de Chardin was found and to link Teilhard's accounts to the new Gospel. And also tell the story of how you and Frankie took possession of the Gospel."

"We understand that," I said, glancing across at Leo to warn him not to say anything else. It was not yet the time to bring up the fact that we were talking about much more than a book about a new Gospel; that we would need a team of writers and media directors for the project of disclosing the information about Jesus' hand and his body buried at Lake Tiberias.

"Then can we shake on this?" Sullivan said, extending his hand across the desk. "We won't need a formal contract, being from the old neighborhood. I'll call Norman Barlow and set up a meeting for you at his office on Madison Avenue. I'll get back to you and Frankie when everything is set. Agreed?"

"Agreed," I answered. "But you understand this is not for public consumption. You tell no one about the Gospel or the deal is off. This book will only be marketable if we maintain the element of surprise. We can't have every graduate student in the country talking about this for months before the book comes out."

"Of course, of course. Agreed."

Leo and I stopped for beers at St. Dymphna's on St. Mark's place after leaving Sullivan. It was one of these new Irish places that caters to the body-pierced and Doc Martens Irish, the crowd that likes to talk of their "pagan Celtic roots" and engage in one-upmanship with the older establishment Irish, poke fun at them for daring to move to Rockland County and keep gays out of the St. Patrick's Day parade, things like that. But we liked the place. Painted a soft yellow and nestled among the occult bookshops and trendy secondhand stores, it looked like just another storefront from the outside. But inside everything was warm and woody, with fresh Guinness on tap.

Not a bad setting to toast what seemed to be the first step on our road to riches. In the past, I had seen Leo score with some of the babes who hung out here by playing up his working-class roots, acting like the Studs Lonigan of the East Coast. One of his funniest barroom monologues of all time was the night he told his firehouse buddies about the complications that arose because of his dental bridge when he made his moves on a girl that he met here—one with a pierced tongue

We moved to a side table, along a stucco wall adorned with an old poster for some Irish product called "St. Bruno Flake." I had no idea what it was. The bar was half full and pleasantly boisterous. No one would be interested in what Leo and I were talking about.

Leo drew long and full on his Guinness, wiping the foam from his mouth with the back of his sleeve. "I think this is going to work, Frankie. I really do. We're on first base and making the turn for second. All we have to do is tease this Barlow at Lantern Press with what we've got. He's got to go for it."

"The problem," I answered, "is that we got *nothing* yet."

"First things first," said Leo. "Once we know how much money they are going to offer, we'll work out the details of getting the stuff out of the wall at Regis. We'll get it if the money is right. Breaking into a bank vault to get a couple of million bucks is a problem. Breaking into your old high school isn't. You'll see—it's a piece of cake."

Chapter Nine

There it is, Frankie. That's the building with Barlow's office." Leo was pointing towards a sleek newer building on Madison Avenue, one of those unadorned columns of black glass that the modern architects seem to favor. It sparked like a jewel in the afternoon sun, which, I guess, is what it is supposed to do. I had taken some vacation time for the meeting. And Leo? I don't know—he always seemed to have a day off available from his firehouse. We were just a few blocks north of the Chrysler Building, the art deco structure that I always thought the best example of Manhattan's older architecture.

It is going to take a lot of explaining to convince me that these modern buildings are a step up from the brawny elegance of the Chrysler Building or Grand Central Station and the stately elegance of the golden steeple of the New York Life Building. The old sky-scrapers always seemed to "belong," massive contoured stalagmites thrusting from the city's bedrock core. The new? Form follows function? What function? Enclosing a whole generation of office workers in laminated slabs with the character of a milk carton?

We rode the elevator to the ninth floor and walked down a long hallway adorned with blowups of the recent best-sellers from Lantern Press. I hadn't read any of them, but can't say I regretted the lapse. A receptionist greeted us and steered us in the direction of Norman Barlow's office, where a secretary seated us on a leather couch looking north toward Central Park. In the distance, I could see skaters circling on Wolman Rink, like figurines in a model railroad set.

"Mr. Barlow is expecting you, but he will be a few minutes. Would you gentlemen like some coffee while you wait?" asked the secretary. She was a matronly woman in a severe gray suit and sensible shoes, all business. Even Leo did not look twice.

"I could use a cup," Leo answered, tapping his unopened pack of Marlboros against the back of his hand and looking around for an ashtray. "I guess this is a no-smoking office."

"I'm afraid you are right," the secretary replied. "Mr. Barlow sometimes enjoys a fine cigar. Perhaps he will permit you to smoke inside his office." She smiled in strained sympathy. "But out here it is strictly against company policy."

"That's OK, no problem," Leo assured her, shoving the cigarettes back into his breast pocket. He glared over at me with a look of dismay.

I declined the secretary's offer of coffee and sat back in my chair, rehearsing what I would say to Barlow. I had worked out the basics of my presentation repeatedly in preparation for this day, but I wanted it to go just right. I had to remember not only what to say, but what *not* to say.

Taking John Sullivan's warnings to heart, I had dressed for the occasion: a gray, conservatively cut Paul Stuart suit with a powder blue shirt and a navy silk tie—my Cary Grant look. The objective was to convince Norman Barlow that I was no yahoo with a conspiracy theory. Leo had donned his Sunday-go-to-meeting outfit, too: gray polyester slacks, white turtleneck, and a blue blazer that must have been purchased fifty pounds ago. The back vent was split as wide as the canvas awning over a gangplank.

"Mr. Barlow will see you now," announced the secretary after about five minutes of waiting. "This way, please."

The inner sanctum was decorated in quiet good taste, lots of mahogany and teak and carefully chosen paintings, abstract splashes of color in the Jackson Pollock–style, subdued yellows and browns that complemented the warm aura of the room. I haven't a clue about the talent of the artists, but the scheme worked, if only in the way the correct selection of vinyl flooring and curtains can make a difference in a room. Everything fit nicely.

Barlow did not look at us as we entered. He was on the phone, looking out his window at the cityscape below. He waved us toward two chairs in front of his desk and continued his conversation.

"The money will be right," he promised the person on the other end of the line. "But I need assurances that you will hold up your end. No more money from us until I see a few more chapters of quality. Of *quality!* You can't stall us indefinitely. You signed a contract to write a book for us, not to ponder a book. If you can't produce, we can't pay. It's that simple. Am I making myself clear?"

He nodded and strode back and forth in front of his window while listening to the response, head down like a politician pondering a question from an earnest voter.

"No, no, it does not work that way," he asserted emphatically. "You are not a proven commodity. We took a chance on you as an author. We put our trust in you. We can't extend the deadline indefinitely. Your theme is one that requires topicality. Topicality. Not only will there be no future payments, but we will take you to court to recover every penny of our advance if you do not start producing. We'll play hardball if we have to."

I began to wonder if this was a staged event to give Barlow the upper hand in his dealings with us. It was clear that Barlow believed in the importance of first impressions. He was a man who worked on his aura with his tailors and barbers, an aging yuppie, getting soft at the edges, probably about 220 pounds—too much for his five-foot-ten frame. Nothing sloppy, mind you, just a Pillsbury doughboy-kind of fleshiness. His expensive charcoal pants were cut to disguise the girth, though, with a pair of red suspenders for dramatic effect. His Rolex sat on top of the fabric of one of his French cuffs, lest anyone miss it. Fashionably long, his jet-black hair was oiled and swept back from his forehead into a dense mass of curls along his collar. He was about forty, I guessed, maybe a bit older, the age where corporate whiz kids begin to fret that they might not move onward and upward into the ranks of company mover and shaker.

"Look, Larry, I have a meeting scheduled," Barlow continued. "I am in the middle of it. I can't talk any longer. It is really simple: Start writing. That's what writers do, not hobnob with the stars. That comes later. And it will, if you just start writing something, dammit. I want to see something on my desk by the end of the month. Do you understand? . . . Good. *Good-bye!*"

He turned and angrily slammed the phone onto its base. It didn't impress. It was like watching a pitcher slam the rosin bag behind the mound. There were traders who performed that move all day on the floor of the Exchange. I stood to shake his hand; Leo followed suit.

I spoke before Barlow got the chance: "Hello, Mr. Barlow. I'm Francis Corcoran. This is my brother, Leo."

"Yes, yes, I'm Norman Barlow. Please forgive the histrionics." He shook his head as if he were trying to forget some unpleasant memory. "I was just on the phone with someone who likes being a writer, but not writing. There are more of *them* than you would think—more than you would think."

"We might understand more than you think. Leo and I have been around Greenwich Village on Saturday night," I answered.

"Indeed," Barlow sniggered a bit, "Indeed. You get the point." He spun his desk chair into place, dropped into it and leaned back. "So you are old friends of John Sullivan's. Good man, John Sullivan. He reached out for us to some of the most creative Native American voices in the country. I would imagine that you have read *Lakota Silence?*"

"Not yet. But it is on my list." I lied.

Barlow continued: "John was the one who brought the author Russell Six-Trees to our attention. His Catholic Worker connections bring him into contact with Native Americans who are able to articulate the exploitation of the Plains nations. I was proud to be part of the project. We were able to prod the consciences of Americans caught up in their harried pursuit of the almighty dollar, make them aware of the great injustice perpetrated upon Native Americans, and with a book that made the *Times* top-fifty list."

"Doing well by doing good," I responded, in what I hoped was a convincing display of sincerity.

"Precisely, precisely," said Barlow. "It is my credo, what guides my every decision. That's not humbug in my case. I have to make money for this company. That goes without saying. But when I leave the editorial wars, I want to leave a legacy that my children will point to with pride." He turned a framed photo on his desk toward us. It was a shot of two teenage boys holding lacrosse sticks. "Those are my boys. When I agree to publish a book, I think of them. It must be something that will sell, but also something with *gravitas*. I want my books to become part of the dialogue that defines the American character."

Barlow made a tent with his fingertips just under his chin. "John Sullivan tells me that the Corcoran brothers have something like that to offer. Is that so?"

"How much did John tell you?" I asked.

"Quite a bit. But I would prefer to hear it all from you firsthand. It is better that way. If you will just be patient a bit, one of my editors, Helen Bergeron, is on her way. She should be here any second. I want her to hear the proposition. If we decide to go ahead on the project, she will work with you. She is excellent in these areas."

There was a knock on the door, followed by the Plain-Jane secretary's head peeping around the door.

"Helen is here, Mr. Barlow."

"Send her in."

What followed took me by surprise. I had expected an editor of religious books to look like, oh, Doris Kearns Goodwin. Not even close. Leo and I stood to greet a tall, great-looking woman in a perfectly tailored tan tweed ensemble. This Helen Bergeron was a dish. Not that anyone would mistake her for a model or one of the barhopping starlets from the gossip columns. Not that kind of dish. She was older than I was, in her mid-forties, I guessed. I doubt that teenage studs would whistle and stomp when she strolled by, but they'd look. And the suits on the commuter train would snap to attention when she entered their car. That was for sure. Every rheumy male eye would be peeping over the top edge of its bifocal lens to follow those long legs to their seat. Quiet admiration would be the order of the day.

How can I put it? Some women are slender, others skinny—a jumble of elbows and bony clavicles, as if what makes them thin is pushing their bodies into a hard-edged and wiry composite, lanky, gaunt, an Olive Oyl—skinny. That wasn't this Bergeron doll. Every contour that Marilyn Monroe ever possessed was part of the package, just in more elegant and reserved proportions.

She shook hands with professional firmness as Norman Barlow handled the introductions, placed her laptop computer on a corner of his desk and then moved to a chair diagonally across from his. When she crossed her legs, her calf, in dark stockings, extended from the pressure of her knee into a graceful orb. Yet, just like the lanky gals, the foot of the crossed leg, in a patent leather pump, nearly touched the floor. Her breasts did not thrust like some military appendage from under her tweed jacket, but subtly buoyed the fabric in a mounded hint of their presence. Soft brown eyes, reddish-brown hair with a few carefully cultivated bands of gray swept back over her ears to the nape of her neck, the facial bone structure they call "chiseled" in the glossy magazines . . . I wanted to ask her for a picture for my wallet.

"Helen," said Barlow, "Mr. Corcoran was just about to give us a precis of his book proposal."

"You can call me Frankie," I said, trying to keep my eyes off Helen Bergeron's legs. "Does Ms. Bergeron know the theme of the book, too?"

"She does," said Barlow, "she does. I discussed with her what John Sullivan told me about your idea. But, again, tell the story as if we don't know a thing. We want to hear it from you. We won't be bored. And why don't we drop all the formalities. You can call us Norman and Helen."

And so I began, the whole story—to the extent that Leo and I agreed to reveal it. I told them about Teilhard de Chardin discovering the Fifth Gospel transcribed by Joseph of Arimathea while working on the Dead Sea Scrolls; that Teilhard had taken the Gospel and hidden it, along with the story of when and how he found the material; about his and Jean Danielou's translation; that this Gospel was an account of Jesus' words narrated by him to Joseph of Arimathea; that this Gospel corrected the miracle stories found in the other Gospels. And that Leo and I knew where it was hidden, and that we would be willing to produce it—if the money was right.

When I had finished, Barlow leaned back and after a few seconds of studied thoughtfulness spoke in earnest tones: "Let me be blunt with you: Helen and I agree that either you have been completely taken in, or you are talking about one of the most important books of our time. I won't beat around the bush. If you can come up with this new Gospel and Teilhard's accompanying narration—something credible, beyond reproach—we are prepared to offer you an advance of well over one million dollars. But we will not pay a penny until you deliver . . . deliver something that Helen and I accept as legitimate. We are not interested in material that will appeal to *conspiracy theorists*. We want something solid, something that will engage the scholarly world as well as the tabloids."

Barlow leaned across his desk and wagged his finger next to his cheek like a scolding schoolmaster: "You realize of course that the deal is entirely dependent upon your maintaining absolute confidentiality with us. No other publisher can be approached with the project. No one else can even know of the theme. To be effective, this book has to hit the public consciousness as a full-bore surprise. Otherwise the impact will be muffled. If we sign with you, you must be absolutely discreet."

"We understand," I said. "And the same on your end. Getting this Gospel to you will be impossible if the word gets out that we are coming for it. There are people who could make it difficult for us."

"Frankie," Helen Bergeron leaned forward just slightly as she spoke, subtly using her silver Cross pen as a pointer, "I trust you are aware that you are talking about something of enormous scholarly significance. We would want a project of this sort to be carried out with the utmost seriousness."

"I don't know how to be any plainer about what we are offering," I said. "We aren't asking you to accept our credentials as scholars. What we will produce is the original copy of the Fifth Gospel, plus a translation by Teilhard de Chardin and Jean Danielou, plus Teilhard's records of when and how he found it."

"How will we know that the Gospel is authentic and that the diaries are truly Teilhard's," asked Helen, "if you refuse to reveal where you will get the documents in question? Why are you being so mysterious about their location? If we knew that you actually had possession of the material, we would be much more enthusiastic about the project."

"We don't have any of it yet. But we know how to get it," I answered. "We won't expect a penny until we produce everything and let your experts analyze it."

"That goes without saying," said Barlow. "I hope I have made myself clear about that. We require a legitimate, verifiable Gospel and Teilhard's account of when and where he got it."

I was tempted to go further; to tell them about the hand and the dagger and the map to where Jesus' body was located. Their concerns about verifiable evidence would become irrelevant if they knew what we actually were going to plop on their desks. And the million dollar advance would be chump change in comparison to what they would have to offer for the complete package. But I held back. There would be a better time to set the hook.

"Frankie," Helen asked quietly, "will you have to do anything illegal to get your hands on the material? Is that why you are reluctant to tell us where the documents are located?"

"Well, you know," I answered, "I expected that question to come up sooner or later. I've thought it over. I think it is best if you and Lantern Press stay out of that part of the project. Some things will have to take place that might break some laws, but only in a technical sense."

"In a technical sense? You will have to explain what you mean by that," Barlow said apprehensively.

"Well, the way I see it, the new Gospel was not Teilhard's personal property," I said. "So no one *owns* it now. Right? Teilhard could not transfer property rights to anyone. Look: we'll just be changing custodians of the Gospel, from someone who wants to keep it secret to someone who will respect the public's right to know. Maybe there will be some squabbling over who owns the original parchment somewhere along the line. We can deal with that, right? Teilhard took it from Israel. I bet the Israelis will want it back, to store it with the Dead Sea Scrolls. But so what? Once the book is published, we can give it to them, no? The book will sell even if the original Gospel goes to Tel Aviv."

"Please be forthright with us: Are you saying that you will have to steal the Gospel from its current location?" Helen asked with arched eyebrows.

"No, I'm not, except maybe the way treasure hunters take treasure from sunken ships. We are going to have to take possession of it, but not from an owner in the strict sense of the word."

Leo spoke up: "Yeah, come on . . . that is not going to be your problem."

"I don't like this, Norman." Helen turned in her chair and exhaled in a mixture of impatience and annoyance. "We cannot participate in the theft of important historical data. The Corcorans are keeping essential information from us. I don't think we should listen to any more of this."

For a second or two it looked as if Barlow's conscience would overcome his yearning for a blockbuster book. For a second or two . . .

"It is a tightrope, Helen, I'll admit that," he said. "But I think we can proceed as long as we are not asked to participate in anything illegal ourselves. Plus, Frankie is right. We will probably be required to hand the Gospel over to the Israeli authorities once the book is published. In fact, we will actually be returning to them material that Teilhard was not entitled to take in the first place. We can even ask the University of Jerusalem to serve as the verifiers of the authenticity of the document. Which might even help sales.

"I don't see the problem. Consider the way the British and the Greeks are quarreling to this day over the Elgin Marbles—whether the Ottoman Turks had the right to transfer title to the British Museum. These archaeological things are never straightforward."

"Except for the fact that we seem to be discussing breaking and entry to get it," Helen snapped. "Is that right, Frankie? Leo? What will be involved in taking possession of the Gospel?"

"We'll tell you after we get it," I answered. "That way you'll have . . . what do they call it in Washington? Plausible deniability?"

"So we are talking breaking and entry?" Helen replied. "You are going to steal this material from *whom*? Church authorities?"

"No," I responded, "not really. We are not talking about breaking into the Vatican's archives. Nothing like that."

Leo spoke: "Ma'am, my brother and me are giving you a way not to worry about any of this. That's the point here. We aren't talking violence or anything that will put anyone in jail. You've got *nothing* to worry about. Take my word. Relax. Chill. There is nothing for you to get in a dither over."

"No offense, Leo, but I don't know you well enough to take your word," she responded. Leo's barroom condescension was not going to work in this venue. I loved it.

Helen removed her gold-rimmed reading glasses and looked across at Barlow, waiting for him to take the next step.

"I think we can do this, Helen," Barlow assured her. "It will be OK. I'm going to ask you to steer this project along. Use your judgement. Choose the ghostwriter you think best. If anything unethical begins to develop, you will have complete authority to end our involvement. You can . . ."

The office phone interrupted his sentence. Barlow frowned in annoyance as he picked up the receiver.

"I told you no calls, Judy," he snapped into the receiver. "What? Who? . . . OK, put him through." Barlow huffed in exasperation, shook his head and dropped the receiver just under his chin to speak to us: "I'm sorry, this will just be a minute. Forgive me." He stood and walked to the far end of the room and continued his conversation while looking out the window.

Helen leaned toward Leo and me and spoke quietly: "If you'll excuse me, I'd like to do some paperwork while Norman is on the phone. I am sure he will be finished shortly." She slid her reading

glasses back into place, reached for her laptop computer, and began to tap away at the keyboard, opening and closing files in rapid
succession, just occasionally looking up to acknowledge our presence with a little smile.

I loved every second of it. She gave the impression that the last
thing on her mind would be the possibility that I might be checking her out, examining the way her clothes clung in all the right
places, as if such a circumstance was merely an unavoidable by-
product of her simple good grooming. Yeah, I noticed the wedding
band, too. I guess what they say about all the good ones being
taken is true.

Barlow spoke on the phone for just a minute or two more, then
returned to his seat, frowning at the trials and tribulations of being
a man at the nerve center of so many crucial decisions. "I don't
know what will hit me first—an ulcer or a nervous breakdown."
He exhaled heavily. "Now where were we?"

Helen closed the cover of her laptop and removed her glasses.

"We were giving me the authority to stop our involvement in
the Corcoran brothers' scheme the moment anything illegal or
unethical takes place," she said.

"Correction," said Barlow. "You are to stop anything illegal or
unethical that goes *beyond the bounds of reasonableness*. We are assuming that the Corcorans are going to take the Gospel from someone who will not be pleased by that turn of events. We have agreed
to leave that problem to the Corcorans."

"I must admit I can't picture how doing that is going to stay
within the bounds of reasonableness," she replied calmly.

"That is what we shall see," said Barlow. "You realize, of course,
Helen, that there are editors with this company who would take
your place in a heartbeat and carry through this project even if the
Corcorans were planning to steal the Gospel from Mother Teresa."

"She's no longer with us," Helen answered.

"You get my point," said Barlow.

"You are not threatening my job if I do not take this project, are
you, Norman?" The tone of her voice made clear that she had little
fear of being unable to find work elsewhere.

"No, simply making it clear to you that you could lose the opportunity to work on a book of historic importance. And that someone far less punctilious about doing the right thing will end up in charge of this project if you back away from it."

Helen looked down at her fingernails for a second or two and then looked up at Leo and me.

"I assume that the two of you are Catholics. Am I correct?"

"You are," I answered.

"*Practicing* Catholics?" she asked.

"More or less. I'm more, I'd say Leo is less." I looked across at Leo to see if I had overstepped the line. I hadn't. He raised his eyebrows and shrugged to assure me that he couldn't care less how I phrased it. "We both graduated from Catholic high schools. Leo went to LaSalle; I went to Regis."

"Regis?" she replied with arched eyebrows. "I'm impressed."

"Don't be," I answered. "I just about made it through the place."

"And college?" she asked.

"None . . . for me *or* Leo."

"I am a graduate of Ursuline Academy in the Bronx," she said. "And then Georgetown."

"I am not sure what you are getting at," I said, puzzled over where she was taking the conversation. I didn't think she wanted to swap Catholic school stories about May processions and parish dances.

"Well, what I am getting at is this—are you troubled about what this book will do?"

"I am not sure what you mean."

"You must know. Does it trouble you to be demythologizing Jesus in this manner? You will be confirming everything Bultmann suggested about the New Testament."

"Who?" I asked.

"I'm sorry. Rudolf Bultmann. He was a Protestant theologian who argued that we should view the miraculous elements in the Biblical accounts as myths expressing religious truths, but as myths nevertheless. Modern Catholic authorities are generally unopposed to this approach when the Old Testament is in question. They don't mind viewing the story of Noah and Jonah and the whale as more symbol than fact. But they do not take kindly to viewing the New Testament in the same way. Bultmann calls for that. With this book, you will be exposing traditional Catholic teaching as erroneous. If I understand correctly, you say that Jesus himself dispels the miraculous elements of the Synoptic Gospels in this new Gospel."

"Well, the truth is the truth. And we aren't theologians," I said. "We'll let them work out those things." I paused for a second. "Are you troubled by the idea that Jesus survived the Crucifixion? Is that it?"

"No, not really," she said, pursing her lips slightly. "I guess I am the type of person that people call a *Commonweal* Catholic."

"Which means?" I asked

"*Commonweal* is a liberal Catholic magazine. People who read it generally think it is more important to live Jesus' message of love than to worry about the supernatural elements in the Bible. They generally favor the social programs of the Democratic Party . . . see them as a way of helping the least of our brethren, of bringing Jesus' words to life in our lives."

"Catholic Worker-types?" I asked.

"No, not exactly," Helen answered. "More upper-middle class in temperament. Professional and academic types."

"Limousine liberals?" Leo asked with a little smirk.

Helen laughed and shrugged her shoulders: "*They* would use different language to describe themselves."

"They sound like the kind of people who would like Teilhard," I said.

"They do; they do indeed," Helen confirmed.

"And that's you?" I asked.

"Pretty much. My position has always been that it did not really matter if Jesus rose from the dead in a strictly physical sense—that his message of love coming to life again in the minds and hearts of his followers is what matters, even if a camera would not have recorded anything unusual on the first Easter morning. Still, I am not sure I like the idea of discovering that there is positive evidence that he did not rise from the dead—of being able to actually *document* that fact. It surrenders an awful lot of Catholicism. I never pictured myself playing a role in bringing that information to mankind."

"But I thought you said the message is what mattered, not where the body is," I said, pondering how she would react when I revealed to her that I could actually show her where Jesus' body was buried.

"Well, that is my point," she said, "but it is easier to be a liberal when you are seeking to liberalize an institution with vitality, a Church that will survive your liberalizing efforts and continue to do the noble things that make a liberal stay within the Church rather than simply stop practicing the faith . . . I wonder if actually confirming that there was no physical resurrection will weaken the Church's prestige to an extent that it will no longer be able to work effectively for peace and social justice around the world? Do you see my point?"

"Yeah, you want the Church to stay strong enough to do the things that you agree with," said Leo. I was not sure if he understood the ramifications of his comment, although he might have. He was no dummy.

Helen Bergeron did though. She raised her eyebrows and lowered her chin as she replied, "Are you accusing me of hypocrisy, Leo?" She was not angry though. There was a smile at the edge of her eyes, those gorgeous eyes.

"No offense, Ma'am," Leo assured her. "Just observing. Hell, I thought Rudolf Bultmann was a wrestler."

"Do you believe that the bread and wine become Jesus' body and blood at the Consecration?" I asked her. I wasn't sure what that had to do with anything, but I was curious about what she believed and what she did not. It could make a difference down the road.

"Yes, I do," she replied without hesitation. "I do. I am a Eucharistic minister at my parish, in fact. I don't believe that I am biting off a portion of Jesus' hand or foot when I receive Communion, but I do believe that Jesus comes to life in the minds and hearts of the congregation at Mass; that when they join in a communal expression of Christian love the congregation becomes one body in Christ in a mysterious and profound way. I think most Catholics work out something for themselves like that to explain what they mean by the Real Presence." She paused for emphasis. "What do you believe happens at the Consecration?"

"I don't know. I believe Jesus becomes part of us—under the appearances of bread and wine, and that it happens only at Mass. I can't give you any more details than that."

"But you remain a regular communicant?" she asked.

"Yeah, I am. I even go to Confession once in a while." I laughed a bit self-consciously. "I need it more than most."

Norman Barlow had been unaccustomedly quiet for the last minute or two. "This is getting interesting," he commented, "but it is over my head. I am not a Catholic, you know. Do these things make any difference for the book we have in mind?"

"It could," Helen answered. "We could find ourselves in heated opposition with Catholic authorities as we go along with this project. I want the Corcorans to realize what is in store for them. They will make enemies of people they may not want to alienate. Maybe their favorite Cardinal."

"Leo and I have thought about that. We know the stakes," I said. "I don't think we have a favorite Cardinal."

"And the fact that you stand to make a considerable fortune with this book is enough to make up for the likely notoriety you will experience?" Helen asked calmly, as if she were a doctor explaining the pros and cons of an upcoming operation. "You have no problem with that?"

"None that we can't handle," I assured her. "We're big boys."

"What do they say? The truth will set you free? Right?" Leo added.

I wasn't sure.

Chapter Ten

Leo and I spent the next few weeks sorting things out, Leo becoming more energized than I had seen him in years, fully engaged in working out our strategy to get into Teilhard's casket. He had all the angles figured. We would find three or four Inwood barflies with strong backs to serve as diggers; lowlifes, but not hardboiled types difficult to control. If we told them that we were looking for some documents that would affect a dispute over an inheritance they would not think twice—especially if the money we offered was right. Leo was sure he could sell the deal.

The dollar amount was important. It had to be sufficient to cover the criminal risks of grave robbing, but not enough to arouse suspicion that they were participating in a boost with a big pay day. And the diggers had to be people not savvy enough to put two and two together once the full story came out. The connection between grave robbing in Poughkeepsie and subsequent archaeological discoveries along the shores of Lake Tiberias would not be obvious, but we didn't want to take any chances.

A two-hour drive from Inwood to Poughkeepsie after midnight, a few hours of digging, and then a drive back to the city before dawn—Leo was convinced that there would be plenty of eager candidates, especially if we gave them a grand a piece. He would take care of recruiting. We would dig in the spring when the ground would be softened up a bit, just a few weeks more.

How would we do the shoveling without being detected by anyone at the Culinary Institute? Leo had that figured out, too. We would drive up to the grounds some night—a week or so before we planned to dig—and ingratiate ourselves with the night watchmen, buy them some beers and smokes, that kind of thing. We would give them some story about why we had to get into the casket and assure them that we would dig up the grave quietly and smooth over the ground meticulously when we were finished; that no one would even know we had been there. That all they had to do was spend a few hours patrolling the opposite end of the campus while our digging was going on—and we would grease their palms with a few C-notes.

They'd bite. Why wouldn't they? We weren't going to damage anything that the Culinary Institute cared about. The watchmen would get no grief. It was likely that the graveyard was technically not even within their area of responsibility. Hell, maybe it was even beyond the Culinary Institute's property lines in a technical sense. Maybe the Jesuits retained ownership of the cemetery. That would be logical. The Institute's activities would go on as usual the day after we were finished. No one would be hurt. No violence. A no-brainer. The odds were that no one would even notice the traces of our work until weeks later. Money might not have the power to buy everything in this world, but it would be enough to convince a few groggy night watchmen to look the other way for a few hours.

I also spent time during those weeks thinking about Helen Bergeron. I'll say. I moped about like one of those lost souls in the Frank Sinatra songs—you know, seeing her face before me, feeling a glow just thinking of her, lost in a dream of her, the beautiful theme of every dream I ever knew—all that weepy drivel. I'm not kidding. I could not get over the way she combined a powerful sexiness with . . . with what? You wouldn't call it innocence. She was no little girl, no cutie pie. There was an air of sophistication and worldliness about her, but a basic decency also, something clean and fresh and forthright, something that made you want to be in her presence, to bathe in her smile and the warmth of her eyes.

These were strange feelings for me. I know lust. I know one-night stands. Love I'm not so sure about. I wouldn't call myself a confirmed bachelor, but I have seen too many aging sorority sisters start the evening nibbling on the crudités and talking about their favorite art galleries and end it snorting coke and looking for edgy sex. The experience has soured my hopes that there will ever be a Sunday kind of love in my future. I know, I know—my lifestyle isn't going to persuade some fair damsel that I come from east of the sun and west of the moon either. I guess that's the point. You had to be good to have a woman like Helen Bergeron in your life.

I wasn't chump enough to think that I could be in love with her on the basis of our single meeting in Norman Barlow's office. But I'll say this: I dwelled upon visions of how great it would be to take someone like her and a couple of young kids to the Macy's Thanksgiving Day Parade or one of the city's museums and then curl up with her that evening on the couch after the kids hit the sack. Chet Baker music, wine, and this Bergeron by the fire. Wooo-boy. I played with the thought that maybe there are better ways to spend a night than at a Rangers' game and beers afterwards.

I spent my evenings wondering what she was doing at her home in Pleasantville, what her children and husband were like, about the way she carried herself on the altar when she distributed Communion at her parish on Sundays, her smile as she entertained friends at dinner parties—whether she ever thought of me at all. And, yeah, I thought of her as I fell asleep, picturing her walking to her bed in a slinky nightgown, while her husband anticipated her warm presence beside him. Part Teresa of Avila, part Princess Diana. (If you're talking about looks alone, Lady Di is one of my all-time favorite foxes.)

I tried to come up with an excuse to call her at Lantern Press, but it wasn't easy. The agreement when we left Norman Bartlow's office was that we would contact them only after the "irregular" aspects of acquiring the new Gospel were completed. Still, I wanted an excuse to see her again . . . just to be near her, see her laugh, hear her talk. I had no intention of trying to seduce her, nothing like that. Seriously. I knew that even hinting at such a thing would sour things between us. I'd have to be a Straight Arrow to make her a part of my life. Any sleaze and she would treat me like an irresponsible adolescent. The irony hit home: The worldly posturing about cars and bank accounts, the whiff of decadence that I used to attract the tawny goddesses of the bar and beach house circuit, would be counterproductive with Helen Bergeron.

So you won't think I'm exaggerating when I say that I almost fell off the couch when she called. It was a Wednesday night, while I was stretched out and flipping the remote control between a basketball game and the nightly talk shows—Bill O'Reilly and Chris Matthews and the like. I bolted up and patted my hair into place when I heard her voice. (I know that didn't make sense; that is the point.)

"Hello, Frankie, it's Helen Bergeron from Lantern Press. How are you?"

My heart began throbbing like a schoolboy's. I started to breathe so heavily that I had to take the phone away from my mouth and take a deep breath to calm down.

"Well, hello, Helen, how nice to hear from you," I answered, my voice cracking a bit. "Are you still at your office?"

"No. I'm at my home in Pleasantville. I thought it would be easier to reach you at home. I know you are tied up all day on the floor of the Stock Exchange."

"True enough. Most days I don't even get a chance to take a break." My voice was calming down. "Is there something wrong?"

"No, nothing wrong *per se*," she answered. "But I do have some, well . . . concerns. I was wondering if there is anything new on your end?"

"If you mean do I have the new Gospel, no. But we will within a month or so."

"Have you thought any more about what will come after that?"

"A lot," I answered. "In fact, I have some additional information for you, something important."

"I wish you wouldn't be so mysterious. What are you talking about?"

I had to tell her about the hand and Jesus' body sooner or later. But I still was not sure if it was time. I hedged.

"Helen, look, let me put it this way: there is more to this than just the new Gospel. There is going to be some additional archaeological information, too."

"What kind of information?"

"I don't think I should tell you over the phone. It won't work that way. It's too sensitive, delicate. I have to make sure that you are the right person to work with."

"I don't know if I like this. You have doubts about me? In what way?"

"About how you will respond to the new things I have to tell you."

"I don't know what you are talking about, but we'd better get this out of the way," she said with a noticeable trace of anger. "Can you come to my office tomorrow?"

"No, I can't. Really. I don't want to sound like a master of the universe, but when I take off things go bad for the company on the floor of the Exchange. I could come after work though—between six and seven some night, if you want."

"That's not good for me, not for the next few weeks. I have obligations at home in the evenings. My children are of school age. What about on the weekend? This Saturday maybe? I'm working at the office until noon," she said. "Could you meet me then?"

"I can. But how about we talk someplace less official. Maybe over lunch." (Yeah, yeah, I was being devious.) "I can meet you at Annie Moore's at noon, just behind Grand Central. You'll be able to hop on your train for Pleasantville afterwards. It'd be convenient."

"I know Annie Moore's," she said. "Just past the taxi stands, between Madison and Vanderbilt, correct?"

"That's the place. It's a mob scene there during commuter hours and at night, but Saturday afternoon is usually quiet. I know some of the waitresses. I'll have them set us up at a table in the back. It'll give us some space to talk this out."

"Fine. I'll be there," she said. "A neighbor is taking my boys to a hockey game in Connecticut for the afternoon on Saturday. I can fit in an hour or so. But can't you give me a hint at what this earthshaking revelation will be?"

"No, I'm serious. Not on the phone. I'd feel funny. I have to ease you into this."

She laughed a clean and unaffected laugh. "This is really beginning to intrigue me, Mr. Corcoran. It isn't something about space aliens, now, is it?"

"Bigger."

"Oh, my, I can't wait," she laughed again. "I'll see you on Saturday. Are you sure that Leo can make it, too?"

"Leo?"

"Shouldn't he be there for this discussion?"

"No, no, he'll be working on Saturday." I had no idea if that was true. Yeah: devious.

Saturday could not come fast enough. I bought a new shirt for the day, a creamy white knit from Brooks Brothers, plush enough for an afternoon at a polo club. I hit my barber for the lightest of trims. I ran three miles through the wind in Central Park early on Saturday morning to get a healthy glow.

What was I hoping for if seduction was out the question? Well, how can I put it? I wanted her to know me at my best, to see me as someone she might be attracted to if she were not married. That's all. I was hoping for something like what the medieval knights used to mean by worshipping from afar. Becoming a meaningful "if things were different" with her would be sufficient, all things considered.

She had arrived at Annie Moore's before me. I could see her at a back table as soon as I opened the door. There were only two or three other tables occupied in the restaurant area where she sat, a raised platform just past the bar, an expanse of embossed green wallpaper, cherry wood moldings and bronze sconces. The bar was quiet too, just a few customers hunched over their drinks and three waitresses gathered near the cash register. One of the waitresses was a twenty-something girl named Marie from my mother's hometown in Clare. I joked around with her whenever I was in the place. She called me the "King of the Narrowbacks," an Irish-American with a back too narrow to bear the traditions of the old country. She meant it good-naturedly. I think.

The melancholy strains of "The Boys of the Old Brigade," sung by the Irish folk group the Wolfe Tones, could be heard faintly in the background. The phenomenon always intrigued me: why so many buttoned down Irish-American account executives and law-yer-types loved to nurse a beer and muse the words of I.R.A. battle hymns while waiting for the commuter train to Scarsdale.

"Hey, hey, Marie, how the hell are you today?" I asked as I neared the waitresses. "Pretty quiet in here." I gave her my naughty wink.

"It is, Francis darlin'," Marie said. "We set up your date in the back. I must say, you are getting up in the world. Classy lady, in-deed."

"Business, Marie, strictly business."

"I know your business," she responded with a tiny smile.

"Shame on you," I answered. "You going to wait on us?"

"I will, luv. I'll be right there."

I walked past the waitresses and toward Helen. She looked down and tried to smother her laughter as I neared the table. I didn't get it.

"What's so funny?" I asked as I removed my jacket and draped it over the chair. (Which was OK. It is that kind of place.)

"The reaction that you elicit from the waitresses," Helen an-swered whimsically. "My God . . . when you passed them they looked at each other as if they had just seen Brad Pitt. Wide-eyed adoration. It must be a burden to be such a dashing fellow."

"I think it has more to do with the tips I leave," I explained, not really sure what Marie and her friends had done.

"No, no, Frankie, that look had nothing to do with tips." She laughed again. "How are you?"

"Fine, fine."

She looked drop-dead gorgeous in the amber glow of the wall lamps. Saloon light became her. She was dressed more casually than when I had met her in Norman Barlow's office: tan cashmere sweater, chocolate-colored slacks and highly polished antique-brown boots. To think there was a guy somewhere in Pleasantville who came home to this every night. Life isn't fair.

The waitress arrived in her spiffy little tuxedo outfit to take our order, her cute butt jutting out under the tightly wrapped cummerbund. I was dying for a frothy pint of Guinness, but went for a glass of Merlot instead. I had stayed away from cigarettes and chewed half a pack of baking soda gum for the last two hours for the same reason. There would be no beer and cigarette breath seeping around this table, not today. Helen had ordered a glass of Chardonnay before I arrived. She surprised me by ordering a refill. We both ordered turkey club sandwiches. If I had been alone I would have ordered one of Annie Moore's sizzling burgers with chili on the side. Helen Bergeron was civilizing me into something unrecognizable.

"I have some interesting news for you, Frankie," said Helen, sipping her wine. "Norman Barlow is playing with the idea of hiring Meredith McCoy to narrate some promotional material for the book. He believes the public has to be prepared for the impact—to assure them that we are not doing anything irreverent."

"Why Meredith McCoy?" I responded. "She is one movie away from selling jewelry on the Home Shopping Network."

Helen laughed in spite of herself. "Frankie, please, she is an accomplished actress, a distinguished woman."

I liked making her laugh.

"But over the hill for ten years."

"She is past her peak, that is true. But actresses at the peak of their careers do not do voice-overs for book promotions."

"Helen, believe me . . . when you hear what I am going to tell you, the most distinguished names in the entertainment industry will be lining up to be part of this project. And it will require more than a book promotion—more like a prime time television special. More people will be watching than the last Seinfeld."

"Go on," she said as the waitress placed our sandwiches on the table.

"Remember a few years back when Geraldo Rivera made a fool of himself by televising the opening of Al Capone's secret safe somewhere?"

"Vaguely," she answered.

"Well, you don't remember much about the show because Geraldo found nothing there. The vault was as empty, except for the cobwebs. Geraldo looked like a turkey, pointing his flashlight around the walls. But the hype had people talking about the show for weeks ahead of time. If he had found something it would have been a big story. People like that kind of thing. What I'm talking about makes Al Capone's buried treasure look like chicken feed in comparison."

She took a small bite from her sandwich, sipped her wine, rested the glass on the table, then leaned back and crossed her arms: "I'm listening," she said, almost smugly, as if I were surely exaggerating.

So I told her.

Everything. About Desmond Carey. The dagger inscribed with INRI. The map to where Jesus was buried. The hand. The fake wall at Regis; the directions hidden in Teilhard de Chardin's grave at the Culinary Institute. The Jesuit conspirators. All of it.

I was surprised by how hard it hit her. The impact was dramatic. She followed my every word, barely moving a muscle, her arms folded in place. When I finished, she dropped her eyes toward her wineglass and twisted the stem between her fingers. She did not look up for what seemed a long time. It was as if she had heard some devastating medical news that she did not know how to handle.

"Hey, Helen . . . are you OK?" I asked.

She looked up somberly: "You are not kidding, are you?"

"No, I am not," I answered. "I'm deadly serious."

She pushed her sandwich to the side with a dismissive thrust.

"What's the matter? Something wrong with the sandwich?" I asked.

"Something wrong? Please . . . you think I can sit here nibbling on a sandwich after hearing that?" She leaned back and stared at the ceiling and exhaled heavily.

"Hey, I don't get this," I responded. "Is breaking into Regis such a big deal? I told you that Lantern Press will not have to be involved with any of that."

"My God, breaking into Regis is the least of my concerns." She leaned forward and spoke in an intense whisper. "You are talking about the hand of Jesus Christ! About digging up his body!"

"And? You told me at Barlow's office that you weren't bothered by the idea that Jesus' body was in the ground somewhere. All I'm talking about is showing the world where."

"I can't discuss this. I need time. Please, I want to go home. I'll call you. Let me give you something to cover the bill," she said while slipping her coat over her shoulders.

"No need for that," I responded. I threw a few tens onto the table. "Come on, talk to me. What's the matter?"

"Not now."

She stood abruptly and walked toward the door. I followed, shrugging my shoulders in confusion toward the waitresses as I passed them. They smiled smugly and waved, apparently thinking that I had said something to set off a lovers' quarrel.

I caught up to Helen as she approached the taxi drop-off at the Vanderbilt Avenue entrance to Grand Central, grabbing her arm more forcefully than I should have. She spun angrily.

"Take your hands off me!" she snapped. "Who do you think you are?"

I let go as if I had grabbed a hot poker. "Helen, I'm sorry. Please, talk to me. What's going on? I don't get it."

"Do I have to draw a picture? I don't want to be part of this," she said emphatically. "Apparently you do not take your faith seriously. I do. I told you I need time. Is that too much to ask?"

"Please," I said. "Come on, let's talk. Let's walk over to Bryant Park. It's just around the corner."

"I know where Bryant Park is, damn it!" she shot back.

"Well, come on then. Walk with me. Please. You have to explain what's got you so riled? We're supposed to be colleagues, no?"

Neither of us said much until we got to Bryant Park. We found a bench near the band shell. The afternoon sun beamed down pleasantly through an early spring breeze. Bundled in our winter coats, it was comfortable enough.

"Helen, you're acting as if I've done something wrong. You've got to tell me what's going on. What is it? Do you think this information should be kept secret from the world? Is that it?"

"I don't know what I think," she answered. "I told you that I need time." Her eyes roamed across the choir of bare-limbed trees circling the park.

I spoke carefully: "Helen, I know I said this already, but you told me that you already thought that Jesus' body was in the ground somewhere. That the physical resurrection was unimportant—that Jesus' teachings are what matter, not the old miracle stories. Why is it so hard to take to find out that you were right?"

"This is different," she said. "What you told us the other day at the office left some ambiguity about what happened after the Crucifixion. I had expected this new Gospel that you were talking about to be something that would be little more than a lively topic for debate. I never dreamed that anything as conclusive as Jesus' body was involved in your scheme."

She shook her head in exasperation, then continued: "I don't know why I'm telling you this, Frankie. You are hardly the right person to be my spiritual adviser, but I pray to Jesus, to a real Jesus, not some symbol," she answered. "I never needed the miracle stories to be a Christian. My God, I have edited books by Jesus Seminar scholars. I have no problem with that."

"The Jesus what?" I asked. "You're going to have to help me out here."

"They are theologians who are considered radical for alleging the things about Jesus that you now say you can prove, prove beyond any doubt. And I am going to be your accomplice," she answered. "One of them, John Dominic Crossan, describes the Gospels as 'powerful metaphorical stories,' as something comparable to *Aesop's Fables*. I never minded the fact that there were some Christians who think of Jesus that way. But I don't. I pray to a personal God, to a risen Jesus. My whole life, my sense of right and wrong, of what is honorable and dishonorable behavior hinge upon his role in my life. I mean that. I pray to a Jesus who could have performed miracles, whether he actually did or not. It is the core of my being. It is who I am."

"And?" I asked. "You can still pray to him—to his spirit."

"Look: I believe in heaven," she said. "Do you get that? In an eternal reward for living life in a moral manner. Not angels sitting on clouds, but I believe that heaven is where Jesus is, not that he is in the ground somewhere in Israel. At least until now. I have always said that I did not care if intellectuals viewed his ascension as a metaphor for a triumphant Christianity—that they should not be called heretics for that. I am open-minded. But it has never been just a complete metaphor for me—not for me personally. I pray to a personal Christ. I have lived my life with the idea that there is a Jesus who loves me. Can you see why I am a bit unraveled by all of this, damn it?"

"No, not really. I don't see the problem," I pleaded. "You can still believe that Jesus is in heaven, but the same way everyone else is—the way the saints and your relatives and friends who passed on are. His soul. As a spirit. So his followers invented the story about the Resurrection of his body and the Ascension into heaven to get people to take Jesus' teachings more seriously. What's the big deal?"

"It means that the Catholic Church has been in error for nearly two-thousand years. That's the big deal."

"So? They've admitted they were wrong about other things."

"Frankie, this isn't meatless Fridays and the Latin Mass we're talking about. We're talking about the Resurrection, the Ascension—the core beliefs of Christianity. St. Paul said that without the risen Christ our faith is in vain."

"There are Protestant churches where the members don't take these things literally, right? They still pray. They still live good lives, better than a lot of Catholics I know."

"You say that so calmly. You think that the Catholic Church will be able to survive the dissemination of information like this? I am not so sure. Not at all. I don't think the Protestant churches will survive either."

"What are you saying? That we should cover all this up?"

She looked at me, then down at her hands, then up at the wall of skyscrapers bordering the park. Then back at me, closing her eyes and exhaling softly. "No, I'm not saying that." She appeared to be reluctantly coming around to the inevitability of the situation.

"Look, Helen, I've thought about all this. Christianity has been around for 2000 years, right? Christians 5000 years from now are not going to believe in the same things we believe in now, not in the same way. Even if we keep all this a secret, probably science will advance to the point where the idea of a physical resurrection and ascension will not be something the average person even thinks about in the future. Probably Christians hundreds of years ago believed the story of Jonah and the whale more word-for-word than modern Christians do. So what? Times change. People adapt."

"Maybe," she answered. "And you see yourself as the one who has a mission to enlighten the world in this manner?"

"No, I'm just the messenger. I didn't ask for any of this. Theologians and scripture scholars are the ones who will study the evidence. I'm just putting it on the table for them."

"And making millions of dollars for your efforts?"

"Look, Helen, the money we make won't make it any less true. The truth is the truth. The world deserves the truth about this."

"Deserves it maybe—is able to handle it, I'm not so sure."

Two of New York's body-pierced leather boys strolled through the park just then, gaunt and ashen-faced, in their haggard mid-twenties, the epitome of heroin chic. Their engineer boots and metal motorcycle jacket buckles jangled in the chill air.

I nodded toward them after they passed our bench. "Helen, come on, what difference is it going to make to them. They're the Americans of the future."

"Not funny," she responded and lowered her eyes. "My children are the Americans of the future, too."

"Will it change you in any way? It won't. Right? You'll be the same person to your husband and your kids, to your friends, to the people you work with at Lantern Press. You'll still be a Eucharistic minister. You'll fit all this into what you believe."

"You say that so confidently, Frankie. You don't know me or my life. There are many things I do, and don't do—things I put up with in my life because I believe that I have duties to God. Take away a personal, loving Jesus who will judge me for my behavior in the next life and I might very well become a different person; perhaps one that I will not like."

"Come on, what would you have to put up with that is so bad?" I asked in what I hoped would be seen as a whimsical manner. "You're the perfect woman. Anyone can see that."

She lowered her eyes in mock anger, like a teacher reprimanding an unruly but likeable child.

"Well, whatever it is I have to put up with, it is none of your business." She wasn't upset with me, but clearly wanted to steer the conversation in another direction.

"So are you saying you want off the project?" I asked.

"No, not for the time being anyway."

"Are you going to tell Norman Barlow about the hand and the body?"

"Of course. It changes the scope of the project enormously. You will want to see him, too. Obviously you are going to ask for a great deal more money."

"I don't know if I like that idea," I said.

"What idea?"

"Telling Barlow."

"You have to do. How else can the money side of this be worked out?"

"How about if we wait until Leo and I get into Regis and take possession of the hand and the map. I don't know if I trust him to keep things secret if we tell him beforehand. He might want to take control of things too early."

"What is it? Are you afraid he might squeeze you out of the project?" she asked.

"Would you put that past him? I don't know him that well, but I wouldn't. I'd prefer to keep control, to deal with him only after we have the hand and the map."

"I am sure that he would be square with you," she said. "He is one of the best at his business, highly respected among his peers."

"I'll tell you the truth: After seeing Barlow operate, I'm beginning to think that being successful in publishing is like being successful as a politician or a football coach. You know what they say about them?"

She half-smiled. "I do not." She lowered her eyes, waiting for my response.

"You know," I said, "that you have to be smart enough to understand the game, but dumb enough to think that it is important."

She laughed louder than I thought she would. I really liked making her laugh. "And a stockbroker is making that statement?"

"Oooh, the pain," I moaned, placing my hand over my heart. "You agree though? We'll keep a lid on this for a while, OK?" I asked. "I've got your word on that?"

"You don't have to worry about that," she replied. "In case you haven't noticed, I am not straining at the bit to make this information public. In many ways I hope you don't find anything . . . Does that surprise you?"

"Not after today."

"Well, in any event, I have to get home." She paused and lowered her eyes in a wry grin. "I am usually a Eucharistic minister at the eleven o'clock Sunday Mass at my church, but I'm scheduled for the Saturday evening vigil Mass tonight."

"Peace be with you."

"Very funny."

Chapter Eleven

Can I help you guys?" The night watchman called out to us as he crossed the Culinary Institute parking lot in a huff toward Leo's van. He was an older man in a guard service uniform jacket and bus driver-style hat, a graying Ralph Cramden.

It was Wednesday night, just past 1 A.M. I knew I'd be a bit groggy the next day at work, but I wanted to be there when we cut the deal with the night watchman. Leo and I had just exited the van and were standing around like tourists under an overhead parking lot lamp.

"Hey, how you doing, pal?" said Leo, lighting his cigarette and surveying the deserted campus. "Nice night." Leo walked towards the spot where he had recently mounted a new United Fire Fighter's union decal on his van window. There are circles where these decals make a difference, as a badge of authenticity, a way of assuring regular guys that you are a regular guy.

"Yeah, it's a nice night," the watchman responded. "What do you guys want? The place is closed. Everyone is asleep in there." He motioned with his head toward the dorms.

"Want a smoke?" Leo smacked the back of his pack of Marlboros with his palm until a couple of cigarettes popped forward in response.

"No, I don't want a cigarette. What do you guys want?" The watchman pointed his flashlight at us. "I told you everything is closed."

"Hey, hey, pal . . . shh, shh, we're harmless. You'll wake the chefs. Don't get riled," Leo assured him. "We bring tidings of great joy. We got an offer for you, a chance to make a soft three hundred bucks. With no risk. No hassle."

"What are you talking about? You got something to do with drugs? *With drugs?*" the watchman demanded, taking two steps back in alarm.

"No, no, come on, nothing like that," said Leo. "Come on, look, I'm a fireman." He pointed to his decal. "From the city. My brother here is a Wall Street guy. We ain't lowlifes."

"So what? I'm a retired transit worker from the Bronx, worked on the Dyre Avenue line for thirty-five years," the watchman shot back. "That don't make us buddies. I still want to know what you guys want around here."

Leo looked toward the ground and shook his head slowly, as if had been caught in an embarrassing situation. "I guess we should come clean. I don't know how to say this, but . . . you know that graveyard out back, behind the main building?"

"The priest cemetery?" the watchman replied.

"The priest cemetery," said Leo. "That's the place. *Well* . . ." He looked up with a self-conscious grimace. "Well, here goes: we want to get into one of the caskets, my brother and me."

"Get the hell out of here," snapped the watchman, "before I call the cops."

"No, no, I'm serious, listen to me," said Leo. "We're jammed up here. Give us a hand. One of those priests up there is our uncle. We think that when he died a relative put some papers in the casket that the family needs now. It's one of those probate things. You know, with the will and all. I know it sounds weird, but we'd be in an out of here in a couple of hours . . ." Leo extended his pack of cigarettes again. "Come on, take a smoke."

This time the watchman accepted the offer. He bent to Leo's match and exhaled into the night air. You could see the possibilities registering with him.

"We'll bring some friends to do the digging after midnight some night next week," Leo continued. "You pick the night. Some night when you're here. We'll be as quiet as church mice. We'll smooth everything over when we're done. All you've got to do is stay away from us for a while. And we'll give you the three hundred dollars before we start. Right? It'll be no problem for you."

"No way. You're crazy," he answered. "They'll have my job."

"No, they won't. Come on, you got no risk, pal. If someone sees us, you can start yelling like you just caught us in the act. Call the police, scream to high heaven. They'll believe you. You'd be clear. This place is deserted. There's nobody from the administration around this late at night, right? Who's on campus now? Give me a break. A bunch of student-chefs sleeping in their dorms? I never saw a more deserted place. You must have a hard time keeping awake around here. And we'll make it five hundred bucks, half a grand. How's that?"

Leo's logic became irresistible. We negotiated a bit more. Five hundred dollars up front for this guy and one other watchman who would be on duty next Wednesday night. They would give us three hours, make a point of staying clear of the north side of the campus where the graveyard was located while we were digging. A done deal.

Leo and I shook hands with our new partner-in-crime and headed back down Rt. 9 on our way to Manhattan. Along the way I tried to get some sleep with my head propped against the side window of the van. I felt good. I could find no flaw in the plan. This time next week we'd be driving back to Manhattan with the directions to the hidden safe in the wall at Regis firmly in our possession.

Chapter Twelve

can't say that Leo's choice of diggers inspired great confidence in me. They were four characters in their twenties who smelled of cigarettes and unwashed denim. But they were sober. Leo had made sure of that. At least for one night.

One was named Vinnie, a wiry guy with long, narrow sideburns and a goatee as wispy as cigar smoke, out of work and waiting for an opening to come up at the phone company. Another called himself Johnnie-boy. He was heavyset and balding, with lonely strands of black hair that swept across his forehead. And there were two Jims: a Jim and a Jimmy.

Jim was older than the others, a man with a face as lumpy as a bowl of oatmeal, in-between marriages and looking for some extra cash to handle his child support payments. Jimmy was a young guy, early twenties, a bodybuilder type with piercing blue eyes and a shaved head. He had just dropped out of college for "personal reasons," which was fine with me.

There were just perfunctory nods as they loaded into the van around 11:30 P.M. on the corner of Broadway and 215th Street. Leo had already stowed six new shovels, a crow bar, and two rakes, still emblazoned with their "True Value" labels from the hardware store, behind the back seat. Next to the shovels were six Niterider

Digital Extreme headlamps I had ordered from a Road Runner catalog, lights with two-strap headbands, the kind that joggers strap around their heads for night running. The small but powerful beams from them would allow us to focus light on Teilhard's grave without drawing attention to us as we dug.

Leo drove across Kingsbridge Rd. and cut onto the Major Deegan Expressway. Yankee Stadium loomed before us among the sea of Bronx tenement buildings. We had made it clear that we were not eager for any small talk, so our four diggers snuggled up inside their jackets and tried to sleep as Leo drove north toward Poughkeepsie.

The two Jims were deep in sleep when we arrived at the Culinary Institute. They crawled clumsily through the van doors like some bizarre birth, scratching and yawning and pulling their gloves into place. The watchmen were there waiting for us. We slipped them the envelopes with their money without saying a word. And then we were off, moving quietly in the shadows toward the Jesuit graveyard. The grounds of the school were silent, streaked in shadows from decorative walkway lamps. A gentle wind swept up from the Hudson, below us and to the west.

We were able to scale the wrought iron fence around the Jesuit cemetery without difficulty. Decorative escutcheons served as our footholds to push up and over the spiked top rail. A few of the diggers grunted as they hit the ground on the cemetery side. But all was well.

The six of us stood staring down the rows of tombstones, barely visible in the darkness. I swept a flashlight beam across the area, shaping and extinguishing shadows of the tombstones with a sweep of my hand.

"Let's go," I said. "This way."

I counted down and across the rows until I came to the tombstone that Desmond Carey had pointed out to us, a small oval about the size of a phone book. Leo and the diggers gathered at my shoulder like mourners paying their respects.

"You sure we've got the right spot?" asked Leo.

"It's the one that Desmond Carey showed us," I answered.

Leo took my flashlight and knelt close to the tombstone. "I can't read this. It's in Latin and streaked with bird shit. Are you sure this is the right grave?"

"It's got to be. It's the one Carey showed us," I replied. "That's all I know. Come on. Time's short. Let's get going. Five of us will dig at a time. The other guy'll rest and watch to make sure no one is coming." I walked across the top of the grave, kicking at five spots with the heel of my boot, the spots that I thought would be close to the perimeter of the casket. "We'll start digging here . . . here . . . here . . . here . . . and here."

Leo and the diggers shoved their Niterider lamps into place on their foreheads. I stood back, serving as lookout for the first shift. The earth cut easily for them, tan and crumbly and pebbly in the shafts of light from their helmets. No big rocks. That's one thing about grave robbing. You can be sure that someone has been there before to work the ground for you.

I was confident that no one would discover us. A row of evergreens separated us from Rt. 9, the highway that ran along the school's eastern boundary. Passing drivers would not be suspicious of the narrow beams from the Niterider lamps, which from that distance would seem part of the grounds' decorative landscape lighting. To the west there was nothing but the Hudson, a strand of black velvet barely visible through the landscaping.

The diggers may not have been candidates for the keys to the city but they worked hard for us. The dirt piled up in four mounds as they and Leo dug deeper into the earth, tossing shovel after shovel over their shoulders. After half an hour, Johnnie-boy started to breathe heavily, so I relieved him. We were about three feet down by then.

I enjoyed the work at first. At first. I ran regularly, but this was a different kind of exertion. I tried to get a rhythm going for myself, throwing my weight into the downward thrust of my foot against the shovel base, then swinging my shoulders as I swept the earth up to the surface. I found a nice cadence, but it didn't make the work any less demanding. My shoulders and back ached, my breathing grew heavy.

Another foot or two down and we found ourselves deep in a chunky cubicle of Hudson Valley earth, its sides scored by our shovel strokes like the insides of a tub of coffee ice cream. The diggers worked methodically, load after load tossed up onto the rim of our excavation. At this depth, beneath the frost line, the earth scooped easily for us.

I eagerly clambered to the top of the hole when the time came for me to be relieved. We had been at it just over two hours and had to be getting close to the casket. I leaned over and beamed my flashlight into the space where the diggers were hacking away. Some of the diggers began cursing under their breath and exhaling angrily with each shovel they heaved to the surface.

"We've got to be close," I encouraged them. "Hang in there."

Finally it happened: a hollow wooden clunk against Vinnie's shovel. He turned the blade upside down and made a scraping sweep. "I think I got it," he said. "Over here, look."

He was right. Another long scrape uncovered a section of the casket top, a curved plank of wood, gray and mottled, but intact. There were sections still shiny with varnish, others as dull and coarse as old barn board. I leaped into the hole and swept across the area with my gloved hand.

"That's it! That's a casket! Clear off the top so I can open it," I exclaimed. Leo was above me, at the surface, peering down into the hole. I called up to him: "Hand me down that crow bar."

A single thrust of the crow bar popped the top of the casket as easily as a cigar box. I kneeled and shoved it back on its hinges and peered apprehensively into the recess. This was not a routine experience for me. Nor, apparently, for the diggers. They pressed back against the walls of the hole we had dug as if they were worried that Boris Karloff would rise to greet them.

I had expected some ghastly odor to emanate from the casket, but I was surprised. There was a smell all right, but it was more a dank and musty smell like that of an untended boathouse than any hint of rotting flesh. Whatever flesh had been in that casket was long gone, the remains wrapped in thick layers of a tattered burlap-like material. There he was: the great Teilhard de Chardin.

I pointed my flashlight beam around the edges of the corpse, hoping I wouldn't have to go probing with my hand to find the metal case we were looking for.

I didn't. It was there, just as Desmond Carey had said: a green metal container about the size of a cigarette pack pressed in close to the corpse. It would be easy to mistake it for a storage box for stamps or office supplies . . . paper clips and thumbtacks and the like.

"I got it, Leo," I exclaimed. I thumbed the container open just to make sure it was what we were looking for. Inside was a single piece of paper, a pencil sketch and a series of arrows and a short paragraph of instructions. "Let's get out of here," I exclaimed as I snapped the case closed. No reason to let the diggers ponder what we had found. "Let's fill this hole and vamoose."

I eased the casket top back into place and clawed my way to the surface. The others followed and began shoveling the dirt back into the hole. They worked hard. They wanted to end this night as much as I did.

It wasn't long before we were pounding down the surface of the refilled hole and raking it back into some semblance of its original condition. It wouldn't fool anyone. If anyone happened to see the spot they would know something had happened here. Nothing we could do about that. But so what? We would be back in the city for weeks before that was likely to happen. We were free and clear, just a little after 4 A.M.

We rushed back to Leo's van, not even bothering to look for the watchmen. They had their money. Probably the last thing they wanted was to see us again. We threw the tools into the back and Leo drove slowly in the darkness down the driveway toward Rt. 9. I could feel the presence of the old seminary buildings looming behind me as he accelerated and headed south back towards the city.

"Good job, guys. We did it. We'll hit that diner on the Deegan near the old Yonkers track for some coffee and eggs. Our treat." I exhaled and tried to sound upbeat. I didn't have to fake it. The adrenaline surge was making up for the fact that I would have to make some excuses for coming late for work on Wall Street in just a few hours. The diggers were excited and pleased with themselves as well.

"We did all that for that little box?" asked Vinnie, rubbing his hands together for warmth. "What the hell is in there?"

"Hey, hey," reprimanded Leo in a friendly manner, "remember, we said no questions. That was the deal. It's some information that means nothing to nobody except Frankie and my family. You got your money."

"No offense, no offense," Vinnie answered. "Just curious."

"Believe me, it's no big deal," I assured him. I didn't want to create any drama that might heighten their curiosity. "I told you, it's a thing about a will in our family. Some heirlooms and what-not. No big deal. We've got some relatives who are making things tough for us."

"Yeah, we know the score," Johnnie-boy cut in. "We know how to keep our yaps shut. Come on, Vinnie." He made a quick zipping motion across his lips.

Chapter Thirteen

After leaving the diner in Yonkers, we drove back to Inwood and dropped Vinnie and Johnnie-boy off at their respective apartments near Isham Park. The two Jimmies opted for a bar on Nagle Avenue instead, some little dive near the subway yards. Not unexpected. We had just given them a thousand dollars each; the temptation of a boozy morning was too great for them to pass up.

Leo accelerated and sped the two blocks north to Baker Field, Columbia University's baseball diamond. He knew it would be deserted at that time of the morning. Slamming his brakes to a full stop in the parking lot, he turned toward me wide-eyed with excitement. It was just after 8 A.M. and we could see the Metro-North commuter train from Westchester making the turn from Marble Hill and across Spuyten Duyvil on its way south toward midtown.

"*OK* . . . let's see what's in there!" He pointed toward the spot in my coat where I had stashed the metal case. "Come on, come on . . ."

I looked around furtively as I slid the case from my pocket.

"Come on, Frankie," Leo exclaimed. "Who the hell are you looking for? You think there are cops looking for us? From where? Israel? The Vatican? Come on, open the damn thing!"

"Alright, alright . . ." I answered, laughing. I thumbed open the container and removed a single piece of paper.

"Let me see . . . what does it say?" Leo asked excitedly.

"Wait a second, will you? Cheesh . . ." I examined the drawing, turning it from side to side.

"Well? What does it say, dammit?"

"Man . . . this is amazing."

"Let me see," Leo reached across and twisted my wrist to examine the paper.

Look . . ." I pointed to the sketch. "It's simple. They built a three-foot high ledge along the wall opposite the school's central chimney. Here, the arrows show where. Down in the basement storage area, across from the north side of the chimney. It says they slid some cabinets, probably for janitor's stuff or books, in front of it. It would look like part of the design of the wall, like a base molding of some kind. No one would think twice if they saw it, except maybe the janitors and they wouldn't give a damn. Probably think someone did some repairs to the wall somewhere over the years. The safe with the hand is in there. Right there." I jabbed at the sketch.

"Does it say that?"

"No. It just has an *X* on the fake ledge. Look: a decorative X, in fancy scroll, European-style writing. But that's got to be what it means. And look: here're the numbers. They've got to be the combination to the safe, right? Plain as day."

Leo whistled softly and leaned back. He became uncharacteristically pensive. "Well . . . *what now?*"

"Now I go to work," I answered.

"What?"

"Drive me home. I've got to get to work. I still have a job. It's a workday. I'm going to be late as is. We can get together at my place tonight if you want and talk things out."

"Talk things out? There's only one thing left: figuring out how to crack that fake wall and get to the safe."

"I'll work on that. You do the same. But drive me home. I've got to get to the job right away. I'm not kidding. I'm late."

I got to my apartment by 8:45 A.M. I inserted the metal case behind some books on a shelf in my living room, called my boss to tell him I would be late, showered and shaved in a blur and was out the door rushing for the subway station by 9:15. Leo? No problem. He was off today and tomorrow. I told you: he's a fireman. I can't remember a time in the last five years when I was with him when he wasn't off "today and tomorrow." I don't know how it works.

I survived the remainder of the day on the floor of the Exchange without too much difficulty. It would not be my first day on the floor without a good night's sleep, although I must admit the exertion that had kept me up on previous occasions was less rigorous than grave-robbing. But whatever problems I was having keeping track of my buy and sell orders that day came more from distraction than grogginess. I still had no idea how we were going to crack the wall at Regis.

The subway ride home at the end of the day was another matter. I was beat by then, nodding off constantly, one time nearly nestling my head on the shoulder of a heavyset woman seated next to me. She woke me just north of Spring Street with a swift elbow to the ribs and an indignant huff.

I stopped off for a Corona at Gabriela's on Amsterdam and 93rd before walking to my co-op. The restaurant was just beginning to fill up, but the bar was packed: a mix of upscale Latinos and local yuppie types sipping tequila cocktails. I loved the aroma of the place, the smell of their pork marinated in Seville orange juice as the waiters rushed by with trays over their shoulders. From my perch at the bar, I looked out at the restaurant, a cheery aquamarine cluster of tables accentuated with tropical plants and flower arrangements in wicker baskets. I thought of how great it would be to sit here with Helen Bergeron, sipping margaritas and peering through the big plate glass window at the pedestrian traffic on Amsterdam Ave. I settled for second best: a takeout order of two soft pork burritos and a quart of corn soup and headed to my apartment. I was ready for a long night's sleep.

Which I didn't get to enjoy as soon as I'd hoped. Leo had been asleep all day. He was on the phone before I had taken the second bite of my burrito, raring to go.

"Frankie, I'm worried," he said. "I'm at a goddam dead end. I've been thinking about getting to the safe all day, and I've come up with diddley squat. There's no easy way. I think I could fake my way to the basement for a fire inspection. You know, I could go there in uniform and con a secretary to let me see the boiler room. I can do that, but I can't figure out how to start hammering away at the wall without raising suspicion. What the hell can I tell them about why I want to do *that?*"

"Don't ask me," I said. "Faking a fire inspection was your idea. Maybe it won't work. Maybe we'll have to figure out something else."

"Like what?"

"I don't know. I'll work on it," I answered.

"But work on what?"

"I told you: I don't know. Give me some time. Leo, come on . . . I haven't slept in over twenty-four hours. I just got in from work."

"How about we get together and see what we can come up with?" he asked. "Tomorrow sometime. After you get some sleep."

"What good would that do us? You've got no ideas. I've got no ideas," I said. "Look: give me some time. I'll go over to Regis tomorrow after work and look around and see if I can come up with something. Then I'll get back to you."

"What are you going to tell them?"

"Tell who?"

"The priests at Regis."

"I don't know. I'm a graduate. I'll figure something out. Maybe I can talk to one of the secretaries or someone, pretend I want to see one of my old teachers."

"Are any of them still teaching there?"

"I don't know. It's been nearly twenty years since I've been back! That's a long time. I'll find out soon enough, though. *Goodnight.*"

The next day I took the No. 4 train north to 86th Street after work, arriving at the station just before seven o'clock. Daylight savings time was a few weeks away, leaving the stretch of 84th Street where Regis was located still cloaked in dusk. Warm lights shone in the windows of the stately brownstones and granite townhouses stretching from the school toward the west and the stone wall and arched street lamps encircling Central Park. There were lights coming from the front windows of the school as well, so I thought I would take a look inside. The oak doors were unlocked, swinging open easily into the vestibule I remembered as a teenager. It was my first time back since I had been a student. Things had changed, but not that much. It was still a classy place.

I've sat through a few concerts and recitals at the modern suburban public schools you find everywhere these days. My mother is always conniving me to escort her to events where my cousins' kids play the cello or perform in the chorus for something like *South Pacific* or *Godspell*. The buildings could all be from the same mold, bland wedges of plastic and aluminum and drab composite floors with the character of the baggage claim area at an airport. That wasn't Regis. Regis was wood, wood and plaster and frosted glass—good wood, old wood, dark polished wood with character; on the doors, moldings, wainscoting, everywhere you looked.

I walked slowly down the main hall, examining bulletin boards with information about SAT tests, Jesuit mission activities, college open houses, posters with little pockets containing brochures about the benefits of attending Holy Cross and NYU, Georgetown and Princeton. It was as if I had never left. I could remember wondering if I was the only one who never stopped to pick up one of those college brochures when I was a student. I had made up my mind by my Junior year that I was going straight to Wall Street after graduation and had made it a point of pride to skip the Joe College scene.

I kept walking. I wasn't sure, but I thought I remembered a stairway somewhere near the end of the hall that might take me down to the basement. I moved slowly, looking for it, but also checking constantly over my shoulder to see if anyone was around. There had to be someone in the building. The front door would not have been left open otherwise. But so far everything was silent, eerily so, my every footstep echoing down through the long hallway corridor. I moved cautiously, trying to maintain an innocent, ambling gait that would not make me look suspicious if I were discovered.

"Can I help you, friend?"

I was startled by the voice and turned quickly to see a short, middle-aged man in overalls and a denim shirt, rubbing his hands with a grimy orange rag. He was Hispanic, but without a strong accent, just a pleasant, rolling glide across the consonants.

"You have business here?" he asked.

"I'm looking for Father Finley, one of my old teachers. I went to school here."

"I do not know the name," he said, pausing, "but I don't know the names of all the priests who teach here. But no priests are around now. School closed hours ago. It's Friday night. I'm doing the last cleaning for the week. I'm going to lock up in an hour or so. I have just one more hallway to mop."

"Ahh, too bad," I said. "I was hoping Father Finley might still be around. But maybe you can help me. My name is Jack Hurley." I reached across to shake his hand.

"I work for a company that renovates heating systems in these old buildings," I said. "We sell boilers and baseboard systems— upgrades—that have saved a lot of money for people who own places like this." I smiled sheepishly. "I hate to admit this, but I was in the area and wanted to see my old teacher to see if I could use him to get an in, get to give my sales pitch to the people who make decisions about the building's central systems."

"I know nothing about these things," the janitor said. "I think the heater was fixed just a few years ago, but I don't know. It was before I began here. But everything works fine, no problem. What-ever—you should come back during the daytime hours next week."

"Just my luck. But, say, maybe you could let me see the boiler. If I knew what they had down there it would help me prepare a work-up—you know, some suggestions for how they might be able to improve what they've got down there. Hell, I think this place was heated with coal when I was a student here."

"That very well could be," he answered. "Downstairs there are places where you can see where the coal bins used to be."

"Come on . . ."

"In fact, I'm sure there are. You can still see the spots on the wall where the bins were bolted."

"No way."

"It's true," he said, nodding his head in confirmation.

"Let me take a look," I said. "Come on, it won't take me more than a few minutes. Once I see what kind of boiler you've got down there, I can figure out what my company can offer that might be an improvement. It won't take but a minute or two of your time."

"I am very busy, my friend. I am mopping the floor upstairs."

"Just show me the way," I pleaded. "I'll go down and take a look and check out the system and I'll be out of your hair."

"By yourself? No way. I cannot do that," he replied. "I cannot let you roam the building."

"Hey, come on . . . what harm can I do? Is there something valuable down there that you're afraid I might steal? Is that it?"

"Some floor wax and Brillo pads, maybe?" He laughed. "But I still can't let you go on your own. I'll go with you. But just for a few minutes."

"Hey, thanks, pal," I said. "Thanks a lot." I reached out to shake his hand again. "What's your name?"

"Roberto."

"Hey, Roberto, you're a good guy."

We walked down a long, creaking staircase into the basement. It was a part of the school I had never seen as a boy, a cavern of granite block, lined with metal storage cabinets, wooden shelves with paint cans and jars filled with nails and screws, coffee cans holding paint brushes. Spans of fluorescent lights ran down the center of the room, lighting the center aisle between the storage areas right up to the brick chimney I was looking for.

The chimney was enormous, a leftover from the days when the school was heated by coal. The opening where the coal fires once burned had been bricked over many years ago, the newer brick noticeably brighter and more crisply mortared than the original. But new cuts had also been opened in the brick surface of the chimney to accept sturdy aluminum exhaust ducts from the building's modern oil burner. Someone had made the decision to tap into the old coal fire chimney as a way of venting the modern heating system. Looked good to a heating and cooling expert like myself.

Roberto and I had made some turns from the stairway to our current position so I was a bit disoriented, not sure which side of the chimney was the side where Teilhard had secreted the hand and the Gospel. It wasn't the side facing me. That was the span where the new ductwork had been inserted from the oil burner.

"So that's the guts of your system, eh?" I asked Roberto. He was standing just behind me. "Not bad. They used the old chimney for the new burner. Good idea." I walked toward the green and gray oil burner, pretending to be interested in the maze of pipes sprouting from its sides, all the while scanning the walls for the fake ledge that Teilhard had built.

"Say, Roberto, which way is north, the 85th Street side of the building?" I asked.

"That way," he pointed over my shoulder. "Behind the chimney."

I strolled casually in the direction he had indicated. Shoulder high, dark green metal cabinets, dented and scraped and streaked with generations of spilled paint obscured the wall directly across from the chimney. These looked old enough to have been the cabinets shoved into that spot by Teilhard, but I realized that might be a stretch. There was no way to tell for sure. But they were old; that was certain.

"What's in these cabinets?" I asked. "They look like they've been here since the flood."

"What flood?" Roberto asked.

"You know, the one that got Noah."

"Oh, a joke," he said. Roberto was not going to lose any sleep over Teilhard's discoveries.

"Do you think they would move them if I wanted to put in some new pipes for baseboard heating?" I asked, moving closer to the cabinets.

"Hey, my friend, that's not my decision," said Roberto. "I don't know. There's just some old paint cans and soaps in there. They might."

"Just old paint, eh?" I asked, opening one of the doors and peering in. Roberto was right. The cabinets were filled with a hodge-podge of old paint cans and floor wax containers, sheets of sandpaper, half-empty tubes of caulk and asphalt patch. As I closed the door, I leaned along the side of the cabinet and examined the back wall behind it.

And it was there, three-foot high, extending two feet from the wall . . . a solid, professionally mortared ledge, melding smoothly with the wall surface behind it.

"What's back behind the cabinets, Roberto?" I asked.

"A wall, just a wall," he said. "But, look, we have to go. I have work to finish. Have you seen enough? You said just a minute or two."

"Hey, Roberto, I'm sorry," I apologized. "I've seen what I need."

As we walked toward the front door I exchanged some small talk and expressed my gratitude to Roberto for his help.

"Are you sure no priests are around?" I asked. "Upstairs maybe? Do any of them live in the building? I'd like to leave my card."

"No priests live in the building. The rectory is around the corner. You can leave the card there."

It was just as I was about to leave that I saw what I needed. I had walked past it on my way in, but paid no attention. A poster near the main entrance: "PARENTS NIGHT: APRIL 15th Contact Your Guidance Counselor for Additional Details." That was what we needed.

The possibilities raced through my mind. It could be done: get lost in the crowd of parents roaming the halls for the teacher conferences, hide in the basement area until everyone was gone, break into the wall in the middle of the night when everything was silent; make an easy getaway before dawn.

"Hey, Roberto, you look like you've got a busy night coming up! Parents night in a few weeks. Going to be busy, I'll bet."

"No problem. I like it. I come in after ten, when the parents are gone. I straighten up the desks in the rooms and lock the windows. I'm gone by midnight. They pay me extra. No problem."

"And then the place is empty all night?" I asked.

"Like a graveyard."

"Hello, Roberto. Almost finished?" The voice startled me, coming from over my shoulder, from the door leading to the 84th Street exit.

"Just a little while longer, Father," said Roberto. "This man is a salesman from a heating company. I was showing him the down-stairs boiler."

"Kind of late for that," the voice responded.

I turned to look into a florid round face with curious eyeglasses, with one smoked lens. It was the priest from the graveyard at the Culinary Institute, glaring at me from the doorway as if I was a frog on the dissecting table. He was dressed in his Roman collar, but with a tan windbreaker rather than a black outer garment.

"He took just a few minutes, Father. I thought it would do no harm," Roberto answered.

"Hello, Father," I said, trying my best to stay calm. "My name is Jack Hurley. I live just on the other side of the Park. I thought I might find someone around. I was in the area. My company sells heating and cooling systems. I thought I might make a proposal to upgrade what you have here."

"We did all that just a few years ago," the priest answered.

"I could see that from what Roberto showed me downstairs," I said. "But, hey, you can't tell until you take a look. Can't blame a guy for trying."

"You are very well dressed for a plumbing salesman," the priest said. I began to suspect that he knew more than he was letting on; perhaps that he even remembered me from the cemetery. My heart began to pound like a tom-tom.

"Well, thank you," I said. "Park Avenue contractors are a like Park Avenue dentists—a world apart. I do well, thanks be to God."

Roberto tried to be helpful. He wasn't. "He wants to leave his card, Father. He went to school here," he said.

"What year?" asked the priest.

"Jack Hurley. Class of 1980."

"I'll take your card," said the priest.

I reached into my pockets, pretending to search for my busi-ness card. "Oh, darn it, I left my cards in my other jacket. I left it at the office. I'll get it over to you on Monday."

"Where's your office?" the priest asked. I was sure now that he suspected something. What?—I wasn't sure.

"In Chelsea, the old meatpacking district, down near Martha Stewart's new place," I answered, trying to find a place far enough downtown to be unfamiliar for the priest. "Argus Plumbing and Heating."

The priest nodded noncommittally, with a cold-eyed stare, clearly trying to unnerve me.

"What's your name, Father?" I asked. "I'll send the card to you."

"Malcolm Rogers."

"Good, good," I said reaching for his hand. "I'll appreciate any help you can give me. I turned to Roberto. "Thanks again for your help, Roberto. I won't take any more of your time. Thanks, Father Rogers."

I strained to smile in a relaxed and jovial manner as I let myself out the door. In truth I was so nervous that I wanted to break into a gallop. I succeeded at walking calmly instead, faking a casual pace as I moved toward the 85th Street transverse through Central Park on my way back to the West Side.

On Saturday morning I took the train from Times Square up to the Bronx Park East station, just outside the gates to the Bronx Zoo and only a few blocks from Leo's apartment. It seemed easier for me to do that than for Leo to struggle against the Saturday traffic by driving into midtown. His apartment was in an older building in the area, one that he and his wife thought would be just a temporary place until they saved enough to move to Rockland County. The divorce ended those plans. Leo kept the apartment in the deal; the ex got a good chunk of the savings accounts and a Honda Accord.

We sat at Leo's kitchen table, next to a window looking across at the Bronx Park East subway yards, drinking coffee and smoking. Leo's apartment was clean, but clearly a bachelor's place now, every chair and tabletop adorned with laundry either on its way to or just back from the laundromat. Leo listened attentively as I went through my plan.

"We can do it, Leo," I said. "I can remember Parents Night at Regis. I used to take Mom to them when I went there. She didn't like to ride the subway at night by herself."

"I know, I know," Leo said, "it was the same with me at LaSalle."

"I'd stay in the hall while she talked to my teachers," I continued. "The halls were always packed with parents lined up outside the classrooms, waiting to see the teachers. And all the priests and lay teachers were tied up meeting with parents. They would have upper classmen acting like ushers to show the parents where to go. I'd bet it's still pretty much the same. I tell you: we could walk around the place all night free as a bird. No one would think twice about us. They'd never notice us—no one."

Leo rubbed his hands around his coffee mug for warmth, his cigarette resting in an ashtray. "OK," he said, "so we mix with the crowd, then go down the basement. Then what? You think no one would hear us if we hammered away to get to the safe?"

"No, no, that would be too loud," I said. "They'd hear us. For sure. What we do is get down there and hide until all the parents are gone and the building is empty. I think it would be safe for us to start banging at the wall sometime after midnight. Everyone will be gone by then."

Leo nodded appreciatively, lips pursed, like a doctor evaluating an X-ray.

"OK," he said, "but are you sure we'll be able to break down the fake wall with just some small sledgehammers? We can't sneak anything much bigger into the building under our coats in the middle of Parents Night, you know."

"Am I sure of that? How the hell should I know? But I think so. From what I could see, it's pretty narrow, just a few feet wide. But what other choice have we got?"

Leo nodded again. "None. Let's do it. Probably the mortar is crumbly by now, seeing as how it was a quickie job they did. If we can whack off a corner block, we can probably pop the other blocks pretty easily.

"But there are things to consider here," Leo continued. "Look, we can't get out of the building that easily in the middle of the night. There are alarms that would go off. Most schools have them now, hidden sensors that spot any motion in the hallways after the place is locked for the night. I see it all the time with the fire department."

"I thought of that," I answered. "What we do is wait until morning, when school begins. The alarm systems will be turned off by then. The halls will be filled with kids shouting and lockers slamming. We move out through all the hub-bub."

"What if one of the faculty sees us?"

"They won't. They all hang out in the faculty room until a little before class time. At least they used to. And if someone does see us, we tell him we're there to drop off something to one of our sons. No big deal. That would sell."

"But what if we have to make a quick getaway?" Leo asked. "Who knows? It could happen? Maybe that priest with the weird glasses will spot us and get suspicious."

"Yeah. That's not impossible."

"Well, we can't just park my van out front. That's goddam Central Park East. Odds are we couldn't get a parking space anywhere near the school. And if we did, the cops would probably tow us. Then what do we do? Roam around with Jesus' hand in a bag, looking for a cab, maybe with half the faculty at Regis screaming after us? See what I mean?"

"All right. We need someone there with a car, waiting for us," I said.

"There you go. With the engine running and ready to go. Someone we can trust."

"You have anyone in mind?" I asked.

"No. There's no one I can think of," he answered. "That's the problem. It can't be anyone like the rummies who dug the grave for us. This time we'll have to tell whoever we get to help us what we're up to. At least, some of the details. They're gonna know we spent the night in Regis and that we're coming out with something that we copped."

"No good then," I said. "I'm not telling some goddam hired wheelman what we're doing. Everything has to stay secret."

Leo shrugged: "We don't have to tell them what we're stealing, just that it's a heist."

"No good. They'll know we weren't stealing final exams. They'll get curious. I don't want anyone asking questions, especially after the headlines begin when we make everything public. We'll have to park your van in a commercial parking lot nearby and hope for the best. That's the only way to do it."

"That'll work if no one spots us," Leo explained. "But what if we have to sprint? What if someone calls the cops? We'll never get to a commercial parking lot and out before they have every radio car on the East Side looking for us. No good, Frankie, we need someone right outside the door of the school, with the engine running so that we can get out of there quick."

I got up and walked to the half-opened window and watched a train pull out of Bronx Park East on the elevated track on its way toward Gun Hill Road. I blew a stream of smoke into the chill spring air. "How about John Sullivan?" I asked. "He already knows what we're after."

"Sully?" Leo asked skeptically. "You think that fat dump will make a good wheelman? Come on."

"It's not as if we're hitting a Brink's' truck," I answered. "He won't have to carry a shotgun or anything. And he's already in on this for a grand. We can make it five once we get our payday."

Leo laughed. "This is getting good. The Corcoran brothers luring good Mrs. Sullivan's boy into a life of crime. The nuns at Good Shepherd will be clucking their 'I told you sos' if this ever gets out."

"Do you think he'll do it?" I asked.

Leo paused. "He might, if we ease him into it. He might. Remember how his eyes lit up when we offered him the grand to reach out for a publisher for us? For five I think he would put *Nixon's the One* bumper stickers on his car."

"And unless something goes really bad all he would have to do is drive us around the corner and through the Park and over to the West Side," I said. "It would be just an hour's work."

"Of course, he'd have to talk himself into why it was all right to participate in a robbery at a Jesuit high school," Leo added. "That could make a difference."

"Maybe we can convince him that the Jesuits are tools of that cash-nexus society he is always complaining about—that he is striking a blow for the oppressed classes."

"You laugh, but, you know, that might work with that prick. We'll make him our goddam Patty Hearst," said Leo. "Power to the people." He lowered his chin and thrust his right arm into the air in the old '60s radical salute.

I chuckled out some cigarette smoke. "Let's call him. I think I can sell this."

"We'll tell him about the hand?" Leo asked, reverting to a more serious demeanor

"No, no, we don't have to do that. All he knows so far is about the Gospel. Let's keep him there. That should be enough to sell him on the heist. That and the five grand."

"OK, I'll call him. We'll set it up for some night after you get off from work. We'll meet him again at the Catholic Worker. Take him for a few beers and let you sell him on the plot. You up to that?"

"Yeah," I answered. "Call him."

Chapter Fourteen

I don't usually drink alone. I started to while waiting for our meeting with Sullivan. I've heard since I was a teenager that solitary drinking is the first step to becoming a rummy. That's one thing that the priests, drunks, and old biddies all agreed upon in the old neighborhood. I have no idea whether it is true. I know a lot of drunks who always have company. But this was a bit of inherited wisdom that I lived by. Used to, at any rate. I began to hit the local gin mills on Amsterdam and West End avenues, alone, for long hours at a stretch.

Was I mooning over Helen Bergeron? Yeah. That was going on. All the time. I couldn't believe how much she had captured my imagination. But something else was gnawing at me, too. The prospect of actually getting to the hand and the map to Jesus' body started to weigh on me. I don't know why it took so long, but I began to experience periods of introspection, something very new for me.

I know how to get over things like sleeping with a married woman or spending the weekend with some coked-up junior partner at a law firm, pretending to commiserate with her about the inequity of the glass ceiling in her life. A few beers and a couple of hours of laughs with my drinking buddies, and I can convince myself that I had caused no one any pain in these—what do the women call them—dalliances? But this was different.

I could come up with no easy way to get over what it would mean to make public the information about Jesus' body. If a woman as sophisticated and well-read as Helen Bergeron experienced distress after hearing the story, what would happen to people like my mother and her cronies, my relatives in the outer boroughs and the suburbs? I had been telling myself that they would not even pay attention. No way. It would transform their lives in dramatic and unpredictable ways. As it would the lives of the old ladies in black shawls at the early Masses in Italian villages, the Irish priests in the African missions, nuns in the cancer wards.

It would change me, too. I began to sulk over the possibility that I might not be able to adjust. Since my teenage years, I had affected a breezy indifference about my religious beliefs. Not that I ever stopped practicing the faith. I went through the motions. But going through the motions as a Catholic means a lot. There is no periphery to that orbit. The Church draws you in.

The liturgical year marked my days: spotting the first Christmas scenes each year in the blustery winds of December, making jokes about giving up beer nuts—but not the beer—for Lent, kidding my mother about the flu she contracted a week after getting her throat blessed on St. Blaise's Day, laughing at the drunks making the Sign of the Cross as they passed the Cathedral on St. Patrick's Day, showing my niece the money that people put under the Infant of Prague statue in the back of their local church; standing at a distance each May to watch the little girls file into church in their First Communion dresses, warding off tears when the pipers marched alongside the coffin at police funerals. These things made me who I was.

It never troubled me that there were Catholic intellectuals who took things less literally than I did. Hell, I wasn't sure how literally I took everything: the Virgin Birth, the Wise Men, driving the devils into the Gadarene pigs, Fatima, Guadeloupe—*Hell itself*. I never thought about it much, actually.

But the point is that I never thought much about anything, other than making a buck and enjoying a steady diet of earthly pleasures. The squabbles among the intellectuals about where the facts end and the metaphors begin in the Gospels were of no interest to me. It was like watching these tweedy characters who rail at each other over whether Shakespeare was Shakespeare.

But there is a difference between knowing that there are intellectuals quarreling over how much of Christian belief should be seen as a symbol rather than a fact—and facing up to a deliberate deception at the very heart of the faith; realizing that there is no irreducible core. Once Jesus' body was unearthed, liberal and conservative Catholics would have nothing to fight about any longer. Perhaps the liberals would win more than they wanted to win. There would be nothing left for them to liberalize.

I am no saint. I have admitted that. But I have a code of behavior that shapes my life, a series of "ought tos" and "ought nots," and they were all instilled in me by the Catholic Church. I live with the idea that Jesus knows what I do, and cares; that I will face him at the end of my days, when I will be rewarded or punished for the life I have lived. I don't know how all that will happen—I don't picture Jesus on a cloud with an abacus keeping track of my escapades—but the understanding that such a judgment will occur governs my life.

I can force that concern to the back of my mind when the temptations become too strong. I give in to most temptations, in fact. But the fear of meeting my Maker is always there. It always comes back. What will happen when it no longer does?

Look: I have passed up opportunities to scam customers on Wall Street and to pocket big bucks on deals like Hillary Clinton's cattle-futures deal. I don't do drugs, except nicotine and alcohol, if you want to count them. I give my mother $1000 bucks a month. Maybe I don't deserve the Congressional Medal of Honor for that, but I know guys with more dough than me who spend their time figuring out how to hide their parents' bank accounts, so that the old folks can qualify for Medicaid coverage at the nursing home and they can inherit the stash.

I am convinced, as well, that the difference between my feelings for Helen Bergeron and some Chelsea hooker springs from my religious beliefs. Why else would my fantasies about her center on sharing the joys of home and family—what someone has called "the sunlit uplands of life," rather than quickie weekends in the Bahamas? There are guys I know who don't know the difference—who wish they could live a life of Bahamas weekends, in fact. I know the difference. Why?

Where do those thoughts come from? The notion that *it is good to be good?*

Jesus makes a difference.

I know that the atheists insist there is no need for the belief in God in order for an individual to live a life of virtue. They will point to atheists they know who are models of compassion and honesty. OK. I know a few. But you have to wonder if the atheists live that way because they live here—in a society formed by Christian values. What would they be like if they'd grown up in a headhunters' village instead, or with the tribes of Genghis Khan? Wouldn't they be as pumped up as the old Mongol hordes over the joys of pillage and plunder? Wouldn't they also yearn to hear the wailing and lamentations of a vanquished foe? No? Why not?

Wouldn't the feminists who reprimand us for not respecting the dignity of women sing a different tune if they were voluptuaries in some Sultan's court, instead of members of a society whose perceptions of women were shaped by Christian notions of chivalry—a society formed by individuals who believe in the risen Christ—in what the guys with the Meerschaum pipes and leather elbow patches used to call the "Christian West?"

Jesus makes a difference.

I thought about what it would be like to actually see Jesus' hand in just a few days, dry and chalky and broken in its plastic bag. It was the hand I had seen all my life, on the crucifix on the wall in the bedroom Leo and I shared as boys, above the altars in the churches where I served Mass, in the paintings of Giotto and Salvador Dali, the tortured clawing hand in Mathias Grunewald's Crucifixion scene. That hand.

I wondered if I could ever pray again. What was I supposed to pray to from now on? Teilhard's "Christofied" universe, some notion of a spiritualized humanity that even a Washington Square Marxist would feel comfortable with, a vague spiritual presence holding the universe together like a magnetic field? The *Geist*? The Ground of Our Being? That might work for the people who say that it does. But it wouldn't work for me; nor for most of the people I know.

The risen Jesus always made the difference for me. The idea of a formless, omniscient deity, who always was and always will be, the Uncaused Cause, all that had always struck me as an intellectual proposition rather than an object of worship, as something too distant and indeterminate to be of concern. Jesus, in contrast, was real, something one could grasp, love, fear to disappoint, yearn to emulate. I always thought that the most God-like thing about God the Father was his understanding that mankind would need the Son, the Word made Flesh, to live lives of virtue. For me, that was the magic of Christianity, what separated it from the religions that preach the reward of a submersion of the individual into the great cosmic pudding, into nothingness.

I know, I know. You are supposed to go through these worries earlier in life, these "dark nights of the soul." Well, I never did. Call me dense, or insensitive—whatever. It was a new experience for me. My dark nights of the soul never led me into a funk over the emptiness of the universe. It was always the opposite for me: I'd sit on a beach or pause on a moonlit ski slope and conclude that there had to be some explanation for the wonders of life, that there was a story being told in the way humans interacted with the world around us. I never brooded about what the Birkenstock boys called the "absurdity" of life.

Now I was. Jesus as a spirit? Who was going to focus on what that might mean after the Gospel stories that teach us about him are revealed to be a web of deceptions? The awe will be gone, the mystery, the sense of the sacred. I thought long and hard about the likelihood that it would be better for the world if Leo and I just let things stand. Yes, I realized the irony: that I had spoken harshly of those Jesuits who knew Teilhard's secret and who concluded that it was their right to keep the world in ignorance, for what they thought was the world's good. But maybe they were right? Was it my right to break the secret? Was it my right to perpetuate it? It was a classic no-win situation.

The night before we were to meet with John Sullivan I sat on my couch, brooding about these things and staring at the spot behind my bookshelves where I had stashed the metal case with the directions to the fake wall at Regis. To the left of the bookcase was a window looking to the west, toward the Hudson and the Soldiers and Sailors Monument in Riverside Park. Usually it was a view that relaxed me, reinforcing my decision to live in Manhattan. I had all that I wanted here: Central Park, Museum Mile and Lincoln Center were all within walking distance to my east, the subway one block from my door, more coffee shops and bookstores and gorgeous churches than you can shake a stick at. And lots of bars. What I feared was that those bars would shortly become even more important to my life, while the churches would fall into the same category as the museums.

I wasn't expecting a call. Certainly not a call from Desmond Carey.

"You bastard!" he snarled. "Your effrontery is breathtaking. You bastard!"

"Hey, Des, Des" I answered patiently, "cool down. What's going on?"

"Don't persist in your perfidy! I know it was you!"

"You're going to have to explain, Desmond," I said. But I knew. He knew. He had been to Teilhard's grave. "Where are you calling from?"

"From my home. Where you violated my hospitality to betray me!"

"Whoa, Desmond—*betray?* What are you talking about?"

"You damned well know what I am talking about. Your mendacity is beyond bounds. You betrayed my confidence."

"Where did you get my number, Desmond?" I asked.

"The phone book. How the hell many Francis X. Corcorans do you think there are on the Upper West Side?"

"You still haven't told me what's got you so riled. Calm down and tell me what's going on."

"Don't you tell me to calm down, you *shanty Irish* trash," he snarled.

"Hey now, Desmond, you're striking some low blows. Shanty Irish? My mother would come after you with the broom. We're definitely lace-curtain Irish."

"Don't try to make a joke out of this," he responded. "You are not going to get away with it."

"With what?" I asked, struggling for some way to steer the conversation in a direction I could deal with.

"I saw the grave. I saw what you did. You will not get away with this!"

"What grave?"

"You know perfectly well what grave! Have you not a strand of decency in your soul?"

"Soul? I thought there was no such thing. Isn't that what you've been trying to convince people for the last fifty years?"

"You have no right to the information you stole from that grave! None!"

"If you're talking about the grave in Poughkeepsie that you showed us, it was the grave of some priest who stole something he wasn't entitled to, if I remember correctly," I said, struggling to sound calm and collected. "I wouldn't get all riled, Desmond. I'm just guessing, but I'll bet if you go back and check, you will see that everything is intact around the gravesite. No permanent damage. The corpse and the casket are in the same shape they were the day the body was buried. I'll bet if someone took a look they would see that."

"So you admit it was you!"

"No, no, Desmond, I'm just saying that you probably are getting excited about something that the local police would say is chicken shit if you went to them to file a complaint. I'll bet the body is undisturbed, still in its wraps. You'd have to come up with some other reason why anyone should be concerned about someone digging around a bit near that grave. You wouldn't want to do that. You'd have to tell them about what was in that casket that you're so worried about. You'd have to tell them the story about your role in all this. That would mean that everyone would know that you spilled the beans. Man, they'd be putting you on the front page of all the papers. Geraldo would be interviewing you, setting up his cameras outside your house if you wouldn't talk."

"You are a contemptible smart-ass, Corcoran."

"Anyway, I thought you wanted the information that was in that grave to be made public. What are you so worked up about?" I asked.

"It is not up to you to make those decisions."

"Seems to me the people who could inform the public are falling down on the job."

"That's none of your business."

"It's somebody's. The public has a right to know."

"Since when did you become an ACLU activist?"

"Is that an insult?"

"You can be assured of that. May your God-forsaken soul rot in hell."

"I thought there was none," I answered. "A God or a hell. Isn't that what you were telling us?"

"Don't engage in your barroom repartee with me," he shot back. "You won't get away with this."

"Get away with what?"

"I will tell the people who will know how to keep you away from the material you are looking for. You will never get your hands on it."

"I don't know what you are talking about," I said, becoming increasingly uncomfortable with the outright lying I was engaged in. I usually try to finesse things through half-truths when I want to deceive someone.

"But if you start telling the Jesuits about what you told us about Teilhard's grave, it seems to me that you will get them angrier at you than at us. You're the one who told tales out of school."

"You will never get to that material hidden at Regis. You can be assured of that. I will guarantee that," he replied angrily.

"I still don't know what you're talking about," I said. "But I wouldn't go shooting off my mouth, if I were you, about some far-fetched things that haven't happened."

I stood with the phone and walked toward my bookcase. I lifted the metal case from Teilhard's grave and studied its plain green surface, wondering what I had gotten myself into. I had a nice, simple life going on until now.

"I don't know what you plan to do," Carey said. "But there are Jesuits who *will* guard the material that Teilhard hid. You will never get anywhere near it."

"I thought you told us that they didn't know where the hand and the Gospel were hidden? That they would have to dig up the grave to get the map to find that out. Maybe some Jesuits dug up the grave to do just that. Maybe that's what you saw. Maybe they decided the time has come to let the world know. Why are you assuming that I was the one who did it?"

"You are a contemptible liar. I know you are the one. And don't count your chickens yet, Corcoran. There is a Jesuit at Regis who knows exactly where the hand is hidden. The people who know the secret go to great pains to ensure that there is always someone in the Jesuits' midtown community stationed near Regis to protect the site."

"What do you think they will do? Move the hand? To where? Come on, Desmond, you're getting all worked up over nothing."

"Mark my words, Corcoran. You will not get away with this. You have ventured into areas far more serious than your sniveling little Catholic school mind can grasp. There are people who will do anything to stop you."

"What are they going to do? Shoot me?" I asked.

"Don't laugh. You should look for the quickest route you can find to get away from all this. Go back to your life of stocks and bonds and tawdry bars. There is more to the Catholic universe than your world of silly Knights of Columbus yahoos and rosary-fingering women. There are people who have died for matters infinitely less serious than what you are about to do."

"You threatening me with Jesuit hit-men, Desmond? Give me a break."

"There are other societies within the Church, groups that over-lap with the Jesuits, with an agenda different from that of the visible Church that you know. They are capable of more than you could imagine to control this information about the Nazarene. Don't dismiss what I am telling you."

"You're right, Desmond. I have no idea what you are talking about. I don't think you do, either. In any event, I don't know what you want me to do."

"You have been warned, Corcoran. That's all I have to say. You will regret what you have done. More than you know. Mark my words."

I called Leo as soon as I hung up the phone with Desmond Carey. He was at his firehouse when we talked.

I was a bit breathless when I spoke: "Leo, Desmond Carey saw the grave site. He knows what we did. I just got off the phone with him."

"No, no, Frankie—he *thinks* he knows what we did. He can't prove a thing. Who'd listen to that old woodchuck? Relax."

"He says he's going to tell people at Regis what we've done. That there are some Jesuits there who know where the hand is hidden. If he's not just puffing wind, they might move the hand. I think I know who he's talking about."

"Who?"

"Remember the guy with the smoked eyeglasses up at the cemetery? The priest that I told you I met when I was over at Regis?"

"Yeah," Leo answered.

"I think he's one of them. I told you that he looked at me funny when I was there."

"So what if he is? What can we do about it?"

"Don't you realize what this means? We could find everything gone by the time we get there."

"Then it will be gone. What can we do? We go home and mope about a missed opportunity. Life's not fair," Leo said calmly. "All we can do is go ahead with our plan and hope for the best."

I exhaled heavily. Leo heard it.

"What is that? A sigh? From my stud big brother?" he said. "I don't believe it."

"Everything still set for our meeting with Sullivan?" I asked.

"Everything is set. Just a few more days. Any problem?"

"No. I can make it. I'll let you go."

"Thanks. There's a pot of linguini and white clam sauce coming out of the firehouse kitchen as we speak."

"It's a good country," I said.

"It's a good country."

I was not ready to sleep a peaceful night's sleep. It was still early enough to call Helen Bergeron. I worked up my confidence and dialed.

"Hello, Helen . . . it's Frankie Corcoran. I hope I am not disturbing you."

"No, no—I'm at my desk. My children and husband are watching television downstairs. There's no problem, Frankie. How are you?"

"Fine, I guess."

"You don't sound too enthused. Has something happened?" she asked.

"A lot. I have the directions to get the Gospel and the hand. Right here, in my apartment."

"You and Leo exhumed Teilhard's casket?"

"Exhumed and rehumed, if there is such a word. All we did was take a small metal case with the directions from the grave. We didn't touch the corpse. No sacrilege."

"I don't know about that," she replied solemnly. "Everything we are doing comes close to a sacrilege."

"If there is such a thing as a sacrilege from now on," I said.

"That's the point," she said.

"Helen . . . I know that. That's what's bothering me. I don't know how to sort out all that's going on."

"A little late for that, isn't it?"

"Maybe not," I said.

"You can't unring the bell," she said.

"The bell isn't rung yet. It won't be until we get the Gospel and the hand and make it all public."

"Frankie, I think you know how troubled I am by what you are doing. I have been going over everything in my mind since we last talked. I have concluded that truth must be served, no matter what. We have no choice. I hope you find nothing in the wall at Regis. I really do. But if someone has been deliberately keeping this information about Jesus from mankind, the deception must end. Thomas Aquinas insisted that there can be no clash between the truth and the Christian faith. The truth must enter the equation about the role of Jesus in salvation history."

"Do you think you will be able to remain a Christian if the body is found?" I asked.

"Will you?" she replied.

"That's what I want to talk to you about. Look, can we meet somewhere—just for an hour or so?"

"I don't know . . ."

"Come on, Helen, just an hour or so."

"I guess I could meet you again at Annie Moore's. I could do that," she said hesitatingly.

"No, no . . . We need someplace more private. I thought we might find somewhere where we can talk without worrying about being overheard. How about meeting me on Saturday on the steps of the museum—the Metropolitan? Are you working Saturday?"

"I am, as a matter of fact. But why at the museum?"

"You can usually find an open bench in the park on the path between the Needle and the Castle on Saturday afternoons this time of year. We can get a couple of franks for lunch if you want and talk freely there. No one will spot us."

"That's over thirty blocks from my office," she said.

"I can meet you in Grand Central instead. We can take the subway together up to 86th Street. It'll take ten minutes."

"All right, fine."

"Meet me at the bottom of the stairs on the south side of the station."

"12:30, OK?" she asked.

"I'll be there."

Chapter Fifteen

Helen . . . *over here.*"

She was standing at the foot of the stairs alongside the passageway leading down to the Oyster Bar, holding her attaché case with crossed arms in front of her chest and surveying the crowds milling about the computer terminals at the central information booth.

"Hello, Frankie. How are you?"

She smiled and extended her hand. It was no longer glove weather in Manhattan. I took her hand and felt her flesh—for the first time. I held on longer than I should have, letting the sensation linger.

"Nice to see you, Helen," I said. "You look great."

She really did. She must have had a couple of outdoor weekends with her family since I had seen her last. Her face glowed in a healthy radiance that provided the perfect cinnamon setting for her eyes. She wore an ankle-length dress in a flowery pattern, topped with a white linen jacket. In comparison, I felt a little underdressed in khaki pants and a tan L.L. Bean windbreaker.

We walked briskly through the arcade toward the escalator to the uptown subway. From my perch one step behind her on the escalator, I studied the way the rising gusts of air from the trains below ruffled the hair brushed into a cluster at the nape of her neck. Half turning, as if to make sure that I was still there, she smiled faintly. The angels sang.

The subway car was not as crowded as during the workweek, but we had to stand nonetheless, amid a crowd of Hispanics, grungy teenagers, and elderly women with shopping bags. Saturday in New York. Her hand rested just beneath mine on the chromed passenger support pole. I studied her clean, well-tended nails, the long, delicate fingers—adorned with a diamond ring the size of a lima bean. I guess I am not the only one who loves her.

The rocking of the train as it moved uptown bumped our shoulders together. I savored the moment. Just past the 57th Street station, a sudden lurch of the train thrust the full length of her thigh into contact with mine. Smiling in embarrassment, I drew my leg back immediately.

"Pardon," I said.

She lowered her eyes and glowered in a mock-reprimand. Leaning close to my ear, she spoke loudly over the subway's roar. "Crowded for a Saturday, isn't it."

"No, not really—not for the spring. I'll bet Bloomies is hopping," I answered.

She nodded and resumed the mandatory subway rider's stare, impassive, vacant, nearly sullen. It provided me with an opportunity to study her reflection in the subway's window without her being aware of my attention. I liked the way she looked at my side. I was a few inches over six-foot; she was an inch or two less.

I played with the idea that a surge of passengers at the next station might force us even closer together, perhaps give me an excuse to put my hand onto the small of her back in an ostensibly innocent, gentlemanly gesture. Only I would know better. Although they say that women can sense when the male hormones are percolating. Mine were.

We exited at the 86th Street station and walked west through the brownstone and granite caverns extending toward Central Park.

"You want to walk past Regis?" I asked. "I'll show you what Leo and I have planned. Maybe you can come up with some improvements to the scheme."

"I guess I can't get pangs of conscience now," she said. "How do you plan to get in?"

"Parents Night."

"What?" she asked as if she thought I was joking.

"Parents Night," I repeated. "It's coming up soon. Leo and I are going to get lost in the crowd, sneak into the basement and hide out until the place is empty. Then we break into the fake wall and get the hand and the Gospel. We make our getaway when they open the building in the morning and all the kids are milling about and things are hectic. We're going to have a driver waiting for us outside the building."

"You're serious."

"I am."

"Is the driver someone you can trust?" she asked.

"I think so. We are going to ask John Sullivan."

"John Sullivan from the Catholic Worker?"

"Yeah. That John Sullivan," I said as we approached the corner of Park Avenue and 86th Street.

"Are you sure he is the right person for something like this?" she asked. "He doesn't seem the type."

"We are going to talk to him on Monday. But I think he'll be OK. It should be a simple deal. Unless something goes wrong."

"Unless something goes wrong."

"Correct. But it shouldn't."

"You're Irish. You should know about Murphy's Law," she said

"What can go wrong, will go wrong?"

"That's the one," she answered.

"Let's hope this time will be an exception."

We walked south on Park Avenue toward 84th Street, where I planned to turn toward Regis and then Central Park.

I changed my mind. To this day I am not sure why. "Have you ever been inside St. Ignatius Loyola?" I asked her. "It's right there on the corner of 84th."

"No . . . why do you ask?"

"I don't know. Just that it is a beautiful church."

"Isn't that the church they call the celebrities' church?"

"I never heard that, but I can believe it," I said. I motioned with my head toward the neighboring Park Avenue buildings. "Not a bad neighborhood. Feel like taking a look?"

"For what reason? To say a prayer?" she asked, raising her eyebrows skeptically.

"Well, something like that," I said. "Make a visit with me."

"A visit? Do you mean it? I don't have that much time, Frankie."

"Just for a few minutes. It might help."

"Help what?" she asked.

"Help us figure out what's the right thing to do."

"My God—you *are* talking about praying," she said, stopping suddenly to look deep into my eyes. "I don't know what to make of you. I really don't. Do you realize what you're going to do to the entire Christian world's understanding of prayer, once you reveal this information about Jesus' body?"

"All the more reason for us to give it a shot—one last try for old times' sake," I said as we resumed walking.

"You know, this is the epitome of cognitive dissonance. I don't know who you are," she said. "The smart-aleck who jokes like that about praying or the man who thinks it appropriate for me to kneel with him in an old church."

"Neither do I. Why don't we go into St. Ignatius and maybe we'll get some clues."

The vestibule at St. Ignatius was empty, as you would expect it to be on a Saturday afternoon, a cool marble and polished stone space separated from the vast arched nave by a span of padded leather doors. Propped against a side wall was a bookrack with copies of the Jesuits' *America* magazine prominently displayed.

We moved into one of the rear pews. Only three or four other worshipers were scattered about, as well as an older woman making her way through the succession of richly painted Stations of the Cross that rimmed the interior walls. A cleaning woman moved about the altar, dusting and repositioning flower arrangements.

"Beautiful, isn't it?" I said.

"It is," Helen answered quietly. "It really is."

I knelt. So did Helen, her shoulder just briefly touching mine as she moved into place. I didn't know if she was praying—or if she was, about what. And I don't know if what I was going through could be called a prayer: I allowed the beauty of the church to sweep over me, contemplating what buildings like this represented in the western world's psychological development.

The expansive dome, the stained glass windows, marble statuary and Baroque filigree that once served as the backdrop for the pre-Vatican II altar combined to create a space at once overwhelming and reassuring, as if losing oneself in the fullness of Christian worship added to an individual's self-worth. All but the most bitter of Marxists would agree that the human race was better off for the idealism expressed in these buildings. The time, money, and energy that went into them were signs of a conviction that life had meaning, that we had an obligation to seek a community of virtue, to strive to lift life to higher levels than Jack London's bloody world of fang and claw.

We knelt in silence for a few minutes more.

"Ready to go?" I asked in a whisper.

She nodded and crossed herself slowly and precisely.

We exited onto a busy Park Avenue, its dazzling array of windows glowing painfully bright in the midday sun.

"Why did we do that?" she asked.

"Do what?"

"Go into the church."

"I don't know. Maybe I'm hoping for a revelation."

"I don't know about that. But it is a beautiful church," she said. "Extraordinary, in fact."

"It is modeled on Gesu, the Jesuit church in Rome. Or so I've heard. Gesu is supposed to be one of the world's best examples of Baroque architecture."

"Baroque architecture? My, my, you really are a Jesuit boy, you know," Helen chided, "in spite of yourself."

I laughed. "I don't think the Jebbies would agree. Those that would remember me. I wasn't a prize pupil at Regis."

"Maybe revealing this information about Jesus is your way of getting even with your old teachers? Did you ever think of that?"

"No, no, nothing like that. You're digging too deep into the psychological stuff. I don't even remember most of their names. It is Leo's and my way of making some money. At least that's what I thought until recently. But I've got to admit—I'm worrying a little now."

We turned and walked down 84th Street toward Regis, stopping in the shadows on the south side of the street across from the school's main entrance.

"There it is," I said. "We're going to have Sullivan park in my brother's van as close as he can get to the corner of Madison. When we come out, he'll pick us up in front of the school and shoot up to Park, turn north and head up to 85th and then turn back across toward the West Side and over to my apartment. I'll stash the Gospel and the hand there until we decide on the next move. That's when we'll tell Barlow and the others at Lantern Press about it."

"It sounds easy enough," she said. "Except that I was the one who was supposed to warn Lantern Press if anything illegal took place. You're talking about an outright burglary."

"You think they would nix the plans? Come on. As long as we keep them in the dark about the illegal stuff, they'll have no problem with what we do."

"What about me? I can't plead ignorance any longer."

"Sure you can. I'm the only one who knows that you know. You know you can trust me, don't you?"

"Yes. I'm not worried about that."

"I'd never do anything that would hurt you. You can be sure of that. Believe me."

Our eyes locked for a second or two. At least I thought so. Perhaps I was caught in a moment of wishful thinking.

"Let's head to the park," I said. "It'll be nice over there."

We found a bench just behind the Metropolitan Museum of Art, within sight of the roofline of the Delacorte Theater. It was a warm enough day for a cluster of twenty-somethings to be flipping their Frisbees and stretching out for some early sunbathing. The damp, earthy smell of early spring seeped from the muddy edges of the Great Lawn bordering the concrete walkways near our bench.

"I promised you lunch," I said. "I see a hot dog cart over there. Can I get you one?"

"No, I'm not hungry."

"Don't say I didn't offer."

"Agreed. But, seriously—it is not too late, you know," she said. "Are you sure about going ahead with this? I presume that is what we are here to talk about."

"No, I'm not sure," I said. "Of course I'm not sure. That's why I wanted to talk to you. But, look, if the hand and the Gospel are really there, shouldn't someone do something? If I don't have the right to release this information, I damn well don't have the right to keep it secret."

"But maybe the proper thing is to bring this information to the Church authorities," she suggested.

"And run the risk that someone will just move everything to somewhere else—and deny everything? No way."

"You think the hierarchy would do that? Keep everything secret?" she asked.

"They might," I replied. "Look how long they waited to release the third Fatima revelation. Everyone was waiting for it to be released back in the 1960s. But someone at the top thought it would be better for the world if the information was covered up all these years. They didn't release it until a few years back. They might decide to do the same thing with the information we have. Or maybe they'd never release it."

She smiled coyly. "Were you surprised when it turned out that the third Fatima revelation wasn't the bill for the Last Supper?"

I laughed out loud. "I'll use that one." I paused. "But, look, Helen, I'm not blowing smoke. It's not just the money I'm after. If it is the truth, it's right to let the world know. You agreed with that, you said."

"I did. And I meant it. But I don't know if that gives you and Leo the right to do what you are planning. You're about to commit a crime."

"I'll tell you the truth, Helen. I'm serious . . . breaking into that wall at Regis doesn't trouble me as much as exposing so much of Christianity to be a fraud. That's what I can't deal with."

I paused, trying to find the right words. "Helen, tell me what it would do to your life. You told me when we talked in Bryant Park that there are things you do because you think Jesus wants you to do them? What were you talking about?"

She smiled: "Please, Frankie, you're acting like my confessor again."

"No . . . come on. Tell me. You don't have to give me all the gory details. But I want to know how people's lives will be changed if I make all this public."

"OK," she said. "I'll give you an example. Look: I am a married, Catholic woman. I have always respected my vows, for better or for worse. But it has not always been for better. OK? I meet men in my line of work who are very successful, engaging men—men who make clear to me that they would welcome a, shall we say, *interlude* with me."

She paused, as if not sure if she should go on. "Would it surprise you if I admitted that there are times when the day-by-day demands of working and raising a family make the thought of a night on the town—with all that implies—sound very attractive? Very attractive, indeed?" she asked.

I wasn't sure how to respond. "I guess not," I said.

"Well, there *are* times like that. But I do not entertain the prospect in a serious manner—because of my marriage vows. The vows give me an anchor, a sense of obligation, a conviction that I am not entitled to enjoy the company of every exciting man I meet. That conviction comes from my being a Christian, because of Jesus and the Church."

"You aren't talking about me now, are you?" I asked. I wanted to take back the words as soon as I had spoken them.

"Frankie, *please* . . . I thought you were being serious."

"I am. I'm sorry," I said sincerely. "I want to keep everything up front with you. You're special to me, Helen . . . the best. Your being so gorgeous is only part of it."

Her smile surprised me. "Gorgeous? What is this? Do you have a thing for older women?"

"Not until now," I replied cautiously.

"I think we should change the subject," she answered with a small smile that indicated she was not greatly offended by my compliments. "But seriously . . . do you understand what I was trying to say?"

"I do," I answered. "I don't know if a love for the Baby Jesus like yours is what makes the difference with me. But the idea of hell does. I never could figure out the appeal of heaven. None of the scenes that people describe ever appealed to me. I have no idea of what a Beatific Vision would be like. But I fear hell, some kind of punishment for living life like a dirtbag. That fear makes me a better person. Believe me, if I ever did everything I'm tempted to do, I'd make the Hollywood slimeballs look like saints."

"You mean hell fires, burning for an eternity?" she asked with raised eyebrows. "Do you take that literally?"

"I don't know about literally, but I picture something that will hurt—hurt like hell. Jesus mentions hell more than heaven, you know. You can check it out. We can't filter it out to make him more politically correct. That fear *is* part of me. Don't you worry about it?"

"No, not really," she answered. "I don't discount it, or mock those who worry about hell. But my real fear is that giving in to sin—to sexual adventures, for example—will do great harm to my marriage, to my hopes for the life I want to live as my children grow and become parents themselves, when I become a grandparent. I want to be able to live those roles in my life without any sense of guilt or hypocrisy. I am willing to deny myself sensual pleasures to safeguard those things."

"None of that would be threatened unless you get caught, you know. The fear of a divine judgment keeps people on the straight-and-narrow even when they can get away with some sleeping around. That makes a difference. Doing the right thing even when no one knows. Your system wouldn't stop every salesman in the country from tomcatting when he's on the road."

"Maybe that's why so many do," she replied.

"Exactly," I said. "That's what I mean. Jesus makes the difference. What's going to happen when he's gone from the picture? When I, Frankie Corcoran, take him out of the picture?"

"But you agreed with me that Jesus need not become irrelevant just because we find the location of his unresurrected body. You agreed that Christians can go on worshipping Jesus as a *spiritual* reality—that a physical resurrection was not necessary to keep one faithful. That wasn't just a line you were giving me, was it?"

"No, I meant it," I answered.

"Well, I agree. I think the fact that people all over the world still try to live by his teachings is a stronger proof of his divinity than whether or not his body is somewhere in the ground in the Middle East." She paused for emphasis, assuming an almost professorial posture. "But—please listen carefully to what I am saying—I still worry that the impact of discovering the body will cause Christianity to unravel, and for me, too. I don't want that to happen."

"Maybe it won't," I said.

"Frankie, I'm a liberal Catholic. I never have had trouble with theologians interpreting certain New Testament accounts, with them not taking everything literally."

"Which means?"

"It means that I have never been troubled by speculation about things like the Virgin Birth or Jesus' walking on water—about whether they should be seen symbolically, whether a camera would have recorded anything out of the ordinary on Easter morning, whether it would have picked up Jesus ascending into the clouds like a space launch on Ascension Thursday."

"And?"

"But I always thought that these modern interpretations of the New Testament were interpretations of a story that was basically true—basically *true*. That Jesus really was the Word made Flesh, the Incarnation of the will of the Creator—true God and true man—that in some mysterious way the Bible stories represented that truth, even if a number of them are more myth than fact. When you uncover the body, it will take away the truth that is at the center of everything. It will make clear that a deception—a deliberate deception—is the basis of Christianity, at the beginning and now. It will transform the Church into the product of an enormous historical lie. Everyone will know that."

"Then you don't really believe what you just said—about the power of Jesus' words to inspire—the fact that they have lasted for so long?" I asked.

"I just don't think that will be enough. I know it won't, in fact. There are weepy middle-aged women who are inspired by the memory of Elvis and James Dean. That doesn't make *them* God. I don't know how the Christian churches can survive this. I think St. Paul was right—that we need the crucified and risen Christ for Christianity to endure."

"So are you saying that I should leave the hand in the wall?"

"No, I already told you that a cover-up would be wrong," she answered. "I meant that. I wish that a burglary were not involved, but a cover-up would be wrong." She reached into her briefcase and handed me a thin book with a dark and ragged jacket adorned with a large white Greek Omega sign.

"I suppose you have read this already," she said. She handed me a copy of Teilhard de Chardin's *The Divine Milieu.*

"No," I answered, taking the book into my hand. "Just the stuff about the stuff?"

"The what?" she said with a little laugh.

"You know, essays the Jesuits used to give us about his theories."

"Didn't you get curious enough to actually read Teilhard once you learned about his secret?"

"A little. But I've been more involved in planning the heist, to tell you the truth. Plus I've always heard that it's hard to figure out what he's all about. Lots of mystic mumbo-jumbo."

"Frankie, take it, read it. Look, it's short, not much more than a hundred pages. Considering what you are about to do to this man's reputation, you owe it to him."

"Owe it to him?"

"You know what I mean," she answered. "You should spend some time with what motivated him to write as he did."

Something caught my eye at that moment. Looking up, I saw a wobbling Frisbee bearing down toward the back of Helen's head.

"Watch, watch," I said, as I reached across and tilted her head to the side. The Frisbee fluttered by harmlessly and plopped on the grass in front of us. My hand was on the side of her jaw, just beneath her ear. The skin was soft and cool and slightly dampened from a facial cream.

A shirtless twenty-something jogged over to pick up the Frisbee.

"Sorry, man. We lost control," he proclaimed, breathing heavily and proud of himself, as if he had just plunged into the end zone at the Super Bowl.

"No problem," I answered, staring at the Frisbee, as if that might give me an excuse to keep my hand resting on Helen's cheek. I turned toward her.

"Sorry. I hope I didn't shove your head too hard," I said. "I might have done more damage than the Frisbee would have. Are you OK?"

"I'm fine," she smiled. "But you can take your hand off my neck now."

"Sorry again. A guy can't get anything past you, can he?"

"Not one who drags me into conversations about hell and eternal judgments," she replied with a sardonic smile. "Read the book, Frankie. Read it and let me know what you think."

"About what?" I asked.

"Ask yourself if it was written by a priest who had discovered that the story of the resurrection was a lie. Was he trying to ease the world into a new understanding of Christianity—a completely secularized Christianity?"

"Is that what you think?"

"No. That's the problem, Frankie. I can't believe that someone seeking to prove that Christianity was a hoax would write a book like this. I have never interpreted Teilhard that way. I find his words inspiring, truly orthodox, if properly understood. And I'm not the only one. Cardinal Maurice Feltin of Paris argued that Teilhard gave us a vision of the universe where matter and spirit, body and soul, nature and the supernatural, science and faith . . . where they all found their unity in Christ."

"And you know what that means?"

"I do—and come on, so do you," she snapped. "Don't play Irish lounge lizard with me."

"But he wrote this book years before he discovered the hand and the Gospel."

"True," she said emphatically. "That's true. But he could easily have rewritten it, or added an appendix if he actually made the discovery that you think he made. He didn't change anything after the date when you think he found Jesus' body."

"Which means what?" I asked. "What do you think I'll find if I read it?"

"Just read it."

"OK, OK—I'll read it," I said, smiling deferentially, with a shrug and a nod, like a husband telling his wife, "Yes, dear."

Before leaving the park, I convinced her to stop and share a hot pretzel and a Snapple while watching the water spout from the top of the fountain in the reservoir. I told her some stories she had never heard about the history of the angel on top the fountain, which she found interesting. And about the time my friends and I threw John Dwyer's pants onto the angel's wings when he passed out after drinking too much cheap wine after one St. Patrick's Day parade, which she did not.

Just for a moment, I considered trying my well-practiced soul-ful stare and tender ear-nuzzle. It worked wonders in the Hamptons. But not now, not here, not with her. I knew that. Every time I thought about moving closer, she seemed to sense my intentions in some mysterious way and raise her eyebrows in an amalgam of a smile and a mock frown, as if to say, "Mr. Corcoran, *what* do you think you are up to?"

It put me in my place. I contented myself with the sight of the sun glistening on her skin and hair, the way she reached up to brush windblown strands of hair from her eyes and glowed with the joy of living as she watched young couples with children stroll past us through the park.

Sinatra was right: There are such things. But not for me.

Chapter Sixteen

I fully intended to hit the bars the night after my afternoon with Helen in Central Park. A few hours with my smokes and some boozy melancholy seemed a good way to deal with my uneasiness. The Charles Mingus Big Band was playing at the new Birdland down on 44th Street, so I thought I would take a listen. The jumbled Mingus sound is not one of my favorites, but I felt that its atonal bluster might suit my mood that night. Actually, it didn't matter too much who was playing; I liked to sit at the dark circular bar at Birdland, staring out at the tables of tourists and aging jazz buffs nodding to the beat in front of the bandstand. It never mattered if they liked the sound; they always applauded the solos enthusiastically. They were out to make a point.

I decided to spend an hour or so with Helen's copy of *The Divine Milieu* before showering and heading downtown. I opened my window a crack to let in the breeze coming off the Hudson and stretched out on my couch and began paging through the book. I knew what Helen wanted me to look for: Was Teilhard trying to communicate a new understanding of Christianity because of his discovery of the secret, a completely secular vision of a world without a personal God and a risen Son? To help Christians accept that Jesus' body was soon to be unearthed? Was this book a way of cushioning the fall for Catholics who prayed to a loving Father and the Word made Flesh in the person of Jesus? A book written to convince Catholics that Christianity could still be something noble and worthwhile, even if all it offered was a way of making this world a better place through the application of Christ's message of love—even if it was founded on a lie?

I didn't expect to be able to understand everything in the book. I had always heard that it was difficult reading. But I wanted to be able to assure Helen, the next time we met, that I had tried. The thought of her was not going to leave me easily. I pondered whether she would be a constant presence in my reveries from now on, even if the day ever came that I settled down and tied the knot with one of the unfairly divorced, thirty-something former debutantes that my bosses' wives were always trying to set me up with. (They tell me the fact that I know Monet from Manet and dress like old money makes up for the fact that I smoke and never went to college; that and my net worth. I'll bet mainly my net worth.)

I worked my way through the early pages of the book.

"Nothing is more certain, dogmatically, than that human action can be sanctified; the actions of life, of which we are speaking, should not be understood solely in the sense of religious and devotional works (prayer, fasting, almsgiving)."

Christians should *"dignify, ennoble, and transfigure in God the duties inherent to one's station in life, the search for natural truth, and the development of human action."*

OK. But *why* should we do that? Should we focus less on prayer and fasting—and more on human action—because God made the world and it is good? In order to "remake all things in Christ," in St. Paul's words? Or because prayer and fasting make no sense when there is no loving Creator who will grant us a life in the hereafter with Him in return for such sacrifices?

"Beneath our individual strivings towards spiritualization, the world slowly accumulates, starting with the whole of matter, that which will make of it the Heavenly Jerusalem or the New Earth."

The New Jerusalem? Is that what the Washington Square Marxists mean by the perfection of the human community, when the state withers away and we all become selfless little comrades? Or is Teilhard describing a world remade in Christ and awaiting his Second Coming?

"The Incarnation will be complete only when the part of chosen substance contained in every object—spiritualized first of all in our souls and a second time with our souls in Jesus—has rejoined the final Centre of its completion. Quid est ascendit, nisi quod prius descendit, ut repleret omnia."

Everything that rises converges. But into what?

"To begin with, in action I cleave to the creative power of God; I coincide with it; I become not only its instrument but its living prolongation . . . I merge myself, in a sense, through my heart, with the very heart of God."

Merge with the very heart of God? How? By becoming a servant of his peace, by living Ad Maiorem Dei Gloriam? Or by becoming one with the physical world, beyond which there is nothing?

Was I reading the words of a priest who wanted to deepen my religious beliefs? Or one who wanted to help me feel better about losing them? The minutes flew by as I reached for a cigarette and moved deeper into the book. The Mingus Band would have to wait for another night.

"We may imagine that the Creation was finished long ago. But that would be quite wrong. It continues still more magnificently, and in the highest zones of the world. . . .We serve to complete it, even by the humblest work of our hands . . . with each one of our works, we labour—atomically, but not less really—to build the Pleroma; that is to say, we bring to Christ a little fulfillment."

There it was: what they say is his central idea—his vision of evolution proceeding under human direction; of a new world constructed by the application of human energy and creativity, with humans, made in the image and likeness of God, now the co-creators with God.

But what did he mean by Jesus' "fulfillment"? Why would Jesus need to be fulfilled if he is true God as well as true man? Is the fulfillment that Teilhard describes the remaking of the world through the love that Christ preached? Is the doctor doing research to find a cure for childhood cancer engaged in a spiritual act? The carpenter volunteering with Habitat for Humanity to construct housing for the poor worshipping? Are those actions prayers? Does thinking that thought disparage traditional prayers said on one's knees in a quiet chapel, the life of the contemplative religious orders? Was it Teilhard's goal to coax us along to that very disparagement? To replace the older notions of prayer with something solely worldly and secular? Or was he looking to expand traditional concepts of prayer into something new and more mature, without in any way demeaning the older understanding?

"Our work appears to us in the main as a way of earning our daily bread. But its essential virtue is of a higher order: through it we complete in ourselves the subject of the divine union; and through it again we augment in some sense, in relation to ourselves, the divine end of that union, Our Lord Jesus Christ."

We "complete in ourselves" Jesus Christ? We become Jesus Christ? How? Does he mean that the human community, perfected through human action, becomes Jesus Christ? Literally? That there is no personal, risen Jesus beyond the human community inspired by his message of love?

"To repeat: by virtue of the Creation and, still more, of the Incarnation, nothing here below is profane for those who know how to see."

No problem. Except if he means that nothing "here below" is profane because there is nothing sacred "above." Is he saying that? That there is no heaven? No place where a personal, risen Jesus oversees the efforts of his followers to perfect the creation of the Father?

"It is part of the essential Catholic vision to look upon the world as maturing—not only in each individual or in each nation, but in the whole human race—a specific power of knowing and loving whose transfigured term is charity, but whose roots and elemental sap lie in the discovery and delectation of everything that is true and beautiful in creation.

"The Kingdom of God is within us. When Christ appears in the clouds He will simply be manifesting a metamorphosis that has been slowly accomplished under His influence in the heart of the mass of mankind."

The plot thickens. Is he playing games with us? Christ appearing in the clouds? The Second Coming? The Parousia? Does he mean that Jesus, the Second Person of the Blessed Trinity, will come again—as an individual, as Lord of History? Or is the "metamorphosis" of the human community inspired by Christ's message of love the only "Christ" the world will ever see again? Is Teilhard's Christ on the clouds nothing more than a metaphor for that perfected humanity? Is Teilhard striving to show us that there is something noble about seeing through the metaphor of a personal Christ coming again? That this is the next essential step in the evolutionary process?

Hell, an atheist could buy into the notion that there is something uplifting about describing the worldly pursuit of scientific and medical progress and social justice as "divine"—if by that you mean the highest expression of human life. An atheist wouldn't even object to someone opting to make Jesus' words the inspiration for his humanitarian concerns. Jesus for some, Buddha for others, John Dewey for still others. Is that the deal? Would someone who knows where Jesus' body is buried think himself in service to the Catholic Church by making the case for Jesus' place in the pantheon?

Would a priest committed to that deception write:

"We have gone deeply into these new perspectives: the progress of the universe, and in particular of the human universe, does not take place in competition with God, nor does it squander energies that we rightly owe to Him. The greater man becomes, the more humanity becomes united, with consciousness of, and mastery of, its potentialities, the more beautiful creation will be, the more perfect adoration will become, and the more Christ will find, for mystical extensions, a body worthy of resurrection. The world can no more have two summits than a circumference can have two centres. The star for which the world is waiting, without yet being able to give it a name, or rightly appreciate its true transcendence, or even recognise the most spiritual and divine of its rays, is, necessarily, Christ himself, in whom we hope. To desire the Parousia, all we have to do is to let the very heart of the earth, as we Christianize it, beat within us."

The "star?" Is that Christ the resurrected Nazarene carpenter, the Word made flesh? Or Christ the human spiritual leader whose message of love will perfect our communal lives? Will the Parousia be his personal return in glory? Or something akin to the hopes for the future you would hear from the slicks in the United Nations lounge while waiting for their drivers to take them to lunch at Nobu or Lespinasse.

"God does not offer Himself to our finite beings as a thing all complete and ready to be embraced. For us He is eternal discovery and eternal growth."

What is "not complete?" God himself, or our perception of him? As humans discover and grow, do we move closer to God, or do we create God—become God, a God who exists nowhere else— in our perfected human communities?

"That I may not succumb to the temptation to curse the universe and Him who made it, teach me to adore it by seeing You concealed within it. O Lord, repeat to me the great liberating words, the words which at once reveal and operate: Hoc est Corpus meum."

Brother, what is there more to say? *"Hoc est Corpus meum,"* the words of the Consecration, the words that Catholics believe transform the bread into the body of Christ. Was Teilhard subtly deriding the notion that anything uniquely sacred takes place at Mass, insinuating that all of the stuff of the universe is as sacred as the consecrated Host? Or was he trying to inspire us to see the beauty and dignity in all of God's creation by comparing it to the highest expression in the Catholic world of Christ's love for mankind, the consecrated Host?

I closed the book, lit another cigarette and stared at the ceiling. I didn't expect to be the one to come up with the definitive explanation of Teilhard's vision, but neither did I expect to be as perplexed as I was. If this French Jesuit was a con artist, he was a good one. I could see why Helen Bergeron believed that he was orthodox and a believer in the risen Christ. His words could easily be interpreted as a prayerful ode to the wonders of creation and the Creator and to the transforming power of the risen Son.

But they could just as easily be interpreted as a cunning ruse meant to disparage the very notion of the supernatural that has been at the core of Christianity from its beginnings; they could be a secular humanist subversion of the Catholic Church.

The kicker was that there were disciples of Teilhard in both camps. I knew that.

It was getting too late to bother with Birdland. Moreover, reading the book had altered my mood. Whatever Teilhard's intentions, blotting out my consciousness with nicotine and Jack Daniels seemed suddenly base and vulgar, the antithesis of "mastering one's potentialities" for the purpose of "Christianizing the heart of the earth and coinciding with the very heart of God." Whatever that meant. I hit the sack and slept like a puppy.

Chapter Seventeen

W hat are you drinking, Sully?" I asked, as John Sullivan slid
next to us in one of the back booths at Ryan's on 2nd Avenue,
a few blocks north from his Catholic Worker office. It was a
little before 6 P.M. and the place was quiet, just a few thirty-something types at the bar, stopping off on their way home from work
for a little lubrication.

"What do you guys have there?" Sullivan asked, a bit breathless and windblown from his walk. He wore a nylon windbreaker
over his usual light blue denim shirt adorned with activist buttons. He brushed wispy strands of hair back across his forehead.

"Some draft Harp," Leo said.

"I can go for that," Sullivan said, nodding toward our glasses.

"Let me get it," Leo volunteered. He walked to the bar to place
the order.

"You know, I wasn't expecting to hear from you guys so soon,"
Sullivan said with an inquisitive look. "What was it? Just a month
or so ago that we talked in my office?"

"About that," I answered. "But things have been moving along."

"Are you saying that you signed the contract with Lantern Press
already?"

"No, not yet. I hope it doesn't disappoint you, but we aren't here to present you with your thousand dollar check."

"Hey, Frankie, don't get me wrong. I wasn't pushing for the money. You know me."

"I know. We're the ones who asked you here. It's something else we want to talk to you about," I assured him.

Leo returned and slid the pint of Harp in front of Sullivan. "Here you go, John. Enjoy." He moved back into the booth next to me. "Want a burger or something? Sandwiches ain't bad here."

"No, I'm good," Sullivan said, patting his stomach. "I had a late lunch."

"Good, good . . . we're not hungry yet either," I said. "Let me tell you what's up, OK?

"I'm all ears," said Sullivan, sipping his beer.

"Well, first thing, we didn't want you to think we forgot you. We want you to know that. Our deal was that we would give you the grand once we signed the contract with Lantern Press. It's just that we haven't done that yet. They want to see Teilhard's Gospel before they give us any money."

"I understand. No problem," Sullivan responded. "Would I be prying if I asked how close you are to getting the Gospel?"

"No," Leo said calmly. "You can ask. We're *real* close."

"We'll have it in a week," I added. I waited to see how he would react.

Sullivan said nothing. His eyes moved from Leo to me, and then back again, as if unsure if he should ask anything else.

"Well . . . do you want to know anything else?" Leo asked, his lips pursed like a jeweler making an appraisal on an old ring.

"Of course I'm curious. I know how to mind my own business though," Sullivan responded. "You guys made it clear when we talked at my office that I wasn't supposed to know too much about how you were going to get this Gospel."

"Hey . . . you got the wrong impression, John. We trust you," I protested. "We're going to get it next week," I said. "It's hidden behind a wall at Regis." I paused, waiting for the impact to hit home.

"You're kidding, right?" said Sullivan.

"Nope," I assured him.

"At the high school?" Sullivan asked. "At Regis High School?"

"At the high school," I said. "Right there. Leo and I have a plan to break into the place. We're going to mix with the parents on their Parents Night next week, then hide out until the building is empty. Once we get the Gospel, we're going to sneak out during the commotion when school opens up the next morning."

Sullivan leaned across and whispered, "My God, you can't do that."

"There's no other way," I explained. "We thought about that. The people who hid this Gospel won't just turn it over to us. There's a bunch of Jesuits who want to keep it a secret."

"That's hard to believe," Sullivan protested. "The Jesuits tend to be progressive on these matters. Teilhard de Chardin was a Jesuit himself."

"Well, that's what we thought," I said. "We were surprised when we learned of the cover-up. But now we're certain that's what's going on."

"How do you know?" Sullivan asked.

"We can't tell you that. Not yet," I responded. "But we have proof solid enough to be risking a break-in to get our hands on the Gospel. That should tell you something."

I paused to allow a slightly tipsy drunk to pass our table on his way to the men's room, then resumed speaking: "The way Leo and I see it, we're doing something technically illegal, but in service of mankind's right to know. No one thinks it's a big deal when an archaeologist violates private property rights when he's looking for some old Mayan vase, right?"

"Lately people do. But what if you get caught?" Sullivan asked. "What then?"

"Well, if we're careful, we won't get caught," I said. "And if we do, what's the big deal? We get caught in the basement of a high school. So what? You don't go to jail for that. We can say we were involved in some stupid alumni prank. If we get caught, the people who want to keep this Gospel secret aren't going to be looking for any publicity. They won't even press charges, I'd bet."

"I don't know," Sullivan said, shaking his head in a mixture of concern and disapproval. "I don't like the sound of all this. Do the people at Lantern Press know what you have planned?"

"Nope," Leo said, putting his hand on Sullivan's forearm. "You're the only one. We have to keep them out of the loop."

"Helen Bergeron doesn't know?" Sullivan asked.

"Not a clue," said Leo. (He didn't know that I had told her everything.) "I don't think she'd go for it."

"You can see why, can't you?" Sullivan replied. "That woman is the epitome of propriety."

"The epitome of legs too," Leo smirked. He had no idea of the intensity of my feelings for Helen. He gave Sullivan's forearm a reassuring squeeze. "But what is it they say? Behind every great fortune is a great crime? We can't get pansy-assed now."

"John, let me ask you a question . . ." I sipped on my beer and leaned closer to Sullivan. "Do you have a problem with the idea of this Gospel being made public? Is that it?" I had mixed motives. I wanted to draw him slowly into the idea of driving the getaway van for us, but I was also genuinely curious about his view of the effect of releasing the new Gospel. "Is that it—you *want* this information to remain secret?"

"No, of course not. It's just the idea of how you are going to take possession of it that troubles me. If this information were being made public in a reputable theological forum, I'd be there with bells and whistles."

"You have no problem with the idea that a lot of the miracles are going to be shown to be fairy tales and that the Resurrection was a con job?" I asked.

"None," he answered. "I welcome it, in fact. It is one of the most fortuitous developments that I can imagine. It will further the causes I have been devoted to for my entire adult life."

"How's that?" I asked.

"It will demonstrate once and for all that Christianity's intrinsic value is in its call to work for social justice in the here and now, not its promise of some heavenly hereafter. I can't think of anything better than having the world realize that Jesus was a social reformer and not some holy-card miracle worker."

"What's so bad about people believing in the holy-card Jesus?" I asked. "The Jesus who healed the sick and raised himself from the dead is the one who taught us to love the poor the way you're always preaching."

"It is a matter of emphasis," Sullivan replied. "The idea of a Jesus up in the clouds waiting to greet us when we die gives the likes of corporate polluters and the hobnail bootboys in the police departments the idea that they can exploit the working poor every day of their lives, and then say a few prayers on Sunday and think they are good Catholics. They think their relationship with some heavenly beings is more important than their commitment to the poor. There are cops who come from their Knights of Columbus Communion breakfasts and then use their billy clubs on the homeless in Tompkins Square Park that afternoon."

"Do you believe in a Jesus up in the clouds?" I asked.

"Not up in the clouds. Of course not," Sullivan answered. He paused for a second, waiting for the rummy who had passed us a few minutes ago to return to his barstool. "What does this new Gospel say about that, by the way? Does it deal with the notion of the Ascension?"

"I don't know. We haven't seen it yet," I said. "But do you believe that there's a place where Jesus and Mary are, however they got there?"

"I assent to the traditional formulations," Sullivan answered.

"You what?" Leo asked with a puzzled squint.

"I accept the Church's teachings—as long as my understanding of metaphor is respected." He sipped his beer and paused to gather his thoughts. "This is not exactly the best place for theological exegesis," he continued, looking around the bar. "But the notion that the body that Jesus was crucified with—dying and coming back and walking around the earth and ascending into a place called heaven, in a three-storey universe—that does not make any sense to me, nor to enlightened Catholics in general. I assume you know that. It will be good for Christians when the notion of a literal bodily resurrection is dismissed once and for all, so that we can get on with building a just society in the world we know."

"Where do you think Jesus is now?" I asked.

"He is here with us, when we care for the least of our brethren," Sullivan answered.

"Anyplace else?"

"Yes. Of course. He is the transforming energy that calls us to follow him by feeding the hungry, sheltering the homeless."

"You didn't answer my question," I said.

"Indeed, I did. We must get beyond the Platonic vision of life. The Christian community in the future will have to live and celebrate its faith in a non-religious world, one which the Christian faith itself has helped to build. Your new Gospel will focus us on that task. Literal interpretations of scripture drain them of their power to transform the world. Teilhard understood that. He understood that our human efforts to perfect our world are the ultimate prayer, and that otherworldly speculation merely diverts us from that task."

"You sure he said that?" I asked.

"Perfectly," he replied.

"Where does he say that?" I asked, thinking of my recent session with Teilhard's *The Divine Milieu*.

"Please," Sullivan protested, "it's been years since I read Teilhard's work. But it is common knowledge that his goal was to end the notion of a separate sacred and secular reality."

"Common knowledge where? Down at the Catholic Worker?" I asked.

"Common knowledge in enlightened Catholic circles," he replied curtly. "Do you doubt that?"

"Just asking," I begged off. I was getting over my head. "But how is that different from what the God is dead people and the Marxists have been saying all along?" I asked.

"I don't play those games," Sullivan responded with a dismissive wave of his hand. "Our goal should be an anonymous Christianity where these distinctions are irrelevant, a Christianity devoted to the struggle which the exploited social classes have undertaken against their oppressors. Christianity must become an intrahistorical reality. Who cares who our allies are? I am not a Marxist. Marx was an enemy of religion, but only because he was mistaken about its potential for catalyzing the political and cultural transformation he sought. He was wrong about that."

"Sounds to me as if you think the Church can do what the Marxists want, only better," Leo cut in with an angry edge to his voice. "You mean the same thing as them, but just use different words to say it. At least the Commies are honest about what they believe. You're the one using weasel words. Maybe that's what you guys like about this Teilhard—he makes it seem OK to have lost your faith."

"Loss of faith? Weasel words?" Sullivan smiled deferentially. "It is not that simple, Leo."

Leo's tone surprised me. He had spent his adult life mocking the religious pieties of my mother and her friends. His derision of the immigrant Irish Catholic was part of his barroom repertoire. But there was no other conclusion than that he too held close to his heart something represented by the risen Christ. It was his compass. I guess that, even when you spend your time off course, it's good to know where there is a safe harbor. Queequeg had his totem, Uncas his amulet, Leo his Jesus and the saints.

"Do you pray to Jesus, Sully?" I asked, sincerely intrigued by what he would say.

"Not if by that you mean adult letters to Santa Claus. If the Catholic Church wants to remain relevant, it will have to move beyond the mythological framework that portrays Jesus as a visiting space traveler, as some saving, divine figure."

"You don't leave a guy much, Sully," said Leo, suddenly with a trace of sadness in his eyes. "You know, Sully, there are a lot of regular people in the pews every Sunday who find all the miracles in the Bible hard to believe, too. You don't have to be a genius to wonder if the story of the loaves and fishes really went down like that, or if Jesus chased devils into some pigs and drove them off a cliff."

"So what's wrong with me doing the same?" Sullivan asked curtly.

"The other people—the cops and accountants and house-wives—they keep their mouths shut about their doubts. They commit themselves to their religion and submit with some humility. They don't think they're so damn smart that they know all there is to know about life. They accept that there is a mystery to the meaning of life, and they believe that Jesus and the Bible are at its heart and that it's best to show them some respect."

"So do I," Sullivan replied.

"Yeah, you say that, but you explain everything away so that you can convince the atheist smart-asses that what you think is no different from them—that you are going to use Jesus and the church to work for the same thing as them. And you go around holding conferences where you and all the other liberals pat each other on the back for selling out like that—for being so much smarter than the average Catholic. You're like some third-grade kid who won't stop telling the other kids that there is no Santa Claus."

"Look, maybe I shouldn't be getting into these things—not like this," Sullivan explained. "You are overreacting. These topics need introductory readings, a proper setting and pace, a familiarity with the lexicon. You will misinterpret me if I talk off the top of my head. You must understand that the Church is important to me. The Mexican Independistas and Emiliano Zapata's followers marched under the flag of Our Lady of Guadalupe. That says something we cannot dismiss. It gives . . ."

"Wait, now . . . *come on*. You've got to explain *this*," Leo interrupted. "You don't believe that there is a heaven where Mary is, but you believe in Our Lady of Guadalupe? How does that work?"

"I believe in what the Virgin of Guadalupe represents," Sullivan answered. "That is real."

"Is that another of those traditional formulations you feel confident with?" I asked.

"I told you that I won't play those games with you," Sullivan begged off. "I believe in the transforming power of the Virgin at Guadalupe. How the image got onto the cloth is irrelevant. Where Mary's body is located now is of no interest to me. The transforming power of her image is real. It lives on."

"So what's your problem with releasing the new Gospel, then?" I asked. "You should be all in favor of it."

"I am!" he exclaimed in an agitated whisper. "I told you that! It is the burglary you are planning that concerns me! I can't believe that the Jesuits would know of a new Gospel and not want to make the information public. It just does not make sense. There must be something more to this."

If he only knew.

"I can't explain why the Jebbies are covering this up," I said. "But you agree that it's wrong for them to be doing it, right?"

"If they are covering it up, it is wrong. Yes."

"Would you be willing to help Leo and me make sure the world learns the truth – to end this deception?"

"I'll have nothing to do with the break-in, if that's what you mean."

"How about just driving us away from Regis after Leo and I do the break-in?"

"Are you crazy?"

"No, I'm serious, John," I said, with a little smile. "Just be outside Regis in Leo's van between seven and eight in the morning with the engine running, shoot up to Park with us when we come out, and then cut across 85th Street to the road through the park and over to my apartment on the West Side. Easy. Like falling off a log."

"You're kidding . . . you want me to become an accessory to this?" Sullivan asked in disbelief. "You think I would do that? *No way!*"

"Sully . . ." Leo reached across and placed his hand on Sullivan's forearm again. "We need you. We trust you. If you leave us hanging here, the world is going to be kept in the dark about this Gospel."

"Plus there's really no risk for you, Sully," I added. "What can happen? If Leo and I get caught it will be while we're inside the school. If we don't come out with the Gospel by eight o'clock, just drive away. You've got nothing to worry about." I paused and gave Sullivan a solemn look. "And if we don't get caught, you will be a participant in one of the most important efforts in human history."

"A goddam mission for mankind," Leo added with an overly earnest nod.

Sullivan looked down his nose at Leo as if he were surveying a carnival huckster.

"Plus, we'll give you another five thousand dollars," I added. "That'll make it six thousand when we sign the contract. Not bad for an hour's work, Sully."

The mood changed.

"Six-thousand dollars? Are you serious?" Sullivan was wide-eyed in disbelief. "There's something you aren't telling me about all this."

"Sully, look," I said, "Lantern Press is offering us big money for this information. We need your help to complete the deal. What's the mystery? We're offering you six thousand so that we can make a lot more. You'll be making a nice buck for doing something you think is right anyway, making this information public. Where's the downside?"

Sullivan breathed heavily and began to look around the walls, studying every piece of Irish memorabilia within his line of vision. Then he looked back at Leo and me.

"Five-thousand dollars?" he asked. "Six all told?"

"Cash," said Leo. "As soon as we sign the contract. We get ours; you get yours."

"Would my name be made public?"

I was about to assure him that we would be models of discretion and that he would remain anonymous, but the look in Sullivan's eyes gave me second thoughts. "John, look, you can have it however you want. If things go sour, no one will know you were anywhere near Regis that morning. But if we get the contract and the book goes well, you can let people know you were involved. If you want them to know you played a central role in the heist, you can do that. If you want to picture your part as something else, as our theological advisor—well, we have no problem with that either."

Sullivan grew pensive. I imagined his mind roaming over the possibilities: becoming a prominent speaker at a long succession of university panel discussions on the significance of the Teilhardian

Gospel, a major player in the world of progressive theologians, maybe even a leading expert on the television talk shows.

"You know, right is right," Sullivan said with a solemn sigh. "Sometimes one must take a risk to do the right thing."

"That's what we're saying, Sully," Leo added. "Sometimes one must. Look, the world will be better when we release the Gospel, no? You just said that."

"I agree," Sullivan nodded.

"So you're in?" Leo asked.

"I didn't say that," Sullivan answered. "I'm just saying that maybe it would be the right thing to do. I don't know what to say."

"What you say is yes or no," Leo replied. "You say yes and collect six-thousand dollars, or no and we look for someone else. Either way the hand becomes public knowledge."

"The hand? What are you talking about now?" Sullivan asked with a puzzled look.

I nearly leaped across the table to shut Leo's mouth, but it was too late. He knew what he had said. He stared across at me as if he had been hit in the stomach with a left hook from Mike Tyson.

"Our hand—you know, our play here," I said calmly. "The hand we're playing with this Gospel."

It worked. Leo emitted an almost audible sigh of relief. He pulled in his chin and stared at me wide-eyed as if to say, "Thank you, thank you."

"Who else would you get if I say no?" Sullivan asked.

"No one we can trust as much as you," I answered. "That's the problem. But if we have to we can get a driver from the old neighborhood for an hour's work for a lot less than five grand. That's for sure. We want you because we know you're honest and a stand-up guy. But if it is too close to the edge for you, we understand."

Flattery and big bucks can get you anywhere. Sullivan closed his eyes and nodded solemnly as if he were surrendering to the demands of truth, justice, and the American way.

"No, no, I guess I shouldn't leave you guys in the lurch," he said. "That wouldn't be right. Look: I'll do it. As long as you stick with the deal that I can leave the area with your van if anything goes wrong . . . if you and Leo don't come out of the building when you're supposed to."

"That goes without saying. No problem. Hell, if we get caught we don't need a getaway driver," Leo assured him. "Just drive away and look in the papers to find out what happened to us. No problem."

"Fair enough. And after I drop you off at Frankie's apartment, what then?"

"You hop on the downtown train and go to work."

"Then what?"

"Then nothing. You wait for your check for six big ones."

Sullivan sat quietly, looking down into his beer. "OK," he nodded finally. "I'll do it." He nodded some more. "Where do I get the keys for your van?"

Leo answered him: "Frankie and me are going into the school during the Parents Night hoopla about nine o'clock. I'll drop the van at your apartment before I head downtown by train. You just make sure you're out front the next morning from between seven and eight when school opens. If you park somewhere near the corner of Madison, you'll be able to see us when we come out."

"How do you know I can get a parking place near enough to see you?" Sullivan asked.

"Come on, Sully. You're not from Kansas. Double-park with the engine running. Me and Frankie will find you. But, look, we're assuming that nothing is going to go wrong. We're expecting to come up to you as calm as on a morning stroll. No big deal. If we come running, then that's something else. Then you slide over and let me take the wheel."

"OK," Sullivan responded pensively.

"You just be outside your apartment on Wednesday night about eight and I'll drop off the van. You still live the same building, right?" said Leo.

"Right."

"Your mom's place, right?"

"Right."

"I'll be there with the keys and a full tank," said Leo. "You got a place where you can park it until morning?"

"I can find a spot," Sullivan answered.

"Then we're in business," I said. "You just make sure that you get to Regis by seven the next morning."

"I'll be there."

"We're counting on you, Sully," said Leo. "We know you won't let us down."

Chapter Eighteen

D id it go OK?" I asked as Leo approached. I was standing, sipping a coffee at Zaro's in Grand Central. Leo had just arrived by subway after dropping off his van uptown with John Sullivan. We turned and walked together toward the escalator to the uptown trains.

"Yeah," Leo laughed, "Sully was out in front of his building with his collar up like he thought he was a spy. His hand was shaking like a drunk's. You should've seen him. I hope he holds up."

"He'll be all right by morning," I responded with a chuckle. "Once he drives into midtown, he'll calm down."

"We hope."

"You have the hammer and the flashlight?" I asked.

He patted his tan raincoat. "Got 'em. You got the combination to the safe?"

I pointed to the inside pocket of my sports coat. "Right here. I guess it's show time."

We took the No. 6 train north to the 86th Street station, saying nothing during the short ride. It was close to 8:30 P.M. and the rush hour was over, but the subway was still crowded, weary men in rumpled suits and limp-haired secretaries in wilted spring blouses hanging onto the passenger poles as if they were on the verge of sinking into a deep sleep. A pock-marked panhandler in a grimy camouflage jacket sat dejectedly and bleary-eyed near where we stood, holding his coffee can at an angle, as if he couldn't care less if anyone gave him a handout or not. We exited up the stairs to the street and walked the short distance to Regis.

And there it was . . . I'll tell you, it was easy to see why parents felt good about sending their boys to this school. The scene outside Regis was an urban fairyland: a misty night cast a damp glitter upon the softly lit windows of the East Side buildings, scrunched against the school like cigarettes in a freshly opened pack. The school was a jewel, every window beaming in welcome to the parents, who were filing in and out of the front door like theatergoers on opening night. My guess was that it was about halfway through the night of parent conferences.

It was a New York crowd in the best sense of that term. Expensively tailored Manhattanites, perhaps after their dinner at one of the neighboring chi-chi spots, mixed with working class couples from the outer boroughs in their Sunday best, a mixture of whites and Hispanics and blacks. Leo and I fit in OK: he in his tan raincoat and I in my Harris Tweed jacket and charcoal pants.

The diversity of the crowd didn't surprise me. Eighth-graders were admitted to Regis on the basis of academic performance, which meant that the sons of postal workers and welfare moms became members of the same student body as the lawyers' and doctors' kids. A blood-red banner emblazoned with the school's name draped diagonally from a pole above the entrance, much the way the prestigious museums in the vicinity announced their presence. Hard to believe that I graduated from the place. I hope that there are enough cultured, socially-conscious yuppie alumni to make up for me—so that the Jebbies who run the place can live out their lives with some semblance of psychological serenity.

Leo and I moved through the doors and ambled about the lobby, trying to blend inconspicuously with the parents moving from classroom to classroom and up and down the staircase toward the richly lit stained glass window on the first landing. We lingered in front of a bulletin board, pretending to be deeply involved in a search of its contents.

"Where's the door to the basement?" Leo whispered anxiously.

"Behind me to the left," I answered with a movement of my head. "Let's walk toward it. Just move slow, casual."

Leo nodded. No wisecracks now. The game was afoot. We moved closer to the basement door, watching carefully to see if anyone had noticed anything out of the ordinary about us. There was no reason that night for any parents to be heading in the direction we were taking, but no reason for any of the parents to know that either. My main worry was that a faculty member or some student-host playing concerned citizen would spot us and get curious. We moved closer to the door to the staircase to the basement. Peering over my shoulder, I jiggled the door handle to make sure it was open. It was.

"OK, Leo, when I open the door, move in. Quick."

I checked once again to see if anyone was watching. It looked good. The crowd near the front door was moving in and out without a glance our way. I nudged open the basement door.

"Go!" I said in an excited whisper.

Leo darted behind the door; I followed so quickly I stepped on the back of his shoes, yanking the door closed behind me. We stood breathless and silent on the top step. The stairwell was pitch black, as was the basement storage area beneath us.

"Stay still just a minute or so," I whispered. "If no one comes by then, we're clear."

"Damn, Frankie . . ." Leo muttered. "I can't see a thing. Where are we?"

"At the top of a stairs . . . *be careful.* It's about fifteen steps down."

Leo reached inside his raincoat and pulled out the flashlight and cast its beam down the stairs and into the storage area beyond.

"OK?" I whispered.

"Yeah, looks OK," he replied. He swept the beam from side to side, across the boxes and storage cabinets lining the basement.

"Just hold on a second or two more and we'll go down."

"OK . . ." Leo breathed heavily and turned off the flashlight. The darkness swept back over us.

I pressed my ear against the door, listening for footsteps in the hallway or some other sign that someone might be aware of where we were. Not a sound. I waited for a few seconds more. Still nothing

"OK, Leo," I whispered. "Let's go down."

Leo led the way, pointing his flashlight into the basement.

"Back there," I said as we reached the bottom of the stairs. "There's the oil burner I was telling you about . . . to your left. The fake wall is back that way. We can hide back there and wait."

We found some cardboard boxes to sit on behind the oil burner. I wanted to be out of the line of vision of anyone at the top of the stairs. I suspected that Roberto, the custodian I had met a few weeks earlier, would appear on those stairs sometime before the end of the night.

"What do we do now?" Leo asked.

"We wait," I answered. "It'll be at least an hour or so before the building is empty. We'll be able to tell by the noise level."

"Where's the wall we got to break open?" he asked.

"Give me the flashlight."

I beamed the light toward the old green storage cabinet that stood in front of the fake wall. "Right back there," I said. "Behind that cabinet. See over there in the back, where the brick is a little different from the wall behind it, a little newer-looking."

"Yeah . . . *that's it?*"

"That's the place."

"Man . . ." Leo exhaled heavily. "You edgy, Frankie?"

"A little," I answered. "More than a little, in fact. But all we can do is wait."

"Yeah, I guess . . ." Leo muttered. He removed the small sledge-hammer from under his raincoat and placed it on top of a nearby cardboard box and leaned back against the oil burner.

I did the same, closing my eyes.

After all this time, it was finally going go happen. Within a few hours I would have the hand of Jesus Christ in mine. I was apprehensive, but not as much as you might think. Come on . . . I have lived most of my life with the thought that I take his body and blood into my mouth at Communion. I've learned to handle the implications, even though I can't put them into words. Same thing now.

I listened to the sound of the building above us, the nervous energy of the parents moving about, friendly chatter and laughter, doors closing, the occasional rumble of the oil burner as it clicked on to heat the building's water system. Every once in a while I would turn the flashlight beam onto my wristwatch. The time passed slowly.

By 10:30 I sensed a change. There was still a scattering of activity in the building, but things were clearly winding down. Instead of a stream of footsteps heading toward the front door, there was now just an occasional patter of feet, followed by the chunk of the door closing on its latches. My guess was that it was the last of the parents, the eager beavers lingering to impress the teachers with the level of their parental concerns. And then came the last footsteps, no doubt the teachers heading home for the night.

And then silence. I kept my eyes on the door to the hallway above. My guess was right. A few minutes later, without warning, the door popped open and light leaped across the basement. I could feel Leo jolt to attention beside me. I motioned with my hand to assure him that nothing was wrong: I peeped through some boxes to see the custodian looking for a broom. He lifted one from a rack near the top of the stairs, turned off the lights and disappeared back behind the door.

"That's the guy I was telling you about," I said to Leo. "He's the janitor. He cleans up after the parent conferences end. It shouldn't be long now."

I leaned back and waited.

Roberto returned the broom about an hour later, nearly midnight. I could hear him moving about in the hall above us for a few minutes more, and then the sound of the door to 84th Street closing as he left the building. If I was right, the building was now empty, except for Leo and me.

In the silence, the building seemed to take on a life of its own: the hisses and gurgles of water moving through pipes, the hum of cafeteria refrigerators, the clicking of clocks and the beeping of computer systems, the creak of old beams and trusses, what I suspected was the nervous scraping of mice scurrying about the cardboard boxes in the basement.

"Stay here," I whispered, as I reached for the flashlight. "I'm going to check to see if anyone is still up there."

"OK, but Frankie—don't open the goddam door," Leo warned. "Probably they've got their motion sensors covering the whole hall area, right up to the front door. That's how it works."

"OK," I answered. "I'll listen from inside the door."

I pressed my ear to the door to the hallway and listened. When I was certain that the building was empty, I turned on the basement lights and returned to the place where Leo was sitting behind the oil burner.

"You think it's OK to do that—put the lights on down here?" Leo asked, standing and squinting nervously as I neared him.

"Yeah, it should be OK. No one can see us from the street. There's no windows on the 84th Street side and just those little windows on the back wall."

"I guess . . . let's go then," he said, exhaling heavily.

We set to work, emptying the cabinet in front of the fake wall of its old paint cans and nails and assorted maintenance supplies so that we could slide it to the side. It clanked and rattled as we shoved it across the concrete floor to give ourselves room to work.

Leo stood, hands on hips surveying the fake wall: "Damn, Frankie, they did a nice job. No one would think anything if they saw this. It looks like something they put up to cover some pipes or some new wiring, maybe something they put in when they computerized the place." He knelt and ran his hand across the upper ledge of the construction. It was about three-foot high, four-foot long, and extending maybe two feet from the wall. He reached for the hammer where he had placed it on the cardboard box.

He looked at the hammer, then at me. "Well . . . what do you think? Time to break some bricks?"

It was too late to turn back, although I was tempted to do just that.

"Yeah . . . go ahead," I said, my voice cracking slightly.

He raised the hammer to about ear level and smashed smartly down on a corner brick. The noise was louder than I thought it would be, a solid thud that filled the basement space. But it was too late to worry now. It took just two blows to crack the mortar around the brick. The next strike popped it loose as if it were a pasta box on a grocery shelf, opening a hole in the brick veneer. Leo then struck repeatedly at the bricks around the opening. They crumbled, two and three at a time. I turned the flashlight beam into the cavity he had opened.

The safe was smaller than I expected, about the size of a liquor box, its gray-green surface coated with dust and mortar thrust up from Leo's hammering.

"There it is, Leo. *There* it is!" I scanned the safe from top to bottom with the flashlight beam. "Hit the bricks in front of it a few times so that I can get to the door."

Leo smacked away at the bricks until the safe sat like a little shrine in a grotto. I knelt before it and wiped the mortar dust from around the combination dial.

"Take the flashlight, Leo. Shine it on the dial."

I reached inside my pocket and took out the paper with the combination to the safe. Left, right, left—and the door opened with a solid little click. I turned the handle and pulled it toward me. Inside was a bundle about the size of an Easter ham, wrapped in white plastic, tightly bound with packaging tape, just the right size to contain what we were looking for. I lifted the package cautiously and drew it to me. I looked up at Leo.

"We've got it, Leo," I said gravely.

Leo shook his head and whistled softly, clearly unsure if he should be jubilant or saddened by the turn of events.

We walked slowly toward the overhead light and studied the package in my hands as warily as if it were a living thing.

"Should we open it, Frankie?" Leo asked. He held his hands under mine, as if he were a fearful parent who had just handed his infant to a stranger.

"No, no . . . let's leave it like this until we get to a safe place— back at my apartment. We don't want to be running around with this stuff flopping around in the wind if we have to run for it later."

"Run for it? Come on, don't even say that, man."

"Look: nothing's gonna happen. But let's just play it safe. We've got to be gentle with what's in here," I explained. "Let's wait until everything is safe and quiet and we can check everything out the right way."

"Yeah, you're right," Leo said, nodding. "What do we do now?"

"It's nearly two o'clock. All we can do is wait until the school opens and the alarms are turned off. We'll be able to hear kids in the hall. Once they're milling around up there, we leave. But look . . ." I motioned with my head toward the empty safe. "First we've got to get things looking as normal as possible around the wall." I nodded toward the pile of bricks around the safe. "They're gonna know we were here sooner or later, but no sense raising the red flag. If we put the wall back into place as best we can and shove the storage cabinet back in front of it, it could be months before anyone knows what happened, years maybe."

I gently placed the white package with the Jesus' hand on top of a storage cabinet and took a broom and swept the dust and debris into a pile, which I then scooped up and dropped into the hole around the safe. Then I helped Leo stack the bricks back into their original place as if we were constructing a jigsaw puzzle. Once everything was as restored to its former condition as we could manage, we slid the cabinet back into place and refilled it with the paint cans and other maintenance materials.

"Damn, Frankie, it doesn't look bad," Leo chuckled when we had finished. "If I didn't know, I wouldn't suspect a thing."

I smiled and nodded in agreement. "You know, you're right. It could be years before anyone looks behind that cabinet."

"How long did you say it would be before the kids start coming in?"

"I'd say we've still got four or five hours. Maybe the faculty will open the building a little earlier. Either way, we've got to wait a while. Let's get back behind the oil burner so that no one will see us if they happen to look down the stairs. We'll be able to hear footsteps in the halls from there as soon as the building opens and the alarm system is turned off."

I turned off the overhead lights and we both returned to the boxes where we had been sitting behind the oil burner. I nestled the package in my crossed arms, against my chest, and leaned my head against the oil burner. "Why don't you try to sleep, Leo. If anything goes wrong later, things might get hectic."

"You think I can sleep now? *No way,*" he said.

"Why don't you close your eyes and try? Who knows? You might surprise yourself."

"What if we sleep longer than we should?"

"Don't worry . . . we'll hear the noise in the hallway. Besides, I've got an alarm on my wristwatch. I'll set it at seven. It'll wake us."

"You serious, Frankie? You can sleep here, with what you've got in your arms?"

"I'm not sure. We'll see what happens. All I'm saying is that if we fall asleep we'll be OK. We've got a long wait."

Leo shrugged and became silent. We sat in the darkness for about half an hour before I heard the heavy breathing that indicated he had fallen asleep. Before long I was nodding in and out of a light sleep as well, mixed with long periods of worrying about whether we would be able to leave the building as inconspicuously as I had planned. There was still the possibility that something could go wrong.

I also pondered whether the package in my arms really contained Jesus' hand. It had to be something of consequence: that was for sure. So far, everything Desmond Carey had told us about the grave, the directions to the fake wall and the safe had turned out to be true. A betting man would place his money on the hand and the Gospel being inside the tightly wrapped package in my arms. Just a few more hours and we would be back in my apartment, and I would know for sure.

It was just before 7 A.M. when I heard the first sound of life in the halls above. It sounded like two or three people moving in the area of the offices near the front entrance—probably the Jebby administrators opening shop for the day. Leo was awake. He whispered:

"They're probably turning off the alarm system right now in the office. They set it up so that they have a couple of minutes after they open the door."

We waited. The footsteps moved back and forth above us. Within a few minutes, more activity could be heard in the hall.

"That's probably the first of the students," I said. "The better boys who come in early to help the teachers get things ready. You remember—you probably were one of them at LaSalle."

"Yeah, right . . . I stayed smoking on Houston Street until the last second before class, even in the goddam rain and snow."

"How'd Mom ever get two dirtbags like us for sons?" I asked with a snicker. "She'd be at Mass praying for us every morning and we'd be at school looking for ways to screw up."

"You laugh," he answered, "but I wonder about that myself. It's like the gods are playing a practical joke on her."

"Well, we aren't dead yet. Maybe we'll turn it around."

"Hell, we'd have to join a monastery to balance the scales for what we've done so far." He laughed under his breath. "And wait until she finds out about this caper. I can see the headlines now: 'The Corcoran Brothers prove Jesus a fraud.' She'll never show her face at the church again."

"Maybe we can built a retirement home for the nuns with part of the money we make," I said. "That might make up for the scandal."

"You think so?" Leo asked.

"No. Jheesh . . . she'll disown us," I answered.

"Even after she finds out about how much money we're making? That could make a difference. The Irish are funny. Look at that slimeball Frank McCourt. He writes books making Irish Catholics look worse than anything the British ever said about them and the Irish make him a hero. They invite him to speak at the ladies club luncheons."

"We don't have a brogue," I added sarcastically. "That makes a difference. It makes McCourt sound authentic. It makes him a smart-ass with charm."

"It's getting noisier up there," Leo noted, nodding with his head toward the door to the first floor hallway. "How much longer should we wait before we try to leave?"

"I don't know. I'm worried that some custodian might come down here for something before school starts."

"How can we tell if that's gonna happen?"

"We can't."

"So let's get going then. Why wait? It's after seven. Sullivan should be out front by now."

"OK." I exhaled heavily. "Let's go." I picked up the package with the Gospel and the hand. "When we get into the hall just walk towards the front door as if we belong there. If anyone asks you what we're doing, just say we had to drop something off and keep moving. Don't stay for follow-up questions."

We walked slowly, following the flashlight's beam toward the stairwell. At the bottom of the stairs we paused, waiting for any indication that anything out of the ordinary was going on in the hallway above. Everything seemed routine: student laughter, lockers slamming closed, bookbags being thrown to the floor. I had just placed my hand on the stairway railing . . . when the door flew open and the overhead basement lights flashed on above us.

Four men appeared in silhouette on the top landing, led by Father Malcolm Rogers, the smoked lens of his eyeglasses gleaming like a black opal in the overhead lights.

"What are you doing down there?" he barked angrily. "Who are you?"

I tried to think of something logical to say, but could come up with nothing. The four men descended the steps robustly and authoritatively. Rogers and one of the other men were in Roman collars and black shirts. I couldn't tell if the other two were priests as well, but they were burly enough to be gym teachers. They showed no fear. It was their turf.

"You heard me—what are you doing here?" Rogers snarled as he neared us.

Leo and I took a few steps backwards, away from the stairs. The four men gathered about us in a half circle, bristling, angry, assertive. My heart was beating like a tom-tom.

"Well, now . . . if it isn't our friendly neighborhood heating system specialist," said Rogers menacingly. He remembered me from our meeting of a few weeks back. He stared at the package in my arms. An outraged look of alarm came over his face. "What do you have there?" he snapped.

"Look, Father, I can explain," I said, playing for time. "I know that this must look suspicious, but I came down here just a few minutes ago to take another look at your heating system. I was hoping to catch you in your office before the school day started with some facts and figures and wanted to double-check a few specifications." I smiled deferentially. "I hope you understand. I guess I shouldn't have come down here on my own, but I didn't see you around." I nodded toward Leo. "This is my technical advisor, Harry Smith. We were just about to come up to talk to you."

"Don't take us for fools," Rogers said impatiently. "I know who you are, Corcoran. You have taken something from us. Hand it over to me," he demanded, pointing at the package in my hands. The four men moved closer to us. I could smell their morning cologne and toothpaste. There was no longer any question that Desmond Carey had spoken to him about me. He knew my name.

"What? *This?*" I looked down at the package. "Hey . . . this is just something I brought to show you—some filter systems and sample valves and electrical switches that would fit in here."

Rogers would have none of it. He glanced over my shoulder toward the fake wall. I wasn't sure if he could see anything in the shadows behind the storage cabinet. It didn't matter. He knew what we had done. We were cooked.

"Hand that package to me and you can leave the building," Rogers demanded. "Otherwise we will call the police. We know who you are, Corcoran. We'll give them your name. You are not walking out of here with that material. Leave the building now and nothing will come of this."

"Hey, come on, this package is from my company," I said deferentially. "Let's go upstairs and I'll show you what's in it."

"Hand it to me," he insisted. "There is no room for negotiations here."

I had no idea what to do next.

Which is why having a brother like Leo can come in handy. He lowered his shoulder and sprang at the four men, his fists flailing wildly. He bowled through them and leaped to the stairs. He turned and began throwing punches at anything that moved.

"Let's go, Frankie!" he shouted back to me. "Let's get outta here!"

I shoved one of the priests to the side, tucked the package under my arm, sprang for the stairs and followed Leo up toward the hallway. My hopes were high. All we had to do was get to the hallway and we could race to the street. I pushed through the door to the hallway and looked across the clusters of students crowding the hall. Leo was already shoving students aside and moving through them like a halfback making an end run. I was just about to follow when a hand reached up from behind and grabbed my arm, ripping the package from my grasp. I looked around to see one of the men who had confronted us in the basement. He had raced up the stairs after me. He was bending over to pick up the package from the floor. I could see Father Rogers and the others clambering up the stairs behind him, eyes afire.

I bolted toward the front door, following Leo through the clusters of students.

"Stop those men!" a voice screamed from behind me. "Stop them!"

I didn't know who was being given the order to apprehend us, but the students in the hall reacted with confusion. They stepped back warily as Leo and I rumbled down the hall. We burst through the doors to 84th Street and raced west toward Madison Avenue looking for Sullivan in Leo's van.

Good old Sully! He wasn't a complete waste, after all. The van was parked with the motor running, about fifty yards to the west, right on the corner of Madison.

"There he is, Frankie!" Leo yelled, pointing toward the van. He began running. I followed him, head down and arms pumping.

We leaped into the van and slammed the doors behind us. Leo pushed Sullivan across the front seat to get to the steering wheel, toppling him like a rag doll. Then he whipped the steering wheel with his palm and floored the van, shooting us out into the traffic heading east toward Park Avenue.

"Oh, my God!" Sullivan exclaimed, trying to gather himself. "I knew something would go wrong!"

We shot across 84th Street, past the entrance to the school, where Father Rogers and the others were standing. Rogers had the package under his arm. He glared and shouted angrily as we roared past.

"What's going to happen? Who are those men?" Sullivan asked nervously.

"Don't worry about it now," Leo urged him. "We'll tell you everything when we get outta here. No one knows anything about you. Frankie, you got the package?"

"No. One of them ripped it from my hands."

"Aw shit, no!" Leo exclaimed.

"What can I say? They got it."

The light was green as we approached the corner of Park Avenue—finally some good luck. It lasted just a second. As we began our left turn around the traffic island that divides uptown and downtown traffic on Park, the traffic slammed to a sudden halt, leaving us locked in place. Something we couldn't see had clogged the traffic north of us.

"Damn it to hell!" Leo shouted, pounding his fist on the steering wheel and twisting his head wildly to see if we were being followed.

I turned to look out the back window, fearing that Rogers and the others would be running up 84th Street, hot on our tail, perhaps with a cop in tow.

I saw Rogers about fifty feet back on 84th Street, the package tucked under his arm, dashing towards a cab. He entered the cab hurriedly, slamming the door behind him.

Chapter Nineteen

L eo, *look!* The priest is in that cab behind us! Look, right there!"
I pointed excitedly toward a taxi approaching us from behind.
The cab was moving in the flow of traffic past the rear of our
van, traveling east on 84th Street. We were still angled onto Park
Avenue . . . at the edge of the traffic island.

"Does he see us?" Leo shouted, staring in his rearview mirror.

"He's got to," I answered. "But he's heading the other way, toward the East Side."

"He's not following us?"

"No," I assured him. "I don't get it."

"I guess we lucked out," said Leo, still staring in his rearview
mirror.

"Where do you think he's heading?" I asked. "He's got the package with him. I'm sure of that."

"What the hell's the difference? It's too damn late to worry about
that now. At least we're clear. For a while anyway."

"Yes, *please*, let's just get out of here," John Sullivan implored.
"I knew I should never have gotten mixed up with this. You two
are crazy." He was pressed back against the passenger side door, as
if Leo and I had some contagious disease.

"Leo, let's follow him," I said excitedly, ignoring Sullivan.
"You've got an opening behind us. Back up onto 84th. Quick . . .
you can do it now!"

"Are you nuts?" Leo asked, turning anxiously to look me in the eye.

"*Do it,* Leo! Back up and get into the lane behind the cab. Let's see where he's going."

"Then what?" Leo argued.

"We follow him. Just back the hell up before someone locks us in here and we can't get out!" I shouted. "Hurry!"

Leo shrugged as if I were a crazy man, shifted the van into reverse, cut hard and accelerated quickly back onto 84th Street, leaving the van facing east. Then, ignoring the red light, he shifted into drive and shot out into the intersection of Park Avenue and 84th Street, waving at the drivers honking their horns in anger as he maneuvered around them. By then the cab carrying Father Rogers was about five cars ahead of us. I had no way of seeing through the cab's tinted back window to determine if Rogers was aware that we were following him.

"You see the cab up there?" I asked, pointing over Leo's shoulder.

"I see it, I see it."

"Don't lose it."

"Keep your shirt on. I've got him," Leo assured me.

"Please . . . will someone tell me what's going on?" Sullivan pleaded anxiously. "You told me there would be nothing dangerous in this. What in God's name are we doing?"

"Relax and enjoy the ride, Sully," said Leo with a wink. "It won't be long now. You'll be at your desk drinking coffee before you know it."

With that, he cut across Lexington Avenue, through the streets lined with busy crowds moving in and out of the midtown coffee and bagel shops for their morning fix of caffeine and sugar.

I leaned across Leo's shoulder. The cab was increasing its lead on us.

"The light on 2nd Avenue might stop them," I said. "He's got only two more blocks before the river. I don't know where the hell he is going. Maybe he's heading toward the FDR Drive."

"We'll lose them if they get on the FDR," Leo answered. "We probably won't even know if they went north or south."

I heard my own angry sigh of exasperation.

We moved forward with the traffic heading toward 2nd Avenue. Rogers' cab was still within sight, on its way toward 1st Avenue. They had to be heading toward the FDR entrance ramp just south of us on 79th. What else was there ahead of them? Just York Avenue and then the grounds around Gracie Mansion and Karl Schurz Park. He couldn't be heading there, I thought.

Wrong. The cab shot across York Avenue and came to a stop where 84th Street ended at the concrete wall that opened onto the promenade that ran along the East River. Leo accelerated across the Avenue and slammed his van to a stop directly behind the cab, just as the cab's door sprung open and Rogers leaped to the sidewalk and darted out onto the promenade. The package was under his arm; he was heading straight to the river's edge.

He wouldn't . . . if he threw the package into the water at that spot it would be gone forever. That stretch of the East River is the southern edge of the legendary Hell's Gate, the turbulent expanse where the East River surges beneath the Triborough Bridge to pour into the vast waters of Long Island Sound, flowing nearly a hundred miles to the east and into the churning waters of the Atlantic off Montauk Point. Hell's Gate—whose fabled currents were the subject of urban legends of sunken treasure ships and mob drownings.

"Let me out!" I shouted to Leo. "I've got to stop him. He's heading toward the goddam river!"

"Jesus, Frankie, you don't think he'd . . ."

I hurled open the sliding door to the van and leaped to the street, running as fast as I could. Rogers was old and fat, but he had a lead on me. I rushed past some elderly men on benches reading their morning papers and staring at the river and the dark steel tracery of the Triborough Bridge, seeming more delicate in the distance than it really was. The broad expanse of the East River stretched before me, gray-green and opaque, reflecting distorted images of the dense stretch of apartment buildings huddled against its banks. There were no rapids or whitecaps like those you would see in some river out west, but the surface of the river throbbed with a latent power, like the back of a rodeo horse in the chute.

Joggers swerved to avoid me as I darted across the promenade. Rogers was leaning over the curved black wrought iron railing that ran along the edge of the promenade about twenty feet above the surface of the water. I was ready to lunge at him like a football player making a tackle.

Too late. The wrought iron railing swept back in a long S-shaped curve designed to thwart foolhardy macho men tempted to dive into the river from the walkway. It succeeded in doing that, but it could not stop Rogers from flipping the package underhanded into the river as if he were dropping an anchor from a rowboat. It plopped, splashed, yawed slightly, and then disappeared. Disappeared. Not a trace. Unperturbed, the river resumed its muscular rush to the sea.

Rogers turned, his face a sweaty mixture of guilt and relief. Whatever I thought, the evidence was gone. If the hand and the ancient Gospel were in that package they would be ground up quickly by the roiling waters of Hell's Gate.

"You son of a bitch!" I shouted.

Rogers was breathing too heavily to respond right away. He gulped as if trying to digest an unpleasant mouthful of food.

"I have nothing to say to you, Corcoran. Get out of my way."

"What? You think you can just walk away after what you did?" I said angrily, stepping into his path. "You call yourself a priest?"

"You don't have to worry about that. Get out of my way or I'll call the police."

He pushed past me and strode briskly back to where his cab was waiting for him. I turned and walked alongside him.

"You can live with yourself with what you just did?" I asked.

"What did I do?"

"You know goddam well. You had no right to do that."

"Do what?"

"I saw that package going under. You threw it in!"

"You're letting your imagination get the best of you. And if I threw something into the river it would be none of your business anyway. Was it something that was your property?"

"It wasn't yours, either," I snapped.

"What wasn't mine? I don't know what you are talking about." Rogers turned before re-entering his cab. "I hope I never set eyes on you again, Corcoran. You're lucky I'm not filing burglary charges against you."

"Burglary?" I responded. "Burglary of what?"

"Just never set foot inside Regis again, Corcoran. Everyone in that building will be warned about you."

He slammed the cab door in my face. His cab turned and disappeared up York Avenue. I have never set eyes on him again, nor stepped again inside the doors of Regis.

Chapter Twenty

We watched Rogers' cab head cross-town back towards Regis. I knew I didn't want to go back to my apartment. Not yet. And I had no intention of spending the day sorting futures contracts and stock options on the floor of the Exchange, not after what we had just been through. So Leo and I headed for Rathbone's on 2nd Ave to drown our sorrows.

John Sullivan didn't come with us. He was not interested in any chitchat. Not with us. He was clearly glad the morning was over. He left us, his face flushed with confusion and exertion, and walked to the 86th Street subway station for the downtown train to his office at the Catholic Worker. I have never seen him again.

Even though it was just slightly after 8 A.M., Rathbone's was not empty. What looked like a couple of cops coming off the night shift were huddled under the canopy at the warmly lit bar, along with two or three yuppie-types juicing themselves up with vodkas. Leo and I sat at the end of the bar across from a large poster of Basil Rathbone in his Sherlock Holmes deerstalker cap and with his Meerschaum pipe, hanging on the scrubbed brick wall. One of the suits got up to play a Van Morrison song on the jukebox. The rumble of the saxes cut through the morning air.

I chug-a-lugged a pint of Bass Ale while tapping on the bar to let the bartender know I wanted him to stay for my refill. Leo was sipping a long green bottle of Rolling Rock and reaching for one of his Marlboros. I took one too as the barkeep walked away to fill my glass.

I inhaled deeply and studied the nice head on my refill. The mix of nicotine and alcohol began to do its work. I exhaled slowly.

"Some morning, brother," I said, lifting the cigarette to my lips.

"I'll say," said Leo, scratching at the stubble of morning beard under his chin. "What comes next?"

"Next? Come on . . . *nothing* comes next. It's over. They can't find goddam pirate ships in Hell's Gate. You think we can find the hand and the Gospel? No way."

"You sure it was the hand that he threw in the river?"

"You mean you think he staged the run to the river to fool us? *Naahh* . . . he didn't even know that we were going to follow him. He got rid of the hand, and probably the dagger and the Gospel, too. He wants us out of the equation when they decide what to do next."

"About what who's going to do next?"

"The Jebbies," I answered, sipping on my ale.

"What can they do? The evidence is in the river for them, too."

"Maybe. Maybe not. Who knows? Maybe Rogers made a copy of the map for where Jesus' body is buried before he left the building. He had time to do that. Maybe he took Teilhard's account of finding the hand and the Gospel out of the package, too, before he ran for the river. Who knows? If he did, nothing is changed for the people who have been hiding this stuff. They can still reveal the secret—when and if they think the time is right. They can still show the world Jesus' body if they want. The fact that a hand is missing won't make that much difference."

"They can keep everything secret too, if they want," Leo said somberly.

"They can, if they want. No question. *Forever* if they want. But that's the way it was before we came on the stage. It's still their call. No one will believe our story without some evidence."

"What if we go to some of these people who are into all this Teilhard stuff and tell them what's going on? They would want the truth to come out."

"You think they would believe you and me instead of those big shots in the Jesuits?"

"I guess not. But maybe we can go up to Poughkeepsie and see Desmond Carey and get him to talk. His story would make a good book all by itself. We can cut him in on the take."

"No way," I responded. "He wouldn't work with us on a book. You should have heard him on the phone when he called me. He's on *their* side. Besides, who would believe him about all this? We thought he was a nut at first. Remember?"

"Yeah," Leo nodded, biting on the filter of his cigarette. "It seems like it was ages ago."

"Besides," I added, "we don't even know if the grave we robbed was Teilhard de Chardin's. You realize that, don't you?"

"Whaddya mean?"

"You couldn't read the inscription that night because of how dark it was and all the bird shit on the tombstone. Remember?"

"Whose grave could it have been then?" Leo asked, confused about what I was saying. "The directions to the safe were in the casket, just like Carey said."

"Yeah, but it could have been some other Jebbie's grave. We don't know. And we don't know for sure what it was that we took out of that safe. We never looked inside the package."

"What the hell else could it have been?" Leo asked. "I don't get your point."

"It was something some Jesuits wanted to hide. We know that, but we don't know that it was Jesus' hand. We never saw the hand or the map."

"What else could some Jesuits want to go to all that trouble to hide?"

"I don't know. But if we tried to tell anyone about all this, anything would be more believable than that it was Jesus' hand and the map to his body—if we tried to tell someone else this story. Six months ago you would have believed that it was a map to where Jimmy Hoffa is buried or the answer to where flying saucers come from before you would believe it was Jesus' hand."

I drained my pint of Bass Ale and motioned for another.

"Look, Leo, it could be records of some financial scam, some secret Jesuit records about how they financed all the land they bought around the country, some records that the Vatican wants secret. Who the hell knows?"

"So you're saying we've got nowhere to turn."

"That's what I'm saying."

"You expect the Jesuits at Regis are going to press charges against us for the break-in?"

"No, I think they just want us out of their lives. I think we're clear there."

"You want to go back up to the Culinary Institute to check out the gravesite?"

"I'll tell you, I am kind of curious about that. But I don't think we should for a while. It probably makes sense for us to stay clear of there. No sense getting anybody asking questions. Last I heard grave-robbing is still a crime."

Leo lit another cigarette and drummed his fingers on the polished surface of the bar. "So we go back to living our lives the way we were—like none of this happened? You going to tell anyone about all this, Frankie?"

"Like who? People will laugh if we tell them."

"You don't think the people at Lantern Press would want to go with the story anyway? About what happened up to this point?"

"Not a chance. They told us they were only interested if we came up with proof. We got diddley-squat for them now."

"What about that Bergeron babe? You and her seemed to be able to talk. You think she'd believe us?"

"Leo . . . believe *what*? I think she'd believe the story about the break-in and that priest dumping something in the river. But we got nothing else to show her. Nothing worth putting in a book. That's for sure."

"So I go back to working in the firehouse. No million bucks. No house in Tahiti, no yacht with Polynesian women taking care of my every need." Leo raised his hands in mock-surrender. "Back to my apartment and my alimony payments?"

"Yeah, back to the firehouse you go," I chuckled. "You got to work tonight?"

"No, I'm off today and tomorrow."

I smiled and raised my hands in mock-surrender.

We sat and drank for about another hour and then headed for a diner on Third Avenue. I was feeling guilty about what all the morning beer would do to my waistline, so I ordered just some coffee and a bran muffin. Leo was less inhibited. He ordered a double order of home fries and a cheese omelet and covered them with catsup and Texas Pete hot sauce. He drank about a quart of coffee. Afterwards, he drove me to my apartment. I slept like a rock until midday.

Chapter Twenty-One

Even though I knew that the book deal was dead, I was not ready to let Helen Bergeron drift out of my life. The thought that I might never see her again was too painful to accept. I searched for some way to keep the door open, just in case. *Just in case what?* I didn't know. Lost causes are no less intense for being hopeless.

I didn't feel guilty about my yearnings. Not a lot, anyway. I had convinced myself that all I was seeking was a way to see her regularly and spend time involved with her in the equivalent of office meetings and coffee breaks, collaborating on projects, sharing pleasantries at holiday time, talking about books and movies and the events of the day, sharing jokes and gossip. No sin there. It would be no more inappropriate than two co-workers who enjoyed each other's company. If I could be with her regularly in that way, I would keep my deeper longings to myself.

I could live with such a relationship—which, after all, would be close to the joy of shared experiences at the heart of a good marriage. Or so they tell me. Everything but the sex. What I couldn't live with was the idea that she would become just a late-night barroom memory, the face in a drunken reverie brought on by some weepy torch song. The question was how to do that, how to work out some excuse to contact her on a regular basis once the book was no longer our common concern.

I had no plan to make all this happen, but the following Sunday I borrowed Leo's van while he was at work and headed up to Pleasantville. I remembered Helen had told me that she regularly served as Eucharistic minister at the 11 o'clock Mass at her parish. It was strange: I felt drawn to her, as if propelled by some uncontrollable force. I didn't know what I hoped would happen. I didn't know if she would be alone at the Mass, or with her family, or what I would say if we met. But the longing to be near her was overpowering, an indefinable yearning that struck at the core of my being.

Even if all that developed was a chance to see her from a distance as she performed her duties as Eucharistic minister, that would be fine. If there were an opportunity to actually talk to her for a while, perhaps share a cup of coffee somewhere . . . *bliss*.

I drove north on the Saw Mill River Parkway to the Bedford Road exit. Holy Innocents Church was just a short drive from the parkway ramp, in a leafy setting of manicured grass and structured evergreens, a massive, precisely cut stone structure, set back from the road. It was the kind of church that you would expect to find in central Westchester. It had the aura of an old W.A.S.P. place of worship, where someone from a John Cheever novel might try to atone for a night of genteel booze and adultery. I didn't worry about fitting in. I had donned my best Glen Plaid jacket and charcoal slacks for the day. My British museum curator look. I wanted to reek of respectability when Helen saw me.

Mass had already begun when I arrived. I parked in the back reaches of the parking lot, leaving Leo's van sticking out like an earthworm on a wedding cake in the sea of Audis and Mercedes. I entered from a side door and took a seat in a pew near the rear of the congregation. The place even smelled of wealth, a mixture of cut flowers, incense, and piney soaps.

I couldn't see Helen, but that was to be expected. The Eucharistic ministers would be seated somewhere near the front of the congregation. The number of children in the congregation struck me. It reminded me of my parish in Inwood when I was a boy, when there would be row upon row of scrubbed-faced schoolchildren reciting their prayers in unison, a sight I seldom encountered any longer at Masses in Manhattan, where young children were few and far between among the double-income-no-kids professional types and neighborhood old folks.

Even after all that had happened over the last week, I tried to pray. Old habits die hard. Jesus remains at the core of my spiritual life. Even if it were true, as the atheists insist, that he is nothing more than a projection of my need to make sense of life, that was nothing to dismiss easily. Without Jesus serving as some omniscient judge and jury, I knew no way to wrestle with my conscience, to draw the lines that governed my behavior. And I wanted that in my life. I didn't want to be the dirt bag that my instincts would lead me to be, if left unchecked. Jesus was the irreducible authority that I couldn't fool with a clever line or strained protestations for mercy when none was warranted. He sees you when you are sleeping, knows when you are awake, whether or not his hand was being ground to pulp at that moment in the currents of Hell's Gate. He remains central to my identity. Probably the psychologists have a word for it all.

I went through the familiar parts of the Mass, following the words of the priest literally in some instances, reacting to other passages as if they were a verbal Rorschach test. I pondered what I would have to change in my life to find myself in a church like this with a woman like Helen Bergeron, with our children next to us in the pew. You didn't get here living the life I was living. That was certain. The Wall Street princesses and Hampton's wonder girls of my world were not the type for churchly pieties. At this hour on a Sunday morning, they were likely to be waking up ashen-faced in some man-about-town's *pied à terre*, wondering if he would want them to stay for breakfast and what they would talk about once they had congratulated each other for their exquisite taste in consumer goods.

Then again, could it be that some of the June Cleaver–types in the congregation around me, whispering to their children to be quiet, were once the hot numbers on the singles' circuit? Some of them looked pretty darn good. Did it work that way?

Whatever. It seemed too late to change what I had become. No Helen Bergerons were going to come into my life. I was beginning to think that she broke the mold.

Then I spotted her, just before Communion in one of the front rows on the right side of the altar. She rose with the other Eucharistic ministers, a hodge-podge of matronly women and pot-bellied men, to take her place in a semicircle around the priest at the altar. She looked like Princess Diana with the kitchen help.

Gorgeous . . . even though she had dressed deliberately demurely for the role she was playing. Loose-fitting skirts and high collars can disguise only so much. The angle-length polka dot navy dress clung perfectly to her legs as she walked up the steps of the altar, hinting at the long, graceful curves beneath the fabric. She bowed her head as the priest handed her the ciborium with the hosts and then moved gracefully to the side of the altar to greet the line of communicants already formed there. An overhead light gleamed upon her hair, carving dramatic shadows across her face. She was wearing her gold-rimmed glasses. They sparkled in the glow. I half-expected every man in the church to rush to her line to get a closer look.

I didn't want her to see me though, not yet. I moved across the back of the church so that I could find a spot in the line in front of one of the other Eucharistic ministers, but I kept my eyes on Helen every step of the way as I advanced toward the front of the church.

When I was a boy, women did not dispense Communion in Catholic churches, but Helen looked as if she were born for the job. Her long graceful fingers held the Host reverently before her eyes as each communicant moved into place before her. I could just hear faint traces of her voice from where I was standing.

"Body of Christ . . . Body of Christ . . . Body of Christ . . ." She repeated the words softly and precisely as she placed the Host into the hands or mouth of each communicant. Talk about having it all! If a guy lived in this parish he could receive Communion and get an erotic jolt all in one experience. *Mea culpa, mea maxima culpa.*

I returned to my seat without her seeing me. After Mass, I moved back to a dark corner of the vestibule that would afford me a vantage point to spot which direction she would take as she left the church. My plan was to approach her in the parking lot and beg for some time to go over what had happened at Regis, and then see what would develop after that.

She walked briskly from the sacristy, the room behind the altar where the priest and other lay ministers had marched in procession after the Mass. She genuflected before the tabernacle and maneuvered deftly through the clusters of worshippers making small talk on their way out of the church, stopping in front of a pew where two young boys were seated next to a balding man in a dark suit. Helen reached to grasp the man's arm at the elbow. He stood and placed her arm around his and allowed her to guide him toward the center aisle. He was blind. The two boys, clean-cut, athletic-looking young men in blue blazers, positioned themselves on either side of their father as the family moved slowly toward the back of the church and the exits.

The man held his head high as if he were focusing on the upper walls of the church, moving his head in an awkward manner that led me to believe that his blindness was a fairly recent affliction. He laughed merrily at some comment that Helen whispered into his ear, taking short steps as if to keep his balance as they advanced up the aisle. The boys spoke quietly to their mother and smiled at her whispered response. I had no idea what she had said to them, but their eyes sparkled with a wholesome joy.

I wasn't the only one who loved her. She fairly beamed in tranquility, a sleek lioness nuzzling her pride toward the den.

Everything fell into place. All this, the goodness of her life, was a consequence of the sacrifices and inner restraints that made these family joys possible. Not a bad trade-off: surrendering the smarmy attention of guys-on-the make like me in order to remain at the center of the lives of this man and the teenage boys who needed her. The self-respect and dignity that made her what she was were a by-product of her commitment to virtue. You couldn't have one without the other.

What I was witnessing confirmed my reaction to her: She was a woman who made men better by her presence in their lives, transforming their baser instincts with her decency, raising them to a higher level of existence.

And I couldn't figure out why she would refrain from smooching it up with me in Central Park . . . There are grown-ups and there are grown-ups.

I may have lost much of my sense of religious obligation over the years, but what was required of me became clear. It was my duty to stay away, to not even hint at inserting something sleazy into her life. I moved further back into the shadows at the rear of the church. It didn't matter if I was certain that my feelings for her were genuinely high-minded and clean, the closest I have ever been to knowing love. It was my obligation to not sully the ceremony of innocence I was witnessing, to not fray the family ties that made her what she was.

She was "taken." I intuited as I had never before what that word meant. It meant she was committed, part of something decent and permanent and ennobling, a family life that gave her dignity and stature, an identity with pleasures and rewards that were world's apart from the sexual acrobatics that they call love on the pickup scene that I inhabited.

It was simple: If I loved her, I would stay away, not complicate her life with the temptations of the baser pleasures of my lounge lizard world. A lot of what the Jesuits taught me as a boy had been lost in the shuffle over the years, but not the disdain for those who make sniveling excuses for their self-centered pursuits. My love for her, if real, would place her happiness over my own.

And what would become of it, this love of mine? That's another thing I retained from the Jesuits: Not every pleasure is meant to be taken. Love is not just an emotion; it is an act of the will. I would stay away. I would phone her during the week to explain what happened at Regis during the break-in. I would tell her that the book deal had no future. I would ask for her understanding, and ask her to convey my regrets to her boss at Lantern Press. And then say good-bye. And I would stay away.

The world would have been a better place if Lancelot had denied himself his love for Guenivere. For Guenivere. For Lancelot. For Camelot. I could try my hand at the knightly thing. I would worship her from afar. As I do to this day.

And what happened with the Jesuits at Regis? So far, not a thing. I never heard a word from Father Rogers or Desmond Carey or any other Jesuit about what happened that night. No one from the Culinary Institute has contacted me about the grave-robbing. My life goes on as before.

I follow the Jesuits' *America* magazine regularly to see if I can spot any clues about what they intend to do about Jesus' body near Lake Tiberias—if indeed the body is actually there. I look for articles about the Dead Sea Scrolls and Teilhard de Chardin's theories to see if they are getting ready to break the news. So far, nothing; not that I can spot.

What about my own religious beliefs? Am I still a Catholic? Well, as much as I was before. How can that be if I am plagued with the suspicion that the story of the Resurrection is a lie and that Jesus' body is still in the ground? First of all, I'm not sure that is the case. If you are an atheist, the idea of Jesus rising from the dead is silly. But if you believe in a God—the Creator of the vast wonders of the universe—who sent his only begotten son to live among us, well, that God could certainly raise Jesus from the dead. That's for sure. I don't claim to have an answer that will work for everyone, but for me the Christian faith remains the key to the mystery of human existence, regardless of what happened to Jesus' body on Easter morning. He is still the Lord, the Word made Flesh.

Look: everybody uses a filter to sort out what's fact and what's metaphor in Scripture. No one takes everything as literal fact. Even the holy rollers who tell us they accept the Bible as the literal word of God will make some exceptions, maybe about Noah and all the animals on the ark or Joshua knocking down the walls of Jericho with his bugle blasts. Or that we have to pluck out our eyes if they are a source of temptation. Know any of the Bible-belt crowd that does that?

A lot of conservative Catholics who view the New Testament as literal truth have no qualms about treating the Old Testament as a collection of myths, more important for the religious wisdom they convey than their factual accuracy. They have no problem with a loose interpretation of the parting of the Red Sea or the manna falling from heaven in the desert to feed the Israelites.

So maybe there is an element of metaphor in the story of the Resurrection, too. Maybe what Desmond Carey told us about Teilhard's discoveries is true. Maybe I held Jesus' hand in mine when I took that package from the wall at Regis. Maybe I didn't. I guess I'll never know for sure.

But what I do know for certain is that Jesus saves. What about St. Paul's insistence that without the risen Christ our faith is in vain? *What about it?* Maybe when he arose from the dead, it wasn't like Dracula popping up from his coffin. Maybe something more mysterious and profound occurred, something that would not be diminished by the physical body still being in the ground in northern Israel. I'll say it again: I don't know.

What I do know is that Christ's life and teachings were what made Helen Bergeron what she was, transforming her and, through her, everyone in her life into something more decent and loving than they would otherwise have been. That's grace at work. That's salvation history. "The phenomenon of man," in Teilhard's words. That's being born again by the blood of the Lamb, a glorious product of "the Word becoming flesh and dwelling among us," the process in time through which the world is transfigured into what a loving Creator would want it to be: a *Divine Milieu*, if you will.

To order additional copies of

THE DEAD SEA CONSPIRACY

Have your credit card ready and call

Toll free: (877) 421-READ (7323)

or send $12.95* each plus $4.95 S&H**

to
WinePress Publishing
PO Box 428
Enumclaw, WA 98022

*Washington residents please add 8.4% tax.
**Add $1.00 S&H for each additional book ordered.